Obloeron:

The Rise of the Dark Falcon

By Sean Sweeney

Obloeron:

The Rise of the Dark Falcon

By Sean Sweeney

Chapter 1

Powder gray smoke rose from modest chimneys just as the sun rose over Cassimina. This small village soon came alive for another day of hard work, the populace shaking a long night's sleep away.

The routine for the townsfolk here was the same, day after day. As soon as the cock crowed, the womenfolk awoke and bathed the young children, prepared the meals, and washed clothes, while the men drank strong coffee and went off to tend the fields surrounding the town. Some worked in the shops, hawking their wares to those who trudged through on a daily basis. The people of Cassimina lived simple lives: It was such that fathers passed their knowledge on to their sons, while mothers taught their daughters how to tend the home and prepare it in the fashion their men liked. It was orderly, and the routine had gone on for generations.

On this day, that routine came to an abrupt end.

While the birds chirped their happy morning songs, extraneous sounds from beyond the hill rose up from the shores of Timber Lake and filtered into town. The sounds of large men singing their tribal hymns, the clatter of hooves slapping on the wet, rocky path echoed into Cassimina. Alongside the songs came the whinny of horses and the sounds of wooden wheels squeaking as they completed their noisy revolutions.

Around the far corner, the first horse, a majestic shire, came into view. Its hoof hair bounced about as it entered, its leather halter attached to a powder blue carriage even larger than the one it had pulled the last time they had visited. One by one the caravan's carriages made their way around the hill, being careful not to tread on the fields. While the travelers brought great items from all over the realms, the people of Cassimina normally paid them in crops or traded older treasurers for newer ones. The caravan was, in essence, a traveling trading post.

The caravan was ten carriages in all, each a different, vibrant color. But as Vossler, the town tanner, looked on from the front of his shop, it wasn't the colors of the carriages or the horses pulling them which drew his attention: It was a boy, a youngster in his teens, walking just to the side of the rearmost carriage, his hands bound. The boy's disheveled clothes looked more like rags than garments. His shoes were worn-down moccasins, his mahogany hair stringy and dirty. The boy appeared malnourished, as he was thin in the arms and waist. The lad kept his eyes turned to the ground, as if afraid to look anyone in the face.

Vossler felt his heart lurch. He kept his watch as the caravan parked itself and formed a semicircle. Within minutes, the young lad, his wrists still tied together, disentangled the horses from their hitches and led them away to a small grass paddock. The muscular gypsy men threw the sides of the carriages open, revealing goods for sale or trade.

The lad returned a minute later, his eyes downward. He occasionally peeked toward the leader of the caravan, who stood next to him. The man inexplicably shoved the boy away with a large, calloused hand.

Vossler's leathery face grew rather flushed, from his scraggly chin to his ears.

No one should be treated like that, not even a slave, he thought. *It's not natural*. But even as the thought came to him, it left his mind with the speed of a puddle evaporating in the midsummer sunshine. Vossler knew, as did everyone in Cassimina, if someone spoke up against this man, his caravan would pack up and depart, never to return.

He sighed deeply, then walked up to the first cart with the intention of browsing, but he had an ulterior motive.

He wanted to see the boy.

The hitch in his step apparent to everyone as he strode forward, Vossler had to wipe the sweat away after his exertion. He peered at the goods in the first carriage with a keen-yet-rheumy eye and saw many treasures he wished he could afford, even if in trade. Over the winter he had worked on several new wheels, knowing the caravan would come looking for replacements. But even his cobbled wheels could not pay for half the items he desired in the first carriage. He went to the second, hoping to find something a little more affordable.

The second didn't offer much more in the way of less expensive trinkets, and neither did the third. But the fourth carriage yielded things Vossler might use in his daily routine—lengths of leather would last him a year, as well as leather ropes to tie pieces together. He haggled with the keeper of the carriage on a price, and they settled for one slightly lower than the keeper wanted. Vossler handed over his goods, and as he walked away, he smiled knowing that he left the caravan with a deal that suited him nicely.

"Find something nice at the caravan, eh Vossler?" a voice called from behind.

With a touch of groaning effort, Vossler turned to see Danith Crassnick standing there, his cannon-like fists balled into his thick waist.

The old man regarded the younger one with a sneer.

"Aye, what's it to you, Crassnick?"

"I need new breeches for me and my son," the brawny, brown-haired man replied. "Piety is growing, and he will need two new pair by his sixteenth summer."

"And you're growing, too, yet not in the way he is," Vossler shot back, shoving his cane toward Crassnick's expanding waistline.

Crassnick's lip curled as he leaned over him threateningly. Vossler didn't back down. Instead, he stared into the man's eyes, holding his gaze.

"Just make the breeches or I'll make you very sorry for crossing me!" he said with a hearty snarl, before he stormed off in the opposite direction.

Vossler sighed and shrugged at the burly man's swagger, but didn't take the threat seriously. Crassnick may have several more inches of muscle than Vossler, but that didn't matter: Vossler's strength came from his experience as a warrior from olden times. However, none who lived here now knew of his life prior to his arrival decades ago. Those that had known were now dead.

In truth, Vossler was a veteran of the long-forgotten Orcan Crusades in the east, far beyond the halfling realm of Deerkin. His wish was to retire in a quiet land where hardly anything happened; he had found Timber Lake forty years prior and, even though illness had swept over the land and killed those quarantined in the log home, took it for his own. The townspeople warned him of germs, but he had assured them he was made of stronger stuff than those who had died. Once settled, he rarely disturbed the townsfolk as they went about their daily routines, and he soon found that he had seamlessly slid into their processes.

Nearly seventy-three years old, Vossler had a shock of long white hair that came just below his shoulder blades; he kept it tied back while working, but now it flowed freely. His face was hard, the lines showing his age to all. His moustache was just as white as the hair on his head, and white stubble dotted his chin. He was lean, the muscles he had developed in the wars atrophied by years of non-use. He had taken up the profession of cobbling and he also tanned leather; the farmers usually paid him in food for leather harnesses that yoked their oxen together.

Vossler had returned to his workshop and deposited the new materials on the ground next to his worktable. He wanted to rest for several minutes, but he remembered the disheveled boy back at the caravan. He recalled the downturned face of the boy when he heard a knock at the door. He sighed and stood, then went to answer it.

Meena Fassel, an older woman who lived several houses down, stood there with a wide smile on her face as he opened the door. She looked at him with her bright brown eyes, as if she took him and the entire house in.

"Hello, Vossler. I was wondering if you could help me bring several things back from the caravan," she said, a light tinge of scarlet rushing across her jawline.

Vossler smiled and half-bowed. He knew the woman held a soft spot for him, and he likewise for her.

"Of course I will help you, my dear. I was just heading back there... to do some additional shopping. Yes, to do some additional shopping." He offered his arm to her as he finished his lie; she took it, and they walked off together.

While she spoke of her life, Vossler thought of the boy, his gaze lingering away from her face. He didn't mean to ignore her, but the boy had ignited something within his subconscious. The young slave looked incredibly pitiful, and Vossler wondered if the youngster would ever break free of his bonds. He escorted her from carriage to carriage, allowing Meena's gaze to linger over each item before he led her to the next. He looked for the boy, but there was no sign of the lad since the caravan leader shooed him away. Vossler wondered what the boy was—

His reverie ended with the sounds of a cracking whip and shrieks of pain filtering over the rear of the caravan, the echoes ricocheting around the clearing. His heart now in his throat, Vossler looked around at the other shoppers. He noticed they, too, heard the sounds, but their wide eyes did not stray from the items they wanted to buy. The wailing continued, and Vossler knew the cries poured from the lungs of a young male.

He looked at Meena and saw her attention drawn elsewhere, not paying him any heed. He promptly slipped away, walking slowly through the throng of customers until he found the end of the caravan. He snuck around the corner and saw what caused the disturbance: the boy had his breeches pulled down, while the caravan master stood behind him with a leather whip. Vossler watched as the whip dropped, bringing scarlet welts to the surface of the boy's bare behind. There were other scars, older and calloused over, while others looked ready to split open with the new assault.

"You'll do as you're told, Krampel! I don't know why we took you on; you've not lived up to the promise your mother made! You slack on us, and we are tired of your bad habits!" the master said as he snapped his whip with each sentence. Vossler noticed the boy tried to stifle his cries. Blood seeped from these new wounds, trickling down the back of his legs.

Vossler clenched his teeth. He wanted to stop the man from harming the boy any further, but he was defenseless. In the old days, he roamed the realms with his master's former sword and several hidden daggers within reach. In the comfort of Cassimina, though, he kept such weapons hidden in his home.

"Hey! Stop your spying! Get out of here!"

Vossler blinked and found one of the master's young assistants barking at him.

"Why are you hurting that boy?" he asked, finding his voice as soon as the assistant came up to him. "What has he done to earn such punishment?"

"That is none of your business, citizen. He is a slave, and we treat our slaves the way we see fit. Now scamper off and buy something before I put the whip to you!" The assistant lifted his own whip, one with little barbs on the sides. The young man, Vossler noted, had an air of haughtiness about him.

Vossler wanted to put his fist through his face.

Swallowing his desires, he looked at the young man and saw his eyes for the first time. Tear-stained and wide, Vossler saw a fire within them despite the beating he received at the hands of the master. For a split second, he thought he saw a twinge of orange wreathing his retinas. He wanted to rub his own eyes and step closer, if only to tell himself he had imagined this incredible vision.

His shock at the boy's expression didn't show on his face; he remained as placid as possible—until the assistant put a hand on his chest. Vossler felt his gut churn; he felt a sudden, strong desire to plant the butt end of his cane in the youngster's breadbasket, if just to show him some manners. The desire left him as he stepped away, his gaze narrowed and fixed on the assistant. The youngster, he heard, said some words in a dialect Vossler didn't understand; it did, however, send the tiny hairs on his arms shooting upward. He returned to Meena's side, trying not to attract attention from the crowd. Only as he returned he heard the crack of the whip again.

With a swallow, he winced as the boy wailed louder.

***

As soon as dusk approached, the caravan packed up and left Cassimina for another year. The womenfolk played their instruments and sang a hasty good bye song as the men shut the creaky carriage sides, before the young slave boy reattached the horses to their hitches. Several of the townspeople witnessed their departure, leaving the same way they arrived.

The next stop for the caravan was the village of Coy, near Deerkin in the Easterlind. It was a three-day trip through smooth terrain.

The slave boy, though, never saw it.

After the caravan traveled for a couple of hours, it had slowed to a halt, the day's travel completed. The men lit fires and the women cooked their meals, using the meat Cassiminian farmers gave them in exchange for grain and feed. They played music and danced their usual nighttime fare as heavily-scented smoke rose around them, mingling with their natural sweat. With the moon surrounded by the matte black backdrop, it was off to sleep. Morning came quickly, and the travel must continue. There were more villages far from the cities they had to visit before winter's snows arrived.

Once he thought everyone had fallen asleep, the slave boy stirred. He walked to the nearest fire and took several scraps from the spit. Rarely did the caravan masters let him eat with the rest of the traveling band; late each night, he stuffed as much food into his mouth before they noticed. His usual meal was a gruel soup, but the caravan masters had forgotten to feed him again. He didn't say anything; he feared the lack of food was further punishment for today's crimes.

He raised the beef to his lips and tasted meat for the first time in what felt like weeks. He savored the taste, chewing as he felt the meat's juices drop on his tongue and slide down his throat. He did not recall anything that tasted so wonderful in all his life.

As he finished the tasty morsel, he licked the juices from his fingers, one by one, smacking his lips together.

It was just a little too loud. Seconds later, and without any warning, the slave boy tasted copper flooding his tongue, as the caravan master had awoken and gave a sharp tug to rope. The boy fell forward, unable to catch himself as his chin slammed into the ground.

"Stealing food, eh? You never learn the lessons we teach you, do you boy?" the master said, reaching once again for his barbed whip.

Before the slave boy reacted, the man cracked the whip against his back, tearing the measly shirt to tatters. The boy knew better than to scream, especially after earlier today; he once screamed so loud during a beating that the punishment for screaming was ten times worse than his original crime. He winced as the barbs tore into his skin, ripping into his flesh. He dropped to his knees and immediately protected the back of his head. Another crack and then another, before the boy felt his skin flaring up, a conflagration set in his flesh. The beatings ceased after a few minutes, but he stayed down just in case the master decided to whip him again.

"Now, no more food for you until you've learned not to take from your betters!"

The boy stifled his cries as he lay face down in the dirt. He had taken many beatings over the last ten months, ever since his mother sold him to the caravan. Each one lit a fire inside him, a fire that tears would not suppress. He dreamed of freedom, and each whipping fueled his dreams.

And as he laid there, his elbows covered in dirt, he made his decision while the tears streamed down his face.

I will run away tonight, he thought. *It has to be tonight. I can't take this any longer. They will kill me if I don't do something for myself.*

He waited until the caravan settled down once again; the others, he noticed, murmured something about stringing him up once and for all. He heard the whistling of a light wind, the chirping of crickets. A soft melody of rustling leaves and the scuffling dirt resounded in his ears. The crackling fire dwindled down to hissing embers.

An hour after the beating, the slave lifted his head if only an inch to see if anyone else stirred.

Nothing. He slowly moved to his knees, trying not to move the rope cutting into his thin wrists. He did not want to move the rope any more than necessary, even though his masters weren't light sleepers by any means; the one holding the whip had the rope tied around his waist, and he would feel the rope rubbing along his midsection. He would shake off the annoyance at first, but repeated movement would certainly wake him. The slave never dreamed of doing this before, for he feared the unknown punishment for disturbing the master's deep slumber. His heart hammered away, denting his breastbone with hard thwacks.

Working slowly, he rubbed his wrists back and forth, trying to get some slack in order to slide his hands out; he wished he had a knife to make this job easier. Within seconds he felt the rope burning his skin, but he didn't relent: the pain drove him further. It felt as if he put a hot branding iron to his wrists.

He didn't care, though. He wanted freedom so badly that he didn't care about the potential costs.

After a few minutes, the lad had worked the rope enough to move his hands less than an inch. Frustrated, he nearly cried. Seeing his quandary, he bit the inside of his cheeks on both sides of his mouth and, with the strength remaining inside him, yanked his hands free.

The rope ripped off a layer of skin, and he immediately let loose a slow, throaty moan as metallic fluid flowed from his mouth. He caught himself a split second later, then opened his eyes and looked toward the sleeping men while the air stung at the raw wounds. They didn't move, and a grin quickly replaced the anguished look he had on his face.

He didn't waste any time. Without a second thought, the slave got to his feet and tiptoed away. Once he reached a hundred feet away, he turned to look back at the camp; the fire had dwindled to nothing. His heart racing, he immediately ran south, running hard and fast even though his bare feet struck multiple stones and outcroppings. He stifled the moans. He found a new strength, a second wind, expanding within him. The wind whipped through his hair and attacked the wounds on his wrists, and despite the pain he felt free for the first time in nearly a year. He wanted to laugh at his luck. He was free of the caravan masters—as long as he kept plenty of distance between himself and them. He ran harder, knowing the easiest way to freedom was through his feet. He crashed through brush and ducked branches, not wanting to slow himself down. The cuts that the sticks and brambles gave him did not compare to the barbed whip, and he shook them off with that knowledge. He used his fear as an ally, and he spurred himself on even faster than before.

As soon as he was a mile away, he stopped running and leaned against a large boulder. He caught his breath quickly, feeling his lungs burn, then looked around. He knew where he was, but it was still too close to the caravan masters. He giggled a little to himself, knowing he had escaped. Tears streamed down his cheeks.

"Krampel Paddymeyer, you are too smart for your own good," he said to the air.

After a few minutes' rest, the former slave known as Krampel pushed off the rock and started to run again, wanting to put another hour between them.

Chapter 2

When the moon reached its highest point in the night sky, Krampel found himself at the top of the hill overlooking both the township of Cassimina and Timber Lake to the south. This was the last group of people that had seen him, and he wondered if the caravan masters might look for him here.

So why am I endangering these good people? he thought.

Because I'm hungry and need bread, his mind quickly answered. The meat he had at the campsite hadn't lasted long. *Besides*, he continued, *they may not come looking, at least not right away.*

Krampel ducked low as he walked down the hill, trying not to attract any attention to himself. Several fires had burned low in the hearths, he saw, the shades drawn in the windows, but darkness had swallowed the majority of the township. He knew that towns usually posted a guard or two at night to stop intruders or to raise the alarm when predators were in the area. A township like Cassimina, one without walls protecting the people, was one of those towns with guards. He knew he'd have to be cautious as he entered.

His knowledge of the town's layout was nil, so he figured he'd have to sneak around and try to use all the cunning he possessed.

Not having the ability to see, he attempted to use his other senses. He smelled the fires burning, the smell of stewing meat, and—then it hit him—the aroma of freshly baked bread wafting on the air! His stomach rumbled with the deepest hunger and his mouth salivated at the thought of tasting something as delicious as fresh bread! Not stale bread like the masters gave him; this bread was fresh, fresh from the oven. He had never felt hungrier in his life than before now.

His nose directed him to the spot where the smell originated: It was as if the scent picked him up off his feet and floated him there. He practically walked with his eyes closed as he visualized himself sitting in the baker's shop, munching on all the bread, sending it to his belly, and then some. He'd been hungry for so long that he didn't know what the words "properly full" meant. Krampel peered into the window of the shop and saw the enlarged hearth lit, the baker standing near it with his back turned. The baker pulled loaves from the hearth, their crusts golden brown.

Krampel slurped and swallowed his saliva. His mouth stayed wet for several minutes.

He tapped twice on the window to get the man's attention, but the baker did not notice; he continued to go about his duties as he pulled another loaf from the hearth. Krampel winced as hunger ravaged his stomach, his insides quaking. Bread was near, and he could not get to it. He rapped his knuckles on the window even harder this time. He hoped he wouldn't wake the entire township from the clatter.

The baker noticed this time, and he looked toward the window and frowned. He moved to the door and, with an annoyed look on his face, opened the door in a rush.

"What do ye want? Who ye be?" the baker barked.

"Please sir," Krampel said, "may I have some bread? I'm a starving lad."

"Aye, I can see that. The answer is no," the baker replied, practically spitting his answer. "These here bread's for me people here, not for strangers that come through in the middle of the night. Now be off with ye."

The door slammed in Krampel's face, and he felt the vibrations meandering all the way into his gut. He needed food, and he didn't know how to go about getting some. His face sank, but then he got an idea. Since he had to fend for himself, he needed to find a way to get what he needed.

And at this time of night, that meant stealing.

When he was a child, his mother taught him that stealing was wrong—but that was before times got rough in Gosnold, forcing her to sell her only son into slavery. He tried to remember her words and the look of her face, but the grumbling in his stomach drowned out everything save his desires.

Krampel looked around and saw no one in the area; he had thought the baker's gruff voice would attract attention from the town's guards. He walked slowly around the left side of the shop nearest the door and found a tall barrel standing there against the wall.

Perfect hiding place, he thought with a grin. He climbed in and waited.

An hour had passed before he heard another noise. As soon as the door opened, he had a few minutes more before it was safe to move again. His muscles had seized as he sat with his legs bunched up to his chest, his arms wrapped around his shins. He heard the door close, then heard gravel crunching under booted soles. The sounds grew softer and softer until he heard nothing save crickets and the sounds of his vibrating sternum.

My chance at last! he thought.

He stood and arched his back; he felt the muscles pop and relax almost immediately. He climbed out of the barrel gingerly and did a few knee bends to get the blood flowing again. Then he walked to the door and opened it. The baker hadn't locked it.

Krampel grinned as the smell of the bread assaulted him, smacking against his nostrils and invading every pore on his face. He rushed around the small counter without closing the door and made his way into the back, where he found loaf on loaf sitting there on the shelves, much like a pyramid, waiting for buyers in the morning.

He reached up onto his tiptoes and grabbed two from the uppermost shelf. He held onto them as if the gods themselves had come down from the seventh ring of the heavens and had handed each loaf to him. Clutching the prizes close to him, he turned and ran from the shop—except that he had rushed headlong into the counter, his weight and speed knocking it over to the ground with a heavy clatter.

The ensuing crash echoed throughout Cassimina.

"Oh great," he exclaimed, picking up the loaves and himself off the floor. "You went ahead and did it now, you idiot."

He ran out the door, looking both ways once in the street and saw the candles coming alight throughout the town. He sighed—he had made such a commotion inside the baker's shop that the whole town was now awake! That was not his intent; he wanted to be far away from here by the time dawn broke.

That's not happening now, Krampel thought, *unless I can get away without anyone seeing me.*

He turned to his right and rushed off, his feet churning underneath him. His hair shot out behind him and he did not look back once, not wanting to see if anyone had taken up the pursuit.

It didn't matter; just as he turned to leave the town and head up the hill, Krampel ran right into a man who appeared seemingly out of nowhere. He held a long pike with a pointed end, and he halted the youth by smacking the side of it against his left flank. Krampel stopped cold and looked up into the hard eyes of the guardsman.

"You're not going anywhere until you tell me where you've been," the guardsman said to the slave boy, looking down with a wide grin.

"I… I…" Krampel stammered, not able to find words. They had caught him red-handed, the bread shaking in his nervous hands, which he didn't try to hide. He lowered his head, his face full of shame. The guardsman chuckled.

"Oy, I have the disturbance here," he yelled to his other mates, who ran toward the pair, their pikes drawn. They circled Krampel, pointing their pikes toward his heart.

Krampel had no idea what to do. He stood there with his eyes wide as he noticed all the guardsmen—there were five of them—surrounding him, a simple, skinny lad. He knew he was in deep trouble if they had every guardsman on this case. His heart raced, thundering against his breastbone, as if it wanted to cut through and escape his chest.

"What's the commotion?" a voice barked from behind him, and the guardsmen closer to the center of the township yielded their positions as a burly man in a sleeping gown and cap strode through.

"We caught the lad stealing bread from old man Willerd, my lord," said the first guard, pointing at Krampel with his right hand. "He was trying to escape."

The large man nodded and then circled Krampel slowly. Krampel felt that he measured him carefully, taking stock in what he saw before him. He made one more pass before he thrust his finger under the boy's chin and raised his head so he can look right into his eyes.

"What do you have to say for yourself, boy?" he demanded.

Krampel glared back at the man, somehow no longer fearful. He was no longer a slave—at least in his mind he wasn't—but he still did not like someone manhandling him like this. He stared right back at the man with hardened eyes, but he stayed defiantly silent.

"Nothing to say, eh? Maybe a night in chains will loosen your tongue," the man said before nodding to the guardsmen, who escorted Krampel away, the bread still clamped in his hands.

The chains won't make me talk, Krampel thought. *I've endured much worse over the past ten months, and I will survive this.*

***

The next morning, word had filtered through the town to those who had remarkably slept through the commotion: a tramp had broken into the baker's shop, and that tramp was now in custody. The townspeople tried to peek into what served as the jailhouse, to no avail. The baker himself wanted to see who had broken into his store and had stolen a portion of the day's profits.

Among those who wished to see the lad was Vossler. The old man had heard about the incident and was naturally curious; hardly anything ever happened in Cassimina, and he had found it laughable to post a guard at all. However, the previous night's events made him bite his tongue, at least for a few minutes.

As the bell in the clock tower of the village square rang nine times, Vossler watched the guardsmen make their way through the crowd escorting the young lad, ropes tied hard around his wrists. He felt a lump rise in his throat as he saw the boy's face, and he immediately knew him.

He remembered the scene as if he couldn't get rid of it; in fact, the memory had kept him up all night long. He saw the pain inflicted on the lad, and then the caravan master wanted to whip him for seeing him whip the boy. His desire to help the lad was strong then, and that desire was even stronger now that he had seen him again, once again a prisoner.

His eyes immediately widened, the breath catching in his throat.

He had an idea, and he only needed to put a few words in the right ear for the idea to grow.

Vossler tried to contend with the crowd as they moved toward the open area of the town square to watch the proceedings. The old man knew these people; he felt their anxiety ripple. He knew they wanted to see justice carried out for a crime that was, in their eyes, committed against each and every one of them.

He darted off to the side to move a little faster. He walked with his usual noticeable limp, his cane propelling him forward faster than he liked. He didn't stop walking, even as the pains rippled across his shins, until he came to a small building where he figured the town leaders now gathered. The leaders would emerge from here in a few minutes.

But Vossler wanted a word with them first, before they dispensed the township's justice.

The door was unguarded, which was a blessing in disguise for the old man; he didn't want to tell a youngster to move aside. He opened the door and strode right in without a second glance.

The leaders turned at the sound of the door opening. The three of them wore ceremonial trappings of red, blue, and gold silken robes, and each looked ready to listen to the day's ordeals.

"Before you listen to the guard, you need to hear me out," Vossler said before giving a formal greeting. "That boy has been wronged by more in his life than anything you three can dish out this morning."

The three men looked at each other with wide eyes, then looked back to Vossler.

"What do you mean, Vossler?" the one in blue said.

"He's a slave, Erig," Vossler replied quickly, "at least he was when he came here yesterday with the caravan. I guess he escaped some time during the night, and somehow made his way here. We can't let them take him back. He deserves freedom, and you can give it to him this morning."

Erig raised his bushy eyebrows at Vossler's unspoken request. Vossler watched as he looked to his fellow leaders for support. They were, surprisingly, noncommittal.

"I don't know what we can do for the lad; we haven't even heard evidence yet. What we have heard, though, was that the baker turned him way when he came around to look for food. Then he broke in after the baker left, so his crime was premeditated.

"We're also going through hard times; theft of this kind is a theft against all, not just one man. We may need to call for the greatest punishment we can dish out," Erig said.

Vossler immediately thought they would put the lad to death, but the next thought didn't exactly calm his fears, either. They would probably sever his hands, which, to a starving lad, was worse than death.

"Let me take him," he said. "The boy has known nothing but suffering in his life. We can protect him."

The leader in red chuckled.

"You must be getting soft in your old age, Vossler. Ten years ago, you would have wanted to chop off his hands, too. What happened to you?"

Vossler ambled a few steps further, his cane rapping on the dirt. The thump echoed through the small room.

"You didn't see what I saw in his eyes yesterday. He has the spirit, gentlemen. It is such a spirit inside him that the caravan hasn't beaten out of him. It's such a natural spirit that has to be nurtured by one with the experience to bring it out of him." He paused and set both hands on his cane. "I want the boy to live with me," Vossler said.

"If we were to grant you that request, do you think the Crassnicks would keep our secret safe, especially if it is known that the lad is an escaped slave? If the caravan came looking for him tomorrow, Danith Crassnick would get as much gold for the information as he could, and then some!"

"That is why we need to make this happen silently and quickly!" Vossler retorted. "We cannot let a case be made against him."

"The entire town has seen him, so it would be very difficult to keep this quiet. And if word gets out that we let the boy go, it would send a message to everyone that they can break the laws of Cassimina whenever they want."

Vossler sighed and felt his body shudder under the weight of his burden. He wanted to free that lad so badly that he hadn't thought about the other side of the coin. By freeing this lad, who had so blatantly broke the law, the council would, in essence, send a message to everyone that breaking the law is okay. They were right.

But, stubborn as he was, he still needed to free the boy. He had no other choice. There was so much potential inside of him. Vossler knew he was the only one around with the power to release it.

"I've seen his eyes," he continued at nearly a whisper. "He is a fighter; with the right person to nourish him, he would be the greatest of them all."

That was all he said. He had said his peace, but as he looked into their eyes before he turned to leave, he noticed the impact his final words had on the three men. They sat there with their eyes wide, apparently dazed by the old man's premonition.

Vossler walked out of the chamber and found everyone looking at him, as if waiting for an explanation. But he paid them no attention; instead he looked to the lad and smiled. He then ambled over to him, his limp apparent, to stand by his side. He kept eye contact with the slave and saw the fire there, still contained within his watery globes.

He knew deep inside that this boy was the one, the one Huckleby had promised him. Vossler needed to make sure he was free.

When he drew next to the boy, he patted the lad's shoulder and said, "Don't worry, it'll be fine."

The boy, he noticed, didn't recoil. He simply kept his eyes looking forward, his gaze on the small dais where the council would eventually decide his fate.

The whispers started, but Vossler easily tuned them out. He had lived here too long to know or care what the gossipmongers thought about his decision to stand next to the boy.

Minutes later, the door opened again. One of the leaders came out by himself and walked over to where the boy sat, keeping his eyes on the lad while he strode out into the open town square. Vossler stood at the lad's left shoulder, and he, too, looked at the solitary man with a quickened heartbeat.

When he stopped and stood in front of them, the gathered throng became silent.

"Come with me, boy. Vossler, you may come, too," the man said, turning back to the small room.

With wide eyes, the boy looked to Vossler. Grinning, he nodded to the boy, then followed as soon as the youngster stood up. The old man felt the eyes of the entire town on his back, and he heard the increasingly raising voices as they made the walk, without guards, together.

Once inside, the leadership wasted no time.

"Sit down."

The boy did as ordered, although, Vossler noted, he did so with a touch of difficulty; he figured the wounds on his buttocks were still rather fresh and painful to the touch. He remained at the boy's left shoulder, stoically silent. The three leaders also sat down and looked at the accused with sharp eyes.

"Tell us about your life before coming here."

***

Krampel didn't know where to begin. He closed his eyes and tried to focus on one starting point, but had trouble doing so. He opened his eyes, then decided to start with the most recent memory first.

"I've been a slave for the past ten months," he began. "My mother sold me into slavery so she could buy curatives. She had been sick for so long; I'm not even sure if she's still alive. Our life together was rough, we hardly had any money for food. I don't know how I survived this long, because the slavers didn't feed me well, either, and I have been hungry for as long as I can remember. Late last night, I took a small bit of meat from the slavers' fire, and they beat me in punishment. I decided that it was time for me to leave, to stop being a slave. I wrestled my hands free of the ropes that bound me, then I ran as fast as my legs could take me. I came here, unaware that I had been here before. I was starving, and I smelled the bread baking. I had asked for some, but the man was gruff and wasn't kind at all. So I decided to hide and take some.

"I'm very sorry for what I did," he finished, feeling that was all that needed to be said.

The leaders paid rapt attention to the boy's history, nodding along with every sentence.

"You know you have done wrong, and for that we accept your apology. But as for your punishment, that is what we will discuss now," Erig said.

Krampel tensed and held his breath.

"There are many in this town who would see you have your hands severed for stealing their bread; the bread in this town is for all, not just one person. A crime of this nature is a crime against the entire populace of Cassimina.

"But we are forgiving where many would be severe in their punishments. We have considered several statements, including the one you just gave and the one given by the gentleman standing behind you. He feels you can be rehabilitated. He says you have promise, and that your potential is very great. So our decision, which is final, is that your punishment will be to serve this man not as a slave, but as an apprentice. You will be given three hearty meals a day; you will not sleep in squalor, and you will be healthy for the first time in your life."

Erig smiled as he spoke, but Krampel didn't. He had never known true freedom—he either worked hard for his mother and father, and then the caravan worked him beyond his body's emotional and physical limitations—but now, he suddenly found himself apprenticed to the man behind him. He was still, however technically, indentured.

The council ordered the bonds from his wrists removed, and Krampel walked out of the leaders' chambers with the old man's hand on his shoulder.

Not for the last time, Krampel wondered if running away from the caravan was worth it.

He wondered, but not for the first time that day, if he would ever truly be free.

Chapter 3

The next few weeks turned out the toughest for the former slave boy known as Krampel. In that time, the only person that regarded him with any civility was his master. They had felt the boy got off practically scot-free, leaving the leaders with a simple warning.

As the weeks turned into months, though, the people of Cassimina slowly warmed to his presence—especially the young ladies of the town, who seemed to enjoy his company once Vossler had him cleaned up and properly fed. Krampel had gained a little weight, helping to fill out his underfed body, and the girls certainly took notice. Once he started to work on the farms, his body developed muscle—even if still on the lean side—which made the girls giggle and blush at the sight of it.

Of course, the girls' attentions to the young newcomer meant several of the lads had grown jealous of him. Some remained friendly with the boy, but as Krampel realized that was only to stick a knife in his back at the opportune time. Some tried to mock him for his background, but once they realized the girls had paid no attention to their snide remarks, they needed to come up with a new plan.

The one who came up with a plan was Piety Crassnick, the leader of the gang.

Piety was Krampel's age, and he quickly turned into his fiercest nemesis. As the son of Danith Crassnick, many of the locals gave him a wide berth and a certain respect—the Crassnicks were bullies, and no one wanted to cross them.

Piety stood slightly taller than Krampel, with blond hair that came down past his ears. His eyes were so gray they actually looked like dwarven whitesilver, and his nose was thin to a point. His jaw, however, was his prominent feature—it resembled his father's so much that people said Piety would turn out just as much the bully as Danith was now.

The son of Crassnick wanted to bring the newcomer down a few notches. He wanted to show him who really controlled the town, and to whom he should pay his allegiance.

He executed his plan while Krampel ran a few errands for the old man.

Krampel had his hands full of meat and bread—the baker didn't even want to look at him, but he took Vossler's money without complaint—and he walked with Rosaline, a pretty neighbor girl. They had passed the village green when Piety leapt out of a tree and landed right on top of the boy, sending the goods flying and Krampel sprawling to the ground. Rosaline shrieked as Piety started to pound on the lad, his fists coiled and going straight for the sides of his head. She turned and ran to find help for Krampel.

But Piety Crassnick had somehow failed to realize that Krampel's constitution was much stronger than he had originally believed. Krampel quickly rolled over, even with Piety's weight resting on his lower back, and fired a punch around Piety's flying fists. His punch landed along Piety's jaw line, sending the bully flying off him.

"So you want to fight, huh?" Krampel asked.

He didn't wait for an answer, as he leapt on Piety and let the blows fall on the now whimpering bully. A fist landed on the nose, breaking it, and one powerful punch landed near the kidneys, making Piety gasp for air. Krampel did not relent for even a second, and soon the other boy cried for his mother. Piety's mates stood aghast, having rushed to witness his intended bullying as soon as he had leapt at Krampel from the tree. They glanced at each other, worry spreading between them, to see who would eventually tear Krampel away from their friend.

Not one of them moved; they apparently didn't want to get caught up in the maelstrom of whirling fists that seemed to attack Piety with mindless abandon.

The fire inside Krampel had ignited, and there was no chance of extinguishing it any time soon. Piety Crassnick's attack was the worst type, and he soon paid for his actions with his blood. The force of Krampel's fists led to bleeding from Piety's nose and mouth; after his punches left Piety moaning, Krampel grabbed the boy's blond tresses and rubbed his face in the dirt, just to embarrass him even more.

"Krampel!" yelled a voice from behind the brawl. "Get off of him!"

Krampel turned and saw Vossler coming out of his home limping rapidly as the walking stick pounded hard on the dirt. His strides came with such precision that it appeared the old man ran toward them.

Reluctantly, Krampel got off the young boy, who immediately got up and ran home crying, his friends trailing him. He didn't even rip off a scathing comment to denounce his rival.

"Get home right now before Danith Crassnick comes looking for you," Vossler warned. "You never should have turned the tables on him like you did."

"You wanted me to let him beat me up?" Krampel said incredulously to his master—just before he felt a sharp crack of flesh against bone.

Vossler had whacked him hard off the side of the head with an open palm.

"Don't you see? By beating on Danith Crassnick's boy, you're putting yourself in his sights. He'll ride day and night, looking for the caravan—or he'll kill you himself," Vossler said.

Krampel's face fell, the blood leaving his face.

"Oh," he simply said. "I didn't think about that."

Vossler snorted.

"Yes, I can see that. Now get home; I'll cut Danith off. Rosaline, you rush off, too."

Neither Krampel nor Rosaline said another word to each other. He simply rushed off for the old man's home and closed the door behind him, while Rosaline went the other way.

***

Vossler looked down at the mess on the ground. He shook his head as he bent down to grab the two loaves of bread that spilled out of the sack Krampel had carried. Groaning, he stuffed them back inside the sack and turned toward his home.

Within reach of his front door, the booming voice of Danith Crassnick filled his ears.

"Here we go," Vossler whispered before he turned around to find Crassnick practically in his face.

"Where is the slave? I'll teach him for touching my boy!"

"You won't teach him anything, Danith. The lad had to protect himself from your son, who jumped him with his back turned. If anything, you should teach your son to fight fairer," Vossler admonished.

That only steamed Crassnick even more. He was ready to push him aside and enter Vossler's home uninvited, but the old man followed through with an earlier threat, shoving his cane into his chest, pushing him backward.

"You are sadly mistaken, Danith. You will not go near the boy, nor will you even think about getting even with him. What's done is done; you can't get involved in their quarrels."

"I have my family's honor to uphold!" Crassnick bellowed. "I can't have a slave beating up a boy with our lineage!"

Vossler sighed, shaking his head.

"You have a stubborn streak in you that I never thought to be possible. Your supposed 'family honor' is nothing more than a group of bullies with an heir that will now be afraid of his own shadow. You can take your family honor and tell it to someone who cares about such things. I, for one, do not. Now leave my doorstep before I really show you stubborn!"

Vossler's eyes grew hot as he spoke, as if he possessed the ability to bore holes into Danith Crassnick's head. The bigger man's lip twitched. Vossler saw Crassnick going through a thought process of stormy upheaval. His eyes, dark with anger, closed briefly. He turned and, even though Vossler noticed that his anger hadn't even ebbed, walked away from the old man.

As soon as Crassnick was away, Vossler let out a long, deep breath and wiped a layer of sweat that had suddenly appeared on his brow. He shook his head, then turned and entered his house.

Krampel sat by the fire, his heaving back to the door. He didn't even turn around when Vossler entered. He just stared into the flames, seemingly deep in his thoughts.

Vossler's cane echoed through the small room as it rapped on the wooden floor. The old man walked toward the hearth to look at the lad. Krampel did not turn his head.

The old man grimaced, then left to let the boy stew. He brought the meat and bread to the kitchen, where he wiped the sand from the pack and the two loaves that fell from it. Vossler then lit a small fire and cooked their evening meal, which they ate in complete silence.

The pair did not speak another word that day, nor did they speak the next.

***

Vossler finally broke the deep silence two days after Krampel had defeated Piety.

He found the lad working in the leather shop, sewing up a pair of breeches for himself. Krampel aggressively sewed, pulling the thick brown thread through the holes with such force that he nearly snapped it.

"You better watch it, there," Vossler said with a light smile, trying to end the tension between them. "You may have to re-sew those again."

"It keeps my mind off Piety," Krampel replied, his tone curt, his voice on a knife-edge.

"Ah, words to the contrary," said Vossler, who had limped forward and rested his body against the table, looking directly at his ward. "Your actions betray your statements. You are still angry by what he did to you that you care not about who you hurt because of it. Your anger should be directed at him, not anyone else—especially not the person who agreed to take you in and protect you from the caravan."

Vossler's words stung Krampel, and the lad felt humbled by them. Krampel went deep into thought about his actions the past two days: He walked around the home like a twister, leaving everything he touched overturned or in total disarray. He had not been friendly toward anyone—especially Vossler and Rosaline, who tried to show her concern for him the day before—and shrugged off anyone who checked on him.

"You're right," Krampel said, looking back into Vossler's eyes, calming himself. "I've been very foolish. I apologize."

Vossler walked around the table and put a hand on the lad's shoulder, walking him away from his work.

"Your apology is accepted, as it always will be, my young friend. Now, do not think about him anymore."

"It's kind of hard not to, you know. The damned coward jumped me from behind!"

"Because that is what he does," the old man countered. "It is how he was trained. He would rather hit from behind, with someone's eyes off him, than face someone man to man. He is like his father; a bully that picks on those lesser in size. You taught Piety Crassnick a lesson without knowing it; you humbled him and taught him not to underestimate those smaller than he." Vossler paused. "You have such great gifts, Krampel. You are a very special young man. You just don't know it yet. I have seen the talent you have, and I want you to see it for yourself.

"Come with me."

Blinking away his confusion, Krampel followed Vossler back into the main house. Vossler brought him to a corner in the southern part of the house and reached down to grab a rope tied around a circlet of steel. It was a trap door. Vossler winced as he bent down, but his hand could not grab it.

"Grab the rope for me, lad, and open the door," Vossler commanded. Krampel and then stood out of the way when the square door finished creaking open.

Below the door was a thin set of stairs, the room below dark. Vossler ambled down the staircase, putting the cane ahead of his feet. Krampel grabbed a lantern, lit it with the twist of a knob, and followed suit. Shadows escaped the light of Krampel's lantern, and when they reached the bottom of the stairs, Vossler turned and took the lantern from Krampel's hands. He lit several torches that hung on the wall, and soon the chamber filled with dancing orange light.

"Welcome to the dungeon," Vossler announced as he turned to face Krampel. His voice bounced a bit. "This is my hideaway, where I avoid the rush of the people above." He spoke in slow, measured tones. "I trained with the weapons in this room, long ago, when I went to war. I brought all of them here under the cover of darkness one night, free of peeping Cassiminian eyes. I brought them here so that one day I could train another to fight like I fought. I wanted to train Danith Crassnick, but he was too stubborn and wretched to follow my teachings. Others came under my eye and went just as quickly.

As I saw it, none of them would ever be committed enough. So, I patiently waited.

"And just when I thought I would never find someone that I could teach, someone to whom I could pass on my knowledge, I heard you being whipped. I saw the fire in your eyes, Krampel, and I thought to myself that you had what it takes to be the next great warrior. If you are willing, if you are strong enough, I can train you to be a fighter; I can train you to be that great warrior. You have the instincts necessary to be a fighter, Krampel. I sense it within you. And yes, the way you turned the tide against young Piety the other day proved to me that you have it all.

"That is why I took you in, my boy. That is why I had to make sure you were not punished all those months ago. You have everything that I have ever wanted in a trainee, and I had to make sure you were able to train. My motives were purely personal and selfish, and I feel no shame in admitting it to you now. But, I also did this for you; you can be great, Krampel. You just need to have your potential unlocked, so the realms can recognize you as being the greatest fighter to ever live. And I want to be the one to unlock it."

Krampel stood in the torchlight and looked at Vossler in complete disbelief. He did not accept what the old man had just told him, but deep within his heart, he believed every single word. He knew he had a fire within him, a passion that burned brightly. The caravan had tried to beat it out of him, unsuccessfully, and now here was a man who had saved him from a life of oppression and wanted to free his fighting spirit.

But while he wanted to say yes right away, he needed to think about everything that was in front of him.

"I don't know what to say," he said.

Vossler chuckled aloud.

"You can start by saying 'yes.'"

This time it was Krampel's turn to give a small, throaty laugh.

"Let me think about it all, then I'll tell you later of my decision."

Then he turned and walked up the stairs, leaving Vossler alone in his sanctuary.

***

The next night, just as they finished their dinner, Vossler called Krampel downstairs to the dungeon. Once again, Vossler asked him the question of questions.

"Yes," Krampel said. "My answer is yes. I want you to unlock what is inside of me. Teach me everything you know. Make me the greatest fighter ever. I am yours to command."

Vossler watched as Krampel went to his knees and bowed his head reverently. This was exactly as he had envisioned, and he found himself surprised that the boy had succumbed to his wishes as easily as he did. He smiled at his new protégé, then instructed him to stand. Krampel smiled and then turned to return upstairs, but Vossler stopped him first with a hand. He limped over to a table and picked up a long scabbard with a sword inside it, the handle gold. He limped back to the boy and handed it to him.

"This sword will be your best friend, your confidante. It will be attached to you over the next few years, as you train hard to be the best of the best. You will have it next to you at all times; when you sleep, it will be in your arms, and when you are bathing, it will be next to you. When you are walking in the streets, it will be on your hip to let everyone know that you are the warrior of warriors. It will make them fear you, but respect you at the same time.

"But most of all, most of all, Krampel my lad, it will be a tool of your growing skill, and you will become symbiotic with it. The sword will be an extension of your arm, and you will learn to fight with it—and without it. You will learn every aspect to fighting, and you will learn how to dissect every situation of a war. You will be the greatest fighter ever—with this sword."

Krampel held the scabbard and grasped the handle, then pulled the sword out. The four-and-a-half foot blade sprawled out of it, and Krampel held it reverently, as if it was the most precious item he ever held. Vossler saw the steel sparkling in his eyes. He smiled at the reflection.

"Yes," Vossler hissed. "Become familiar with this blade. It will be the blade you will forever carry, the sword that brings you your destiny.

"Now, think of the power you hold within you, and channel it through the sword."

"How do I do that?" Krampel quickly asked.

"Take a deep breath, and ask your heart to unlock what is within you. Then swing the sword in a curving arc," Vossler said.

Krampel swallowed, then looked up at the blade. Then, Vossler noticed the boy's skin now rippled with a feeling he knew Krampel had never felt before. He swung the sword with an amazing intensity, bringing the sword down and around in an arc, a long, blazing trail of kindled fire flying behind the blade's wake. The fire evaporated as soon as he stopped the sword, then held it up. Vossler saw a small trickle of smoke curl up from the edge of the blade.

Krampel whistled.

"Wow!" he exclaimed. "That was incredible."

"Yes it was," Vossler said. "You will learn how to do that at will, without even thinking about it. This is the sword you will carry—as soon as you learn how to wield it properly. Until then," he said, before he took the fiery blade away and handed him a smaller sword, "you will use this."

"You must master the others," he said, his eyes looming dark in the torchlight, "before you can master *Flad-rul*."

Chapter 4

Before he came to Cassimina, Krampel thought his life had been a living hell.

The truth, he discovered, was far different than his perceptions. He also discovered that he didn't know what a living hell meant—until he started sword training with Vossler.

The first day, the old man woke Krampel before the roosters even had the chance to crow. Three successive whacks to the side of the head did it, too, and sometimes a bucket of the previous night's rain followed. He ran laps around the farms: Vossler said he had once trained in a large city in the east where the walls encircled the whole area. He explained that he and a friend ran around the city until he dropped, and his master, seeing the considerable pain Vossler suffered, made him run it again.

"It builds stamina, young one," he cried. "Once more, around the field!"

Krampel rolled his eyes as he took off once again. His legs, already like rubber, churned the dust about as he ran. Sweat poured off him following four laps around the farm: if he tripped and fell, Vossler made him wear the dirt all day until it was time to wash.

His chest heaved as he ran, but as the days continued, the heaving lessened. His stamina increased with each time around the fields. Vossler ordered him to run in the cold, the heat, and the rain. With each passing day, he grew healthier.

Once he finished with his run, Vossler brought him down to the dungeon. As soon as they had the torches lit, the old man put him through his paces, working on sword form with both one-handed and two-handed grips. Krampel grew more proficient with the blade as the sessions grew longer, and deep into the evenings.

Vossler made him pay for mistakes. A crack of a whip across the room nearly came close to breaking Krampel's skin, and once again the fire ignited in the lad's eyes. The memories of the caravan came to him, but the boy pushed those away; he was no longer there, and the old man wanted him to focus on his future. He gritted his teeth, took a deep breath, and then, after resetting his posture, he executed the move correctly, only to get a small grin from the old man in response.

Krampel let the breath out, and that, too, received a crack of the whip from Vossler.

"Don't become lackadaisical!" Vossler warned. "That is the fastest way to getting your head chopped off! Now, do it again until you are flawless in your stance!"

Krampel blushed as Vossler admonished him. The old man was right, after all. It was indeed possible a warrior's first mistake ended a sword fight. Krampel certainly didn't want all of Vossler's training to go for naught because he breathed at the wrong time.

He half-bowed to the old man, then set his feet accordingly. He then ripped off a flurry of moves, first right, then left, then straight down the center, turning his back so his shoulders rolled into a spin. Steel rippled against faux steel, and Krampel then brought the sword around, only to find it stopped by the sword Vossler held. The blades clanged together, leaving a sharp ringing in Krampel's eardrums. He stared at his master, wide-eyed, one that matched the stare his master gave him before Vossler pulled the four-and-a-half foot sword off to the side. Krampel relaxed.

The old man then began his lecture.

"*Flad-rul*," he said, referring to the blade in his hand. "The greatest of all the greatswords. Five there were in olden times, all lost, save this one. All had magic that would give the bearer of the blade immense fame and power. The others are known only by the names the gods gave them; they know no other name. Their names are *Karan-thul*, the Storm Creator; *Thulan-ra*, the Bright Blade; *Seron-pi*, the Blade of Disasters; and *Melan-don*, the Cyclone Summoner.

"But all of them paled in comparison to *Flad-rul*, the Flame Thrower, the blade of my former master, the high elf Tyrence Huckleby. The blades held by kings were no match for this sword. In order to wield it properly, to even carry it, one must be agile enough, cunning enough, and smart enough. All throughout the realms there are those who would wish to see the wielder of this sword dead, only to be slain by its point. This sword, while hot, does not cauterize; it slices victims apart and scalds them. In order to wield this blade, you must be impervious to their screams as you take their lives from them. Their terror can be used against them; you will find that their fear is your greatest strength."

Krampel listened to the old man's words and felt his own terror flood through his mind. He never thought he would take someone's life, but he realized Vossler's training had set him up to do just that.

And since Vossler planned on giving him *Flad-rul*, Krampel knew that one day, he would slice into another human for the first time, ending his life.

He shivered at the thought.

"I received *Flad-rul* from my master before I went off to war on my own my first time. That was coming on fifty-five years ago. I was young, a little older than you are now, and my master told me how this sword caused people to run for their lives. None wanted to face it in battle, for the effects of losing were too great. They would have rather faced *Flad-rul*'s brothers instead: Being drown or blind was better than being charred from the inside."

Krampel let a grin tumble off his lips.

The old man continued.

"This is a special sword, Krampel. This sword will gain you the respect of many and will make you a hated man by those who do evil deeds, but holding *Flad-rul* will show all that you are the best fighter in all the realms. You will get to that point someday, but it takes the dedication that I know you have locked away deep inside you. Now, step back and show me what you have learned."

Vossler snapped *Flad-rul* back into its scabbard and laid it on the bench before grabbing another sword, this one slightly worn. He brought it up to an en guard position, then stared at Krampel, who had yet to raise his own rusted blade.

The boy looked at the old man as if he were mad.

"You don't expect me to fight you, do you? You're half-crippled," Krampel said incredulously.

"Do not be lulled into complacency by my handicap," Vossler said, nearly snarling his words. And just to prove his point, his limp lessened with each step as he circled the boy.

He stalked Krampel, and the boy, with a sharp intake of breath, quickly realized his mistake.

"Your handicap is a façade," Krampel mused. "A feint used to trick people into believing something you're not."

This time, it was Vossler who grinned.

"Precisely, my boy. My deception is my strength. I'm as hale at seventy-three as I was when I first held *Flad-rul* back in the summer of my youth," he said, before he rushed in and tried to lay a heavy blow on Krampel's left flank. The boy reacted, deflecting it with ease. Vossler brought his sword around quickly, trying to strike at Krampel's right side. But the boy was a second quicker, as he noticed the move before it happened. He kept the blade parallel to his body, waiting for a chance to make an offensive counter.

Vossler didn't let him have it. The old man snapped off a flurry of moves, and the smile on his face as he locked eyes with the lad in front of him showed that he greatly enjoyed this sparring.

When Vossler made a hard, swinging cut that brought his sword parallel to the floor, Krampel dropped to the floor with the speed of a guillotine blade—a rolling guillotine blade. He came up behind his mentor, then smacked the side of his own blade against the backs of Vossler's knees, ending the duel then and there.

"Ha! Very good, lad! Positioning is very important—you used your position to your advantage. You created an offensive move when I tried to end it. Remember that the best offense is a good defense, and proper positioning can be the difference between living and dying," Vossler praised, chuckling and smiling all the while. He patted Krampel on the back as the youth stood all the way up.

"You must also remember to memorize all of the major moves; that way, you will be an intuitive fighter, a fighter that is unstoppable."

Krampel nodded. He knew he still had a long way to go to be a great fighter, and knew the opening was one Vossler had given him, to boost his confidence. The lad knew the openings would be few and far between from now on, and that he would have to work especially hard to wield the great sword with the honor that Vossler had when he was younger.

"Master," Krampel asked, "how did *Flad-rul* come to be in your possession?"

Vossler, who turned to put his sword back on the table next to *Flad-rul*, stopped suddenly at Krampel's question. He turned back to face the boy with a grave look on his face. His brows had furrowed, his eyes full of sadness.

"It was my master's sword once, as I have already said," he said, looking at the dusty floor. "Back then, masters handed their apprentices valued possessions the young ones would need in their daily lives. Some gave potions to young clerics, others gave tomes to young wizards. Generally, older warriors who trained younger ones gave a coat of mail, since the young warrior already had a sword. My own master gave me a coat of mail and steel shin guards, but in one battle, orcs cut my master down, slicing his throat. He couldn't even yell to me, they were on top of him so quickly. I cut my way to him, but I was too late. He had bled to death. When the battle was done, I pried *Flad-rul* from his cold, dead fingers, buried him, then departed the area where we had camped. I haven't been there since."

Vossler walked silently toward the staircase, leaving Krampel alone in his thoughts. Krampel looked down at the floor after hearing his master's words.

He didn't want to do what Vossler did so long ago. He already thought of the old man as a surrogate father, one who looked out for his best interests. Vossler did his best to teach Krampel everything he knew to keep him alive in a fight.

Krampel made a promise to himself at that moment that he would train as hard as he ever had trained before now. He needed to push himself beyond his physical limitations. He knew he had to, because he believed that was the only way he would carry *Flad-rul*—with the honor that Vossler had wielded it for so long.

***

Over the course of a few weeks, Krampel's skill with the sword improved to such a great level that the old man praised him more than he scolded. It got to the point where Vossler looked at his protégé's rising talent with fresh eyes. Seeing Krampel's skills grow made him realize that he made the right decision in saving his life.

Vossler watched as the lad went through his sword movements, watched as the boy's muscles moved with each pass of the blade. He studied the boy, watching as he moved fluidly, as if he danced with the sword. He watched for any flaw that would turn deadly in a fight, any flaw that needed correcting.

He couldn't find one, and with that knowledge, he grinned inwardly. The boy's skill had grown so great that he had failed to find anything to comment on, anything to tweak. He had taught him well, and he knew that Krampel would be his greatest success story.

He looked back to the boy's performance and marveled at his perfect balance, the perfect footwork, the intense look on his face as he swung and cut and jabbed with his practice sword. Vossler deemed his apprentice ready to move up to another level of combat, and he had no doubt in his mind that his ward would easily succeed at the next stage.

"Krampel, come here," he ordered, and without hesitation the lad stopped shadow sparring. He walked over to where Vossler stood.

"Yes, master?"

"You have exceeded all my expectations these last few weeks."

"Thank you, master. It is all thanks to your training." Krampel bowed.

Vossler allowed himself a tight grin. A slight flush came to his unshaven cheeks.

"No, my lad. You have natural skills. Everything you have done so far is because of your own ability. Now it is time for you to move on to the next stage of your training. You have mastered—quite quickly, I might add—the two-handed fighting style, which is, by far, the easiest of the fighting disciplines. You will now learn to fight one-handed—and with this," Vossler said, before he walked over to the training table and picked up a package. An animal skin covered it, and the way Vossler labored slightly to bring it over to Krampel, it looked to be very heavy.

Krampel took the package and felt its circular edge. His eyes widened slightly.

"Is this what I think it is?" he asked.

"Open it, lad. It will help you in the next level of your training and beyond."

Feverishly, Krampel opened the package and found a golden shield inside. Its raised edges resembled flames, painted green, with a dragon breathing fire etched into the center of it. The sight of it had Krampel mesmerized, unblinking.

"Master," he said breathlessly, "it is gorgeous."

"It is yours," Vossler said. "It is yours to wield in battle. You have earned the right to advance in your training, and this is the next step. The shield will protect you more than it will hinder you, Krampel. You will find it constricting in your battle stance at first, but as you grow in skill, it will become a part of you."

"I don't know what to say, master. This is... this is the most wonderful thing anyone has ever given me."

Vossler looked hard at his apprentice.

"Don't be so naïve, young one. A trinket such as this is not as wonderful as the gift your mother gave you."

Krampel furrowed his eyebrows and looked at Vossler.

"My mother?! That wench gave me to the caravan because she couldn't afford to keep me, and I ended up treated worse than a common mule! My mother gave me the foulest existence one ever thought up!" he yelled. The dust from the ceiling fell to the floor in his rage.

Vossler understood the lad's fury and why he felt justified in his rage, but it was time to knock just a little bit of sense into him.

"Your mother did not know what she was doing when she gave you to them, so do not even think to blame her for what happened. Your mother thought she was doing what was best for you; she was in a desperate situation. She gave you the most precious gift of all—your life. You should do well to remember that without her, you wouldn't be alive.

"And if it weren't for me, you wouldn't be standing here today. You will remember that the next time you want to raise your voice to me in my home," Vossler said. "We will begin the next stage of your training tomorrow morning. Perhaps by then you will have matured enough to train with a shield. Perhaps by then you will have learned to shield your tongue."

Vossler walked away from the youth, his cane thundering away, even on the dusty floor.

***

Ashamed, Krampel looked to the floor as he heard the sounds of his mentor's footsteps heading up the stairs, and when he heard the door shut, he dropped the shield to the ground, the steel colliding with a sudden, hard thunk. He felt the emotion rising in him, and without a second thought, he hit his knees. Bone thudded off the floor, but the pain there didn't compare to the pain in his chest.

He felt the tears slide down his cheeks, tears he couldn't stop even if he wanted.

He cried for his mother and for all the time that he resented her, and he didn't think the tears would ever ebb.

Chapter 5

A light rain fell on Cassimina the next morning. Children splashed in puddles while the womenfolk covered their heads as they walked from shop to shop. The men, out working in the fields and tending to the cattle, barely acknowledged the rain as they tirelessly went about their daily chores.

Sweat coursed down Krampel's broadening chest as he moved around Vossler's training dungeon. He held the sword in his right hand and strapped the shield on his left forearm as he went through his exercises, most of which he adapted to fit his new style of fighting. Krampel started early in the morning, even before Vossler awoke.

The thoughts of what happened the day before haunted the lad, and it had kept him awake half the night. He figured the only way to make up for it was to train harder than he had ever trained before. That's the reason why he drove himself to a healthy sweat this morning. He worked on cleansing his body of the thoughts he had stewed in over the past twelve hours.

He quickly learned that keeping his breathing even was the key to learning the new style. With the two-handed style, he breathed with every thrust and parry; with the new style, he breathed with every block, thump with the shield, and jab, which was, at first, difficult to insert into his arsenal of moves. But as soon as he had that skill pinned down, and that did not take as long as he had originally thought, it became second nature to him. He instantly set to work on sparring, imagining opponents on all sides, with each ghost trying to cut into him. He slashed and bobbed and weaved and thumped the skulls of invisible attackers with the golden shield, all while keeping his feet moving, never trying to hem himself into a corner. He spun left and then right, bringing the sword around as the lead on every even turn, using the shield as the lead on the odd turns. It got to the point where his movements had grown so fluid that he actually felt like he stood in a heavy battle scenario.

The torchlight helped his imaginary scenarios, too. The flickering flames cast different shadows throughout the dungeon, making it easy for Krampel to envision attackers in every corner. With several easy swipes of his sword, he dispatched them all with victorious yells.

A new set of shadows emerged when the trapdoor opened hastily. Krampel turned and awaited the telltale footsteps of his master to come down the stairs.

Instead, it was his voice that echoed into the dungeon.

"Krampel, come outside quickly and be armed. Bring *Fladrul* to me!" Vossler ordered sharply. Without another thought, Krampel sheathed his blade, rushed to the table and grabbed the greatsword, then bounded the stairs two at a time. He swept through the room and out the door, where the rain continued falling on the township. It matted his mahogany hair and plastered his bangs to just above his eyes.

"Here!" Vossler called, and Krampel ran over to him, trekking through the puddles with a light crash. He handed the old man his sword, and Vossler strapped the scabbard to his belt with a quickness that amazed the youngster.

"What's going on?" Krampel asked.

"Orcs have been sighted by the watch over the hill yonder. They are getting antsy; they have been underground for far too long. The cloud cover and the rain gives aid to their attack," Vossler answered. "We're joining the defense of the town; the women and children are going down into an underground hideout.

"This is going to be the greatest challenge of your young life. Remember everything that I've taught you, and you should be all right."

Krampel swallowed and nodded, then looked toward the small hill that overlooked Timber Lake. He hefted the shield in his left hand and pulled his sword out of the scabbard, ready to fight the bloodthirsty beasts. The sound of the steel shaft coming out of the covering echoed throughout the township; it sent the tiny hairs on the back of his neck reaching toward his once-flowing mane with invisible fingers.

He felt a slight breeze blowing against his wet skin, followed by a stench he had never smelled before. It was a rancid stink, like rotten meat mixed with the smell of stale milk and old, spoiled cabbage. The scent assaulted his nostrils and made him recoil.

"Steady lad," Vossler said. "That's the orcs' ghastly smell. They are close. Be on your guard."

Krampel raised his right hand to his face, but he found he couldn't pinch his nose to stop the vile aroma from overpowering his senses. If he pinched his nose with his right hand, he would drop his sword. If he did it with his left hand, he would knock himself out with his own shield. It wasn't the way to start his first battle. He soon put the orc smell out of his mind and concentrated on the upcoming scrum.

Soon, several other men joined the pair, and every few seconds passed before another man joined the throng. Then, without warning, an arrow flew over the hill and landed inside the chest cavity of one of the defenders. He fell backward as the arrow pierced his heart.

Krampel looked down at his fallen comrade and wondered, *That could have been me.*

"That's it, men. Let's get the devils and blast them from the realms!" one of the men said, which preceded a hearty bunch of encouraging yells from the others. They rushed off toward the hill, their swords raised toward the heavens, each singing a song of praise to their war gods.

"The idiots are going to get themselves killed," Vossler said, spitting to the ground.

"Yeah, if the smell doesn't kill them first," Krampel replied. He tried once again to move his hand to his face, but thought better of it. He caught Vossler grinning slowly, before the old man motioned for his apprentice to follow him. "Get ready. The orcs will come in great multiples. Be ready for anything."

"Don't worry about that. I'm ready for anything they can dish out."

Krampel slowly jogged ahead of the old man, ready to slay this band of attacking orcs. Within seconds, he had started a full trot toward the hill, and by the time he made it to the bottom, the lad was in a full-blown run—yet he stopped cold. He looked up and saw the others had stopped, as well, right at the top. He watched as they simply stood there, and it left him baffled. His mind had turned devoid of thought, but he wondered why they stood there when they had started to attack—

Krampel soon saw why they stopped. A split second later, five of them fell to the ground, arrows protruding from their guts. One hefty man rolled down to where Krampel stood, and with his foot, he stopped the body from rolling further.

It was Danith Crassnick, Piety's father. The crags in the dead man's face told the story; he had died in extreme pain.

While Krampel showed no remorse for the man's death—he had not forgotten what Crassnick had threatened to do if he ever came near Piety again—he now realized this might turn into a long and arduous battle for the defenders of Cassimina. He backed up, inhaled, and awaited the rush of the orcs.

Seconds later, the snarls of the bloodthirsty orcs came over the crest of the hill, flashing their deadly, evil blades across the bodies of those who had not retreated.

With wide eyes, Krampel got his first look at the orcs. They were deformed with the pointed ears of elves, but all with dark skin, as if evil flames had burned them over the course of eternity. Some of their bodies seemed sinewy, and some looked like they had swallowed a whole cow, but each carried a sword that had the ability to penetrate skin at any speed, with any amount of strength backing it.

Krampel took two steps up the hill and quickly engaged the first orc, which held its sword above its head. He got his blade up to parry and heard the shrill clang of steel against steel ringing in his ears. He then thumped the orc in the gut with his shield as another orc came up from behind. He saw the first orc double over, the wind leaving its lungs. He fought the second orc one-handed, then flashed his sword left then right, each time hearing the sharp collision.

The orc wound up and swung hard, trying to take Krampel out with one swing. The lad raised his shield in time and, with a spin to the right, cleaved the head off the first orc before he continued the spin and pushed the second beast's blade aside. Krampel's blade came in at a speed resembling terminal velocity on the reversal, and carved a deep gash in the flesh of the evil orc.

A devilish scream curdled the air, but it did not last long—Krampel corrected his swing and plunged the point of his sword right into the orc's heart. It skewered the orc and silenced it, but as Krampel tried to yank his sword loose, it would not budge, not even an inch.

"By the gods!" he swore, repeatedly tugging at the blade until he gave up, instead ripping the curved, scimitar-like blade the orc held out of its hands as another three orcs nearly ran him over. He got it up in time to parry the one on the right while he blocked the beast on the left-hand side with the shield. That left the orc in the middle, and it held its sword two-handed above its head, dagger-like, and ready to stab.

Krampel stared wide-eyed at the blade, then decided to make his move. He spun left and swung the cold, unusual sword with as much strength as he had within him, slicing the middle orc across the chest. The orc stopped in mid-stride and looked down at the long cut across its pectoral muscles while Krampel's blade sailed toward the orc on the left. He severed its left arm, just as his shield came around and smacked the orc on the right on the side of its head. It fell to the ground in a heap while the other two screamed.

Krampel then brought the sword over in an arc, beheading the orc to his left before he reversed the motion to open the other orc on his right from shoulder to hip. It, too, fell dead where it had stood.

"This is easier than I thought," he breathed. He sought out more prey, his blade not sated in the least.

He ran to his left and swung hard after three steps, deflecting the oncoming strike of an orc and knocking its sword askew. Krampel took the opening and shoved his sword into the orc's sternum. It dropped hard, only replaced by another, then another, and then another.

"Where are they all coming from?" Krampel asked.

Instead of an answer to his question, he only heard the growl of the orcs. He slashed horizontally from left to right, cut out the voice box of one while raising his shield to deflect the blade of a rather thin orc. Sparks flew off the shield, and Krampel brought his sword over the shield and engaged it.

The orc's blade crossed Krampel's steel, going back and forth with the young human. When he tried to shove his shield into the orc's gut, it bent itself out of the way. As soon as he noticed that his own poor positioning gave the orc an opening, he turned quickly to the right, bringing his blade around to parry the orc's thrust. The swords met with a hard clang. The orc sneered as its opportunity vanished.

Krampel wanted time to wipe the beaded line of sweat that now saturated his brow. He tried to forget it was there, as Vossler's teachings of distractions suddenly flooded his memory. With a quick breath, the fear and sweat disappeared from Krampel's consciousness.

He then twirled the orc sword he held through his fingers and gave a hearty exclamation as he returned to his attack, the sweat rolling down his forehead and flying off his eye socket. He chopped first, attempting to cut the orc's right flank, before he thrust his sword toward the orc's midsection, and at the same time, brought the shield in from the left, the steel sphere flying toward the beast's skull. The orc made a futile attempt to parry, but any chance of recovery was nil. The force of the shield caved its skull in and snapped its neck.

It fell to the ground with an equally resounding thud that resembled steel against bone.

Krampel breathed easier for a second, as he turned and looked for another orc to fight. But as he saw, the rest had scattered from the hillside, beaten back by the men of the town. The attack was for naught, the townspeople seemingly too ready for them. He looked back and forth, then found Vossler holding his forearm. Crimson stained his fingers.

His eyes widening, he hurried to retrieve his own sword from the corpse of the dead orc and then rushed over to the old man, sheathing his sword as he ran. He grabbed hold of Vossler's upper arm as soon as he was close enough to touch him.

Vossler winced.

"What happened?" Krampel asked.

"An orc got me a little; it's just a scratch. Nothing to worry about," Vossler feinted, but Krampel wasn't having it.

"Yeah right, a scratch that has your fingers stained with blood. Let's get this cleaned and bandaged."

"It's okay, I'm not dying; these orcs' blades weren't poisoned, which I'm surprised at, actually. I'd be dead already if their witches' brew was on their edges. Damn it, I can walk, Krampel!" Vossler said, clearly agitated. He shook off the boy's hands and managed to walk over to a stool near the baker's shop. Soon, the town had grown alive with the sounds of crying women; they saw the bodies of their husbands, murdered in the scuffle. Several women came over to check on Vossler's injury. As Krampel watched, Vossler's expression softened as the women looked at the cut—which was not a scratch—and applied a heavy dose of cleaning liquid over it. Vossler crunched up his face as the heavy waves of a not-so-pleasurable sensation passed through him before the women applied a bandage large enough to cover the wound, the bandage treated in medicinal fluid to stave off infection.

A minute later, Vossler stood, the medicine going to work on his arm quickly. He sheathed *Flad-rul* with a snap.

"Let's go. We need to see the leaders and see what they plan to do about our security over the next few days. The orcs will return, and next time they'll come at us in greater numbers. They are like the drow; they were a scouting party, nothing more. They were gauging our strengths and weaknesses. If this were a full-fledged orc invasion, none of us would be alive right now," Vossler rationalized. "I've seen plenty of them to know that I'm right. Let's hurry!"

The duo walked to the town square where the leaders usually met. They used every ounce of speed they pulled from their tired legs.

The room, they found as soon as they barged through the front door, was empty.

"Where could they be? We're in a crisis and they aren't around!" Vossler exclaimed. "This is not like them." He turned to Krampel and then asked, "You didn't see them fighting the orcs, did you?"

Krampel shook his head.

"No, master. And even if they were, I was busy fighting, so it's not like I had the time to know who was around me," Krampel replied.

They walked away from the square, the old man muttering to himself. He pounded on the door of Erig, who did not answer. The next on his list didn't answer, either. The third time, however, was the charm, and he found all three of them holed up with their families. They gave a flimsy excuse as to why they sat here while everyone else fought for the township.

"And if the orcs had gotten past our front lines and burned this home to the ground, what shape would the town be in then? Can you answer me that?" Vossler snarled.

The three leaders looked at each other with blank stares etched across their faces, but Vossler didn't notice them. He paced the floor, the cane long forgotten; he had taken charge of the town's defenses without even a peep from these three governmental buffoons.

"We need to make sure the orcs cannot break through our defenses again. They will come back under the cover of darkness and slaughter us to a man if we are not vigilant. Our guard did a good job the first time in noticing them, but this time it will be different. Their eyes are much sharper than ours, and they will be on top of us before we know it is too late.

"Therefore, all the elder men should maintain a post tonight on the outskirts of the town, holding a torch, awaiting the evil that intends to descend on us. We have to beat them back before they penetrate the town's borders; we don't have walls like the big cities in the south and west. We are out in the open with hardly any defenses, so it is up to us to provide our own defense.

"With your permission, I will instruct the men to ready themselves for the evening watch," Vossler said as he finished his pacing, turning to look at the three men. To Krampel's eye, they seemed shellshocked from the last attack, their clothes rumpled and their hair twisted, and they didn't question Vossler at all. They simply nodded, and that was it. They huddled their families together and held on to them as though for the last time as the two men left them to their own misery.

Vossler's pace quickened as he left the house, and Krampel nearly had to jog to keep up with him. His master led him toward the town square once more.

"Their problem is that they are too concerned with a small group of people, not the entire bunch. If we are to survive as a people, we will all have to work together. It's a fault of many; they care only about themselves, not the whole community of which they reside. It's a pity; they are leaders, and the only thing they are doing is leading their people into a hole in the ground.

"As long as there is life in my lungs, I won't be like them," Vossler said, before reaching for the rope that sounded the bell in the square. He tugged it hard three times with his left hand—not the arm that the orc blade had damaged, which he continued to favor even though the medicinal wraps had started to kick in—and the bell chimed its gong-like tones for all to hear.

The murmurs rose as soon as the vibrations of the bell faded. The townsfolk, some with tear-stained cheeks, others with grim looks of determination, all came forward and wondered why the old man and his lad wanted to speak: It was common knowledge throughout Cassimina that the one who rings the bell wants to say something important to the masses, and usually only the leaders rang the bell.

When they all arrived, Vossler cleared his throat. They looked at him, awaiting his words.

"My dear Cassiminians, we have been brutally attacked; we all have lost loved ones and friends. The orc scouting party will report to their leaders that they have weakened the humans, and they will lead another charge against us in the night. I tell you that we are not as weak as they think we are; our strength is diminished emotionally, but our real strength is coming from those who we fight to remember. We need to stand together and fight them back, tooth and nail, with everything we have inside of us! We will not go lightly, and we will teach those orcs that the village of Cassimina is not ready to be wiped off the map! Who is with me?"

The men gave valiant cries, shooting upward from all around the square, with the sounds of swords sliding out of scabbards echoing all the way down to Timber Lake. The women, Krampel saw, wore agonized expressions on their faces while the rain, which had slowly abated through the battle, came back in heavy torrents and washed the despair from the people of Cassimina.

The boy let it flood his thoughts as the people dispersed.

***

The next few hours felt grueling to all involved.

Vossler's plan on how to ambush the beasts if they broke through the defenses meant every resident in Cassimina had a role to play in its defense. The men dug several ditches near the hill where the orc battle had taken place, working the soil with their spades, turning over mud in great amounts. The children rushed off to Timber Lake with pails: Vossler ordered them to fetch as much water as possible without spilling it, having them bring it to the ditches. The women cooked feverishly, keeping themselves busy at the fires to keep their minds off the upcoming battle.

Yet while the townsfolk worked, Vossler held Krampel back. Instead of having him toil with the others, Vossler brought him into the dungeon and made him continue his exercises.

"We're going to need you at your sharpest," Vossler said, "which means you won't be wasting your time in meaningless work the ordinary folk will be doing. You're a special lad, and you will realize this soon enough. I am proud of you, lad. You fought incredibly hard today, just like I knew you would.

"Now train hard, because we'll need your sword and shield before the night is over."

"Yes, master. I won't fail you again," Krampel replied.

Vossler looked at him with narrowed, inquisitive eyes.

"Why do you feel you've failed me?"

"I dishonored your good graces last night." He swallowed. "I apologize for what I said about my mother."

The frown the old man wore—the one he knew he wore—softened him for a brief moment.

"You haven't failed me, lad, and I forgive you for last night. You're a strong individual in sword, mind, and especially in tongue," Vossler said in the way of a mild reprimand, delivered with a soft smile. "You spoke out of turn, yes, but you had great reasons for saying what you said. I understand now that you're angry with her for what she did, but remember this: Direct your anger elsewhere so you can benefit from it. In addition, try to channel your anger away from your face so that it keeps your blade steady. The worst thing you can do is reveal your anger to an opponent, for he'll take that anger and use it against you. Your anger is an ally to him, and vice versa. I'll check on you in a while. Work hard, my boy."

***

Krampel bowed, and the old man left him to his own devices. As soon as the door to the dungeon had closed, he immediately busied himself with the sparring that he had started all those hours ago. With the words of his mentor echoing through his mind, he soon felt the sweat course down his skin again, felt his heart race in eager anticipation. He worked on the moves that had nearly cost him his life in the battle, and tweaked others that he knew the orcs had not seen yet.

He wanted to give the beasts a surprise they would never expect from a human. He wanted to show Vossler another reason why he was worthy of the old man's training.

He would show the old man his worth the next time the orcs attacked.

Chapter 6

When night fell, the tension throughout the town had grown palpable. The children had asked their mothers innocent questions about their fathers, wondering when they would come home. The mothers had to choke back their own tears, then told the children they would be back soon.

The men, too, appeared nervous and anxious about the night. They thought about their families' safety, their own safety, and the safety of the man next to them. Each held a torch in their non-sword hand, keeping the flames aloft so they saw the surrounding area as far as the light of the fire reached. They also took their swords out, for they did not want an orc to catch them unawares if it came into their sights.

The flames, though, had turned into a beacon for the evil beasts.

Vossler had dispatched the men—and several of the older, stronger lads—to various points surrounding the township. He did not know from where the orcs came, so he decided to cover all potential angles and entryways. The more men he had spread out across the territory, the better.

Besides, he reasoned, if a scuffle broke out, the sounds of swords clashing would echo throughout the dell where Cassimina lay. Everyone would know about it, and Vossler instructed everyone to follow the sounds of the fight to offer backup. He had mapped his plan out to the letter, even though in the back of his mind a nagging feeling slowly lingered. It was a feeling which told him about things going horribly wrong in a short amount of time if they were not careful. That happened in war.

The air felt ripe and heavy with stifling humidity, even though the rain had finally passed through, heading east toward the land of the halflings. Every man wore a coat of heavy chain mail, and they all felt the extra weight bearing down on them. Every man stank with sweat—and especially with fear.

Vossler walked through the town, checking behind buildings, in barrels, in the fields. He wanted to make certain no orcs had slipped through the town's nets.

Then he heard it—the faint sounds of swords clashing in the distance. His eyes widened immediately.

Alarmed, he yelled as loud as he could: "Orcs! Come on! Follow me!"

As quick as his elderly legs carried him, Vossler rushed to where the sounds had come, a small hillock west of the larger hill where the first battle occurred. By the time he had arrived, he breathed heavily and the telltale limp had returned. He saw no orcs. Only two youngsters—both of which had been friends of Piety Crassnick and had been present when their friend jumped Krampel—who seemed bored with their guard duty and had decided to practice against each other.

Vossler's anger surged.

"You two should be ashamed of yourselves. We're in a state of war, and you two are horsing around like a couple of children—" Vossler said, but the taller lad cut him off.

"We are children, old man. We shouldn't be doing guard work."

"You'll do as you're told by your elders."

"We can think for ourselves!"

"Yet you use your brains for foolishness!" Vossler countered. "You stand here, as guardsmen, and yet you play like children! I've never been as disgusted as I am now!"

"Who cares what you—" the taller boy began to say, but a slight squelch cut his words off. At that exact moment, the boys' fathers approached, and they noticed a pained look on the boy's face.

"What's the matter, Von? Why are you looking like that? Vossler, what is going on here?" the boy's father asked.

Before Vossler even acknowledged the man, Von dropped to the ground, a knife sticking out of the back of his neck.

"We'll discuss it later," Vossler quickly said, knowing the boy was dead but didn't have the heart to tell his father. He drew his sword, the great *Flad-rul*, and immediately called its powers to the blade. It ignited, the flames sending light into the entire glade.

The orcs streamed into it seconds later, not afraid of the flaming sword the old man carried. At least fifty orcs came into the glade, each carrying a scimitar or a short sword. Their growls rang in the Cassiminians' ears, threatening them to fight if they dare.

"Draw your swords and prepare to fight!" he ordered, and soon Cassiminian soldiers filled the glade, all of them ready to defend their town to every last man. Von's father, Vossler noted, had realized his son was dead. He stood over his son's body, sword drawn, protecting the corpse from the bestial creatures. The snarls of the orcs did not deter them at all; they formed a semicircle behind the old man.

Surprisingly, the first Cassiminian to move forward was Von's friend. Vossler watched as the lad rushed ahead, sword drawn, ready to claim an orc life as revenge for his friend's death, ready to prove his worth as a man of Cassimina. Vossler tried to stop him with a word, but the boy had not heard the order. Vossler knew the blood rushed in the boy's ears right now, drowning out everything but his own thoughts of getting even with the evil beasts. Several more men sprinted ahead, also ready to get the battle engaged. The orcs waited, then came forward en masse.

Von's pal sliced left then right, cutting the orc immediately in front of him along the sternum before he moved to his left, spinning his sword and stabbing the next one in the throat. He did not muster any additional offensives as an orc slashed him across the throat. The teen dropped his sword and pawed at the gash as tears ran down his face. Swords jabbed into his trunk as the orcs mauled him.

Vossler watched helplessly as the boy fell, even though the men of Cassimina swarmed toward him. With *Flad-rul* in his hands, he once again called the innate powers of the sword to the fore. Then, with a burst of speed that belied his age, he ran into the fray, swinging the great blade right then left. He caught an orc in the upper arm before he spun and swept the sword low, knocking the next orc off-balance and giving the lads behind him an easy kill.

The old man then raised himself upright, not feeling any pain as his joints didn't even creak. He moved the sword up to parry an attacker's blade and caused the orc to shriek as the sword ignited once again. The beast's exclamation was all Vossler needed, as he pushed the orc blade downward, then came back in an arc to relieve it of its head. The corpse fell slowly, but Vossler didn't step over it and move on to the next creature—he waited for their insatiable lust for destruction to come to him.

And that it did. Within seconds he dealt with two more orcs, and Vossler alternated strokes between the two. Another man came to help, cutting into the orc's chest from behind and twisting his sword, just as Vossler slashed the sword hand away from the orc's body. Vossler turned to thank him, and the man's face contorted as an orc came around from the rear and gave him the same treatment.

"Tha' was me brudder," the orc snarled into the human's ear, before Vossler stepped forward and swung mightily, taking the orc's head off.

"And you can join your brudder in death, maggot!" he said, before he went off to engage another.

The battle raged around them.

***

Several of the orcs attempted to duel the men, some getting lucky enough to cut a few of them down. Their feral screams and snarls echoed throughout the dale, the sounds of steel meeting steel ricocheting off the trees.

One of the villagers isolated an orc over by a small copse of trees at the rear of the glade where the orcs had entered, crossing swords with it. He ducked an arcing swing, but the orc corrected, moving the blade to block a strike at its legs. The orc flicked its wrists and deflected the villager's sword out of position, then jabbed its own into the man's throat, skewering his voice box. The villager hardly let out a whimper as the blood rushed from the wound.

The orc pulled its sword from the man's throat and grinned wickedly as it raised the blade for the final attack. But as it prepared to strike the death blow, a blur of brown tunic dropped from the branches above. The creature did not register the new presence at all, as Krampel—who had heard the bell toll, then rushed to the nearest tree and had climbed it to find the best position to join the oncoming battle in his own way—moved his golden shield up to block the orc's sword. He then swung his own sword, slashing down from the right, opening the creature from shoulder to hip.

Krampel looked down at the fallen man. He knew Vossler's teachings were to never turn your back on an opponent, especially one with the numbers of the orcs, but he didn't want to abandon a wounded comrade.

The man, unfortunately, had died.

Krampel then turned and entered the fray, his sword leading his strides. He ducked one orc who advanced with its sword held like a dagger over its head, rolling into a somersault and coming back up behind the beast. He didn't wait for the orc to turn; instead he buried his sword into its guts, right up to the hilt. With a flick of his wrists, he sliced the beast open to the flank, its steaming entrails spilling onto the ground below.

At sixteen summers, Krampel fought with the dexterity and confidence of someone much older. He kept his feet moving, slashing his sword one-handed as he easily batted away attacks by the orcs with his shield. He spun and carved a line though a pair of orcs that stood next to each other, then ducked a heavy blow before sending his own sword up through the orc's groin.

Seconds later he found himself back-to-back with his mentor, who swung *Flad-rul* back and forth, blocking the orcs' thrusts with a simple twist of his wrists. Their stationary position and style wasn't necessarily a prudent course of action, but it was effective nonetheless as the orcs continued their assault on the duo. The pair turned the orcs into corpses piling on top of each other.

"This is getting too easy," Krampel said over his shoulder. "I'd like a little bit more of a challenge."

"You say that like you're not challenged by them," Vossler replied with a hint of sarcasm.

The young man's smile shone through the look of determination and concentration on his face.

***

Vossler parried an orc blade, but the beast pinned the old man's blade with its own, twisting its wrists to prevent Vossler from countering. Another came up from the left side, swinging its sword parallel to the ground. Its swing was true and right to the mark.

Vossler gasped as he felt the sword make contact with his chest, the point of the blade burrowing just under the breastbone. The pain surged through him like nothing he had ever felt before. His knees buckled and sent him stumbling backward, right into Krampel's backside as the lad sliced one of beast's wrists off.

***

Krampel turned at the nudge and watched helplessly as Vossler fell to his knees. He glanced and saw the orc standing over him, the sword held low and still connected to Vossler's chest cavity. Krampel heard the orc snarl, saw the orc's lips pull back from its deformed and decaying teeth, and watched as the beast yanked the sword out from the old man's body. Vossler fell forward to the ground. Blood coursed along the last five inches of the blade, dripping onto the old man's back.

The next second felt like ten years to Krampel. As if everything moved in slow motion, Krampel saw the old man, his mentor, lying prostrate on the ground, cut down by an orc blade. Gasps rattled the man's chest as disbelief rushed through his mind. A flood of emotions dulled his senses. Vossler had trained the lad to be independent, to make him grow as a person, to help him unleash the talent within him, to make him the greatest fighter the realms ever saw. But everything about becoming the greatest fighter didn't seem to matter now. Vossler lay dying in front of him.

Even through the building grief, Krampel's rage surged through him. This felt worse than his mother selling him to the caravan, worse than the beatings the masters had laid on his back. This felt worse than Piety Crassnick jumping him from the trees; this cut deeper than any sword. Vossler was a surrogate father, a mentor, a friend. To see him cut down brought tears to Krampel's eyes, but he fought them back with everything he had. There would be a time to grieve, but this wasn't it.

It was time to fight.

The fire that Vossler first noticed in Krampel's eyes long ago quickly ignited, and the orcs simply stood there with the same dumb expression. Krampel let loose a primal scream as he brought his sword around from the right. The orc on the right parried his blade just as the orc that sent his bloody blade into Vossler's innards moved to strike the frenzied human. Krampel moved his left arm up to parry, the sword striking the golden shield with such force that made the shield flame. Krampel felt droplets of Vossler's blood strike his face; he snarled in response. Then, with incredible quickness, he spun on his heel and brought his sword around to the right, not stopping until his blade caught a piece of the orc's right flank. It howled in agony.

Good, Krampel thought, *howl away. There's more where that came from.*

Krampel engaged the orc next to him once again, twisting his body around and lunging to catch it in the gut. He ran the blade through, yanking it out immediately after the orc went rigid, its death looming over the horizon. The orc then fell, clutching his bleeding, gaping stomach, but as it hit its knees, Krampel leveled it across the throat with a vicious backhand.

With a flourish, Krampel twirled the blade in his fingers before going back for the orc that had stabbed Vossler. His steel flashed twice, cutting left and then back the other way, leaving two lines across the orc's chest and belly before severing its sword wrist. Krampel didn't care that he had just maimed the beast. He wanted to dish out the greatest amount of punishment to exact full retribution for Vossler's injuries.

It fell soon after, but Krampel's rage was far from sated. The fire in his eyes continued burning, fueling his desire for revenge. He rushed off with his blade practically smoking, looking for another orc to destroy.

He found one quickly, dispatching it with ease, slicing it open with a hearty uppercut from the right hip to the left shoulder, before he spun and brought his shield up to block an attack. In the same movement, his sword went low, swiping underneath and taking the orc's legs out at the knees. Its death squeals came from the fiery pits of Hell itself.

Krampel had turned into a whirlwind of destruction, spinning and jabbing and thrusting with such perfection and fluidity that he grew oblivious to his surroundings. A torrent of wind echoed and pounded his ear drums, so much so in fact that only his concentration for the task at hand kept his mind off what—who—lay in the town square.

He hacked at the evil ones that came at him, and soon he left the glade a mess of orc corpses. Pieces of orcs lay strewn about, the black blood painting the ground. One last orc stood to Krampel and ten of the Cassiminian defenders, and it turned to run before the humans went after it.

Krampel didn't let it get far.

He raised his sword, holding it by the bloodied blade. Then he pulled it back and hurled it forth, making it appear like a silver and black disk hurtled toward the orc. Krampel admired the spin and the rotation so closely that he finally smiled when the disk reached the target, imbedding itself into the orc's spinal column, dropping it hard with a squelch.

Krampel ran up to the beast and yanked his sword out of it, before he remembered Vossler's body. He rushed over to it, instructing others to look after the first human he had protected when he bounded from the trees; they rushed off in the direction he indicated. He dropped his sword and his shield and knelt next to Vossler's body. He turned him over with little effort and looked into the old man's face.

It was a white he had never seen before. It was pasty and translucent, as if Krampel looked into the face of a ghost. His breathing had turned incredibly shallow, but the light in his eyes appeared as bright as the boy had remembered it. Somehow, someway, Vossler had fought to stay alive, holding off the orc poison that laced the evil blades. Krampel felt incredibly proud of his mentor, even though his heart had turned to lead.

Vossler raised his right hand to Krampel's cheek and stroked it once. He looked into the lad's eyes and smiled, still seeing the fire there.

"I'm sorry," Krampel said. "I'm sorry I did not stop them."

"You did, though," Vossler replied, his voice ragged. "You stopped them from hurting anyone else. I'm very proud of you, my boy."

"Thank you, master." Krampel felt tears in his eyes now, and he knew that Vossler would soon breathe his last.

"Keep your mind on the battle, my son," Vossler said, choking the words out. He smiled once again at his protégé, and then, seconds later, the light left his eyes. His body slumped, his head went slack.

Holding the dead man in his arms, Krampel felt a weight fall on his shoulders. Millions of thoughts ran through his head. He did not know if he would ever be the man Vossler thought he would be, and he did not know if he would ever live up to the old man's expectations. Could he stay in Cassimina, now that he was an orphan yet again? Did he have enough training to be the fighter Vossler said he would be? Did he have the power to wield *Flad-rul* effectively?

Krampel looked to the blade that Vossler held and slowly cried. The old man was dead, and the lad remembered the story of how it had come to his mentor: Prying it from the dead hands of his own mentor, Tyrence Huckleby, when he was killed in a battle so long ago. Suddenly Krampel didn't want to hold the blade his master held. He knew if he held onto that blade, it would be a harsh reminder of this battle.

Yet even as he felt his eyelids grow tight in an effort to block the memories, Vossler's voice, stronger, more potent, came to his ears.

People die in war, my lad.

Vossler told him that in his many lessons.

We are to look out for others while in a battle, Vossler had instructed, but we cannot look past the fact that sometimes people die in war. Anything can happen once one's back is turned.

The words vibrated in his skull, coming through so loud and clear now. Vossler's words had become reality, and no matter how hard Krampel closed his eyes, he made himself accept the fact the old man would no longer speak to him in person, only through his memories.

He sobbed openly.

A few minutes had passed. He felt a strong hand on his right shoulder, and a voice that sounded incredibly familiar.

"Come, young one. There will be a time for grief later," said Erig, the counselor. He looked just as disheveled as the last time Krampel saw him, with Vossler, several hours ago after the first attack. "You need to get your rest. Vossler wouldn't want you to grieve for him so quickly. We'll take care of him. Go rest."

Krampel quickly dropped his mentor's body and reached for *Flad-rul*, spinning in the same move to point the sword at Erig's face. In an instant Krampel called the powers of the sword to the fore: the blade ignited immediately, orange flame springing into the councilor's face. The man blanched, his face as white as Vossler's death mask.

"You of all people will not touch him!" Krampel screamed. The fire that gleamed brightly in his eyes seemed just as terrible as the flames spouting along the sword's length. "You will not be privileged to go anywhere near him! He is a hero of this town and will be treated as such; no sniveling coward who hides with the women, behind their skirts, will touch his remains! Anyone who is not worthy will certainly be struck down by my blade!"

Erig slowly regained some of his arrogance as soon as Krampel stopped speaking, and tried to move closer to the body. But Krampel thrust the point of *Flad-rul* several inches closer to face, causing additional flames to spill forth. The counselor moved back and out of the way of striking range.

"You will not touch him! Never mind, I'll do it myself," Krampel said, removing the point of *Flad-rul* from the target, the flames extinguishing immediately. He bent down and picked up the old man's body, placing it over his left shoulder. He grabbed his old sword and his shield, and rose with his incredible burden. He didn't look at anyone as he carried the corpse back to his home, but everyone saw the line of tears that flowed freely down the lad's cheeks.

***

Krampel cried himself to sleep that night, while Vossler's body lay on a workbench in the tanner's shop. Delicately placing the body there, Krampel promised to take care of everything by himself in the morning, which slowly attacked the night from the east. When he awoke, the sun streamed into his chamber as the birds, like normal, chirped their long morning songs.

Normal would not exist on this day.

He stretched his sore muscles, raising his arms and twisting the pain aside. He then got up and walked into the workroom, where he saw Vossler's body, already stiff with the throes of rigor mortis.

Krampel removed the blood stained clothes and washed Vossler's face and hair. He cleaned the wound and tried not to look at the charcoal-colored veins as he worked, instead looking into the dead man's face. The thought of burying this great man gnawed at him from deep inside. He didn't want to do it, but he owed it to Vossler: The old man had saved him from a life of torment and taught him skills he never knew resided inside of him.

Owed it to him? I am indebted to him, he thought.

When he finished dressing the body, he placed his own sword on Vossler's chest and wrapped his hands around the handle. The sword was so small that he managed to hook the little finger of Vossler's left hand around the pommel.

The lad walked outside and looked around Cassimina. The people worked as if nothing had happened the previous day, but Krampel knew the tasks had infinitely doubled. Fewer men worked the fields, and several of the younger boys worked them instead. Krampel noticed them almost immediately, and his swollen heart went into his throat. He knew several of those boys and fought next to their fathers yesterday. Several of those fathers had died. The boys, some as young as twelve summers, had turned into men overnight, and they now made sure their families had food on their tables.

Krampel now understood: It was part of growing up early in Cassimina.

Other men had the painstakingly difficult chore of separating the corpses—the humans for proper burials, the orcs for burning. The task turned even harder to do when those men found their sons, or their neighbors, or close friends they've known their whole lives, as their emotions flooded their souls and overflowed from their eyes. But if they found someone who had simply been knocked unconscious and left in that state overnight, there was a great deal of celebration. One less burial was for the better of Cassimina.

Krampel finally found the courage to smile. He accepted the condolences of several of the women as well as the men, and he seemed to take it all in stride.

Until he saw Erig.

His cheeks suddenly flared scarlet, his anger brewing, as if *Flad-rul*'s powers had suddenly erupted on his face. But with a calming breath, the lad pushed the urge to swat the counselor's face off with his sword. He then walked up to the man and looked him directly in the eye.

"Counselor, my master's body is ready for burial. You may take it when you are ready."

Erig nodded to him, then nodded to the three men standing next to him. They let Krampel lead the way while they carried a makeshift stretcher large enough for a full-sized adult male.

Krampel led them to the front door of his home and brought them inside to the workshop. The three men carefully placed Vossler's body on the stretcher and were nearly out the door when Erig stopped them.

"Wait a moment," he ordered, stopping the men. "Where is his sword?"

Krampel looked to the body and saw the sword—his old sword—still placed on top of the body.

"It's right there, lord," he replied, pointing at it.

"No lad, not that one. The one you brandished at me yesterday. I know that blade was his, you pulled it out of his hand. It belongs to him."

"He gave it to me," Krampel said, raising his voice slightly. "He told me that blade would be mine when I was ready for it. And he no longer needs it; he's dead."

The admittance made Krampel's throat bounce.

"That is of no concern to me," the pompous councilor said, waving Krampel's words aside with a sneer. "Vossler was a warrior, and he is befitting of a warrior's burial. That means in armor, with his sword. Not this pathetic steel blade he gave you to use."

Krampel's anger, simmering for the last few minutes, had hit the boiling point.

"It was my sword—that sword, the one Vossler holds—that saved this town, not *Flad-rul*. It was Vossler—not you—that organized this town's defenses and made sure we had a chance. That sword deserves to be buried with Vossler; it is a part of this town's history!" Krampel gestured madly with his hands as he spoke, even shoving his finger into Erig's face demonstratively.

"It matters not to me, and neither do you, child," Erig said, interrupting. "Produce the sword. It is his, and it is to be buried with him. Produce it now!"

Krampel stared hard at the man, whose menacing stare equaled his own. It was a fight Krampel knew he would not win, as Erig held too much power over the township. Begrudgingly, Krampel grabbed the sword and placed it in Vossler's hands after taking his own blade out of them. He gave the counselor a look of loathing as the older man smirked with pride at humbling the youth. The four men departed with Vossler's body, leaving the youth alone in the house, which suddenly felt large and empty. His gut was also empty, and it suddenly dawned on him that he had yet to eat that morning: He hadn't eaten since the previous afternoon. He did not know how he managed to stay on his feet; he figured he had operated purely on adrenaline and emotions these last few hours, and that is why he never noticed his aching hunger. He swooned where he stood.

He found some meat, bread and cheese in Vossler's stores, and noticed that quite a bit remained. It would last him for several weeks, but after what had just occurred, he did not know how much longer he would stay in this village. He was an orphan yet again, and it was just a matter of time before he had to earn his own keep.

The question for him was whether he would earn it here or somewhere else.

As he ate, it was the last thing he wanted to think about. For so long, someone else cared for him: His mother, the caravan masters, and then Vossler. Now that he was alone—he winced at that thought—he was now responsible for himself, and only himself. Cassiminians looked after each other, but right now, after Erig's last comments to him, he certainly did not want to be where he was not wanted.

He recalled that his existence in Cassimina wasn't exactly the greatest. His first trip here, he had been beaten by the caravan, then imprisoned, then beaten up by a bully who, now that Krampel thought about it a little more, hadn't been seen since before his father's death, then scolded like a child after his mentor had been killed. Everything about Cassimina stank to him at that moment. He knew what a hard life was; to him, the Cassiminians knew nothing about a hard life.

The boy's anger surged through him as he thought of the pompous councilor and his arrogance. The man showed his true colors just a few moments ago, and all because Krampel had embarrassed him. Krampel had the right of it, and did it with good reason; Erig had not assisted in the town's defense, and there he was, trying to maintain order after everything had calmed down.

He had no right to do that, Krampel thought. *He was one of the people that they had been trying to defend. He had no right to question them, had no right to tell a warrior not to grieve for his fallen mentor.*

He tried not to think about the last battle, but little by little, the visions of it came streaming into his head. He squeezed his eyes together, trying to blot out every little detail. He didn't want to think about it right now, though, seeing as he now had his entire life to think about it. It wasn't that he didn't want to remember the battle—it was hard to forget fighting back-to-back with his mentor, only to feel Vossler's body slump against his...

He shot up from the table as the thought entered his mind. His breath had grown ragged, his heart hammering away at his breastbone. Hearing horses whinny hard outside, Krampel reached up and felt his forehead and found it slick with sweat.

Wiping the perspiration off with a cloth, he grabbed a flagon of mead—after all, he was an adult now, in his own eyes —and swallowed the heavy brown liquid in one swallow. That brought a little bit of color back to his face, yet his hands still shook. He needed to rest.

Krampel brought a hunk of cheese and a large portion of bread to his bed, where he nibbled them until his belly fit no more. He wiped his mouth on the sleeve of his tunic and wanted to fall asleep.

Wood rattled as a fist repeatedly pounded the door.

Now who could that be, Krampel thought. He rose and went to answer it.

When he opened it, he suddenly saw a flash of white and heard a crack of bone and cartilage. Krampel fell backward, his head banging against the wooden floor with another resounding crack. Shaking his head to clear the fuzziness, he looked up and half-expected to see Piety Crassnick standing there, or even Erig, trying to exact a little revenge for Krampel's actions from yesterday.

But it was the last person Krampel expected to see the day after his mentor's death who stood there—the master of the caravan.

"Well, the rat escaped the pen, and now we have him caught," the master said, reaching for his whip.

Krampel stared at the man and knew that his service to him ended long ago. He wouldn't be cowed by him ever again, he promised himself this. He escaped in the first place for that very reason.

But now they had tracked him down. He did not want to become a hostage again.

He quickly found the strength in him to avoid that situation.

Krampel scurried away and reached for his sword, pulling it from the scabbard. He stood up and, as the caravan master uncoiled the whip, Krampel raced in and struck hard.

This caught the caravan master off guard. Krampel easily recalled his servitude, that of a submissive life. He felt more confident now, and he had a weapon in his hand.

The master raised the whip and wanted to crack it over Krampel's back, if just to remind the lad where he came from, but a flash of steel from the master's right caused a sparking light to come across his face. Krampel severed the rope, which sailed over to the wall. The master looked to the rope with an astonished look on his face: His eyes were wide and his mouth hung open slightly. He looked over at the boy, then the rope, and then the boy again.

Krampel simply smirked in his direction.

The caravan master's bravado returned a few seconds later, his recovery quick.

"You've sure grown in ability, rat. But I'm sure my abilities outreach yours by a great stretch," the master said, reaching for his hip. Krampel wanted to sever his wrist, but wanted to show the man how badly he had erred in trying to find him. Krampel shifted his weight and twirled his own sword between his fingers while the echoes of steel sliding out of a metal case bounced off the walls of the modest home. He looked right into his eyes and didn't flinch, even as the taller, broader man started to chuckle. "I've always hoped you'd develop a talent so I can drum it out of you. Prepare to meet the gods."

Krampel didn't say a word, only offering a cold stare in return. He did not ignite the fire within himself yet, though: He wanted to give the caravan master the illusion that he had this duel won.

The master moved in first and chopped at Krampel's left side, the lad tilting his blade down to parry with a twist of his wrists. He turned that move against the taller man, as he spun quickly to his left, bringing the two swords up and around and knocking the other away. He then executed a flurry of moves, crossing over right then left, before he tried to drive the edge of his sword into the caravan master's scalp. The man blocked the strike to his head.

"Maybe it is you who should prepare to meet the gods," Krampel finally said with a rasp, his mouth dry despite the mead. The master gritted his teeth and yelled a frustrated exclamation, then raised his blade. He tried to chop at Krampel but missed, as the youngster rushed forward and rolled past him, somersaulting his way out the door and into the town proper. He got up and turned, swinging his blade as he moved. The caravan master blocked it.

Krampel moved backward, letting the man in front of him go on the offensive, slashing and chopping. Even though he heard the screams of fright coming from the women, he blocked them out of his mind; he couldn't afford a distraction. Krampel turned his wrists just slightly to keep him from coming anywhere close to striking a killing blow, always moving his sword to close up any openings Krampel possibly gave him with a feint. The master also kept his feet moving, which kept him off-balance.

Krampel blocked the master's two-handed chop and quickly started his offensive. He let the fire within him explode, and with frantic swipes and slashes, made the caravan master back away. Krampel surged through his zone, slashing, hacking, slicing. The master expelled quite a bit of energy during his offensive, and at that moment, he yearned for a respite of breath. The lad did not give it to him; Krampel wanted to exact quite a bit of revenge for the months of torment he had suffered and endured at the hands of the master.

Using a two-handed grip, he found more power. The flames burning in his eyes fueled his attack with a never-ending supply of energy, and Krampel rained blow after blow on the master, hammering with precise strikes that left the man in front of him breathless and baffled. He crisscrossed the blade in front of him several times, going for the left leg. The caravan master moved to parry, but he did not see Krampel go into a spin, raising his leg to deliver a kick. It was the master's turn to see a white flash as Krampel's foot connected with the side of his head.

The master stumbled and Krampel grinned at the sight. He stalked in and, as the master regained his balance, slashed at the man's left shoulder. The master got his blade up to parry the strike, but the move was just a feint for what Krampel really wanted to do.

Krampel then spun and laid a hearty slash on the master's right thigh, gouging a good inch or two into the flesh. The caravan master howled in pain, and as he reached for the wound in an attempt to stop the bleeding, Krampel sent the sword flying back to the left, slicing through skin and bone, sending the master's hands flying away. The master hit his knees, holding up the bloody stumps of his wrists, looking for mercy.

Krampel gave none; his mood wanted full payment.

"Please, spare me!" the man cried out in a whimper, and as he looked around, he noticed that Cassimina as a whole intently watched Krampel.

"Spare you? Spare you!? After all the pain and agony you caused me over those ten months? I don't think so," Krampel sneered as his internal fire consumed him completely. His anger rushed through his body and gave him new life. He pointed the tip of his sword right underneath the man's breastbone. All he wanted to do was plunge the tip inside him, and he'd pierce his heart. It would be all over, and the months of abuse would be washed away in a split second. He pressed the point against the man's flesh, then reached up and grabbed the topknot of his hair. "Where is my mother?" Krampel asked.

"How in the nine hells should I know?" the man replied, the pained expression digging deeper, just as Krampel pressed harder. The man took in slightly more air than he should, and he started coughing. "I don't know," he continued, "we took you on in the northeast. A village called Cosumelle. I wouldn't know where she would be now. She's probably dead for all I know."

That was not the right thing to say. With the fire burning hotter, Krampel plunged the tip of his sword deep into the man's heart. The master's eyes widened with a sharp gasp, his body rigid. A few seconds of agony passed before he slumped.

"No, she may not be dead, but you sure are," Krampel said, feeling a bit of relief wash over him. He breathed hard and kept his hands on the sword, half proud, half in disbelief. He took a heavy breath, closing his eyes as he stepped on the caravan master's chest for leverage. The sword came out of his chest with a slight pop.

Krampel wanted to celebrate his final break from the caravan, but thought quickly caught up to him.

He didn't have Vossler there to congratulate him, and that saddened him greatly.

***

The town buried Vossler the next morning.

Even though Krampel had bathed the body himself and dressed it in clean clothes, his dead mentor looked incredibly peaceful—a look Krampel had never once saw on the old man's face—as men carried his body into the tomb. It must have been the angle of the sun, because the lad never once saw the perfect shade of pink in Vossler's face before. He clutched *Flad-rul* as if he still lived.

As Krampel thought about the life he took yesterday, his heart told him he had done the right thing. He felt no remorse for killing the caravan master; far from it. The man gave Krampel so much grief for every little thing he did, and for the first time in his life, Krampel felt powerful; incredibly powerful. Just thinking about that fight excited him, even though the hate he felt for the caravan master overwhelmed any other feeling in his mind. After months of the master pressing him under the heel of his boot, Krampel had soared above him and made him pay for the life of misery he had unleashed on him.

He sneered under the hood and cloak that he wore to hide his face from the other mourners. He grinned because he had finally escaped the caravan master's clutches. There had always been a chance of the master returning to find him and return him to the caravan in bondage. That was because the man whom he watched disappear from this world forever gave him a gift—the gift of freedom.

And now, another gift was about to disappear from Krampel's life forever.

Krampel's face went from a sneer to a hardened shell in less than a second. He watched intently as the pallbearers brought

Vossler's body into the tomb, *Flad-rul* on his breast. He felt the bile rise into his throat, suddenly despising Cassimina and all of its inhabitants at the same time.

There was nothing left for him here. He was sure of it, and that made his decision all the more easier.

He watched as the tomb closed and remained standing there as the residents dispersed. He ignored the few offers to sup with Vossler's friends, instead choosing to stare at the tomb door and hold a sentinel's vigil. As he stood there, Krampel vowed to himself not to let that sword get away again. He needed it, because as Vossler once said, he would become the greatest fighter ever with that sword.

He had a plan, one that he needed to execute under the cover of darkness.

***

He saw no one else the rest of the day. No one came to his door. He stayed out of sight as he methodically prepared for his last evening in Cassimina.

It would be, if he pulled everything off, a memorable one.

He stuffed plenty of food into a rucksack, and he did not leave a crumb of bread or a slab of meat or cheese behind. He gathered all of his personal possessions, which amounted to clothes, his own sword, and his shield, and filled a second rucksack with the clothes. He slung the shield behind his back.

He went downstairs into the training dungeon one last time and grabbed the scabbard of a four-and-a-half foot sword. He attached it to his belt, then rushed back up the stairs and into the main room proper. He didn't let his eyes linger on the dungeon; he felt his master's presence here, even though his body was some distance away.

He didn't see the need to write a note to anyone, either; as far as he was concerned, he owed nothing to anyone here. His heart had hardened so much, so quickly, that he turned into an unfeeling individual. All that had happened in his young life—the betrayal of his mother, the torture at the hands of the caravan, the mistreatment by Piety and the other lads of the town, Vossler's death, Erig's condescension to him after

Vossler's death—seemed too much for one young man to handle.

And taking the life of the caravan master had weighed on him just as heavily.

The mixture of emotions—his love and respect for Vossler, tied in with his utter hatred for the master—confused him. While Vossler taught him to protect himself, the caravan master taught him just as much. The beatings he endured echoed in his mind, and the memories of his mother, while fading, seemed to burn his soul.

The only person that truly cared for him lay in a nearby tomb. He cared not about anyone else.

And as he placed the two rucksacks over his shoulders, he grabbed the sword, shield, a cloak, and two lanterns, and then exited the house for the last time. He looked around and saw no one, not even a member of the town guard, walking the streets, looking for enemies that wanted to attack Cassimina in the night.

This is going to be easier than I thought, he thought.

One of the lanterns was lit, the other dark. He walked around to the rear of the house and, with a mighty toss, threw the lit lantern against the corner of the building. The glass cracked and the flames spread, igniting the dwelling. He did not wait to see the conflagration spread any further, as he gave himself limited time with which to accomplish this one, final task.

He quickly lit the other lantern as he walked with all the speed possible to the tomb where Vossler's remains lay. It pained him to think of Vossler as dead, but he steeled his nerve. He needed to get over that fact. He turned the corner and went to the tomb, turning the knob to the door and found that it was unlocked.

The fools, Krampel thought. *Didn't they think I would attempt to go after the sword? This is where I will expose their folly.*

Once inside, he lifted the torch to look around. Inside the remains of Cassimina's greatest citizens rested. Vossler, he saw, lay closest to the door.

He soon heard the screams of the people as they had discovered the fire, which meant time slowly evaporated on him. He knew his diversion only bought him a set amount, so he quickly went to work. He removed *Flad-rul* from Vossler's hands, before he laid his own sword on his breast. He finished clamping Vossler's stony hands around the blade, then, without a second's thought, placed his lips on his mentor's forehead. He then extinguished the torch and left it inside the grave.

With the Flame Thrower now securely in his grasp, he slid it into the scabbard and walked out of the tomb, closing the door behind him, more potent and more powerful than ever before. He looked toward the city and didn't see anyone paying any attention to the tomb. He saw people running about, trying to organize a fire brigade down to Timber Lake to extinguish the blaze. Some screamed to the others, wondering if Krampel was still inside the home, while others put their arms over their faces to shield them from the extreme heat that now poured off the building.

Krampel smirked.

Let them worry, he thought. *I have more important things to do with my life now.*

Without a second look back at the town where Vossler rescued him and turned him from a slave into a great fighter, Krampel threw the cloak about his shoulders and turned away from his old life, beginning his new one with every step that led him away from Cassimina. He disappeared into the trees beyond the fields where the caravan had once traveled, knowing that like the time he escaped the dreaded gypsies, he wanted to get as far away from this place as humanly possible before he stopped for rest.

Rest did not come soon.

Chapter 7
Five years later

A brisk fall afternoon turned into a chilly fall evening. In the towns throughout the middle of Obloeron, smoke curled from the hearth in many homes, the light breezes swirling the gray smoke about. It was late in the season of the harvest. About a month prior, farmers moved their sheep into the corral for shearing, and now many people wore warm, woolen sweaters to keep the cold away. Some gathered in front of their hearths and told bedtime stories, while others prepared the next day's meals, complete with sweet cider from the nearest orchard.

In the forests of the realms, those who took shelter there did not have the comforts of man-made homes. The small animals gathered food for the long, cold winter that quickly approached, that was true, but the humans in the forests just tried to stay alive. They were the outcasts of society, the dregs of humanity.

They also happened to be wanted men, and none wanted to be found.

They knew it was only a matter of time before a bounty hunter found them, and none stayed in the same place for longer than a night. They left little trace of their presence, but they always forgot one thing—they did not have the ability to disguise their footprints, no matter how hard they tried.

It was one of the tricks the man known as the Dark Falcon used in his surveillance—and subsequent capture—of every bounty he took.

Now twenty-one years old and the summer of his youth behind him, Krampel took the ominous name while he hunted down the most wanted individuals, whether murderers or debtors. Over the past five years, Krampel's star rose, and many of the affluent asked him to fetch someone who had defaulted on a loan of gold, someone who had escaped from a prison, or someone who had taken the honor of one's daughter. It was a messy business, but Krampel did not care about those he hunted or those who had hired him to hunt. Those who wished for him to hunt paid handsomely for his services, and those whom he hunted usually deserved their penalties. He even assisted the poor, taking food in payment instead of gold, for it was all they could afford.

It had been the closest Krampel came to being friendly with anyone in years.

Since Vossler's death, Krampel had withdrawn from society, preferring to walk in the wild instead of staying in one place for the rest of his life. He had become one with nature. He had grown in size, his body slowly filling out, his muscles larger than they were when he had first lifted *Flad-rul* in his mentor's dungeon. Now he lifted the sword with ease and snapped it out of its scabbard so many times that its leather covering had grown worn. He had taken to wearing a dark forest green pant-and-tunic set, which helped him blend in with his surroundings: he liked to camouflage himself when on a hunt, as he felt it gave him an advantage over his prey. His skin, especially in the face, had browned and bronzed from time spent in the sun.

And he now wore elven moccasins that hardly made a print when he trod on wet ground or heavy sand. He considered the boots his best investment during the five years that he traveled the realms on his own, as they kept enemies away from his own trail. Like the falcon above, with deadly stealth he patrolled the treetops throughout the forests of the realms. A silent sentinel, he stood ready to swoop down on his prey at the most opportune moment.

His travels took him across many different locales that his former bondage to the long-forgotten caravan wouldn't allow. North, south, east, west; he visited many places, and many criminals blanched on seeing him, running for the nearest hiding place as soon as their eyes fell on his fierce face. He had gone as far north as the boundary that set the northlands apart from the rest of civilization, that several thousand-mile stretch of wilderness where no one dared to travel at night, and as far east as halfling country, where no human, dwarf, or elf was now welcome. He had logged many miles on his feet, for he did not travel by horse or cart. He rested only when necessary, for he feared that one day, a criminal would get the drop on him and end his hunting days—and his life.

Now, he traveled southeast to the township of Hanlin, a quaint town twenty miles as the bird flies from Arborway, a wooded realm bounding the rest of the realms from Myrindar, with a summons in hand. Arborway loomed ahead as Krampel walked as far from the watch as he could, for he knew the archers of the tall trees were excellent shots which reached some two hundred axe-lengths of the entryway. The trees of Arborway stretched to the heavens, their gray-brown bark shimmering and reflecting the moonlight, making it appear like thousands of tall candles standing still. Krampel glanced over toward the trees, and with his keen vision he saw the archers and those on the watch keeping their own tabs on the visitor.

But Krampel's destination was far from Arborway, so he paid the archers no mind. He lowered the cowl of his cloak to show those in the trees that he meant no harm to them or those they protected.

On he walked, covering the twenty miles in what seemed like no time. He constantly shifted his eyes back and forth, always aware of his surroundings, just in case he needed to draw *Flad-rul* and call its powers to the fore. He had his shield, the golden dragon shield that Vossler gave to him, strapped to his back, ready to slip onto his forearm when needed.

As it turned out, his trip to Hanlin was as easy as could be.

He traveled there to take on a new job, as someone had robbed one of the lords of the town. The fellow he sent to find Krampel—never an easy task, for starters—gave few details to him, and after careful interrogation of the messenger, he had decided to see the lord.

As soon as he saw the home of the lord, Krampel's eyes widened. It was huge for the town's size, as if half of the town's population fit inside. It was clearly the largest of the homes for miles, Krampel knew. He also knew that for this job, he would deal with someone who commanded a great deal of power and prestige. A dark look came over his face as he approached the door; he had summoned the power of the Dark Falcon, where none penetrated his defenses, not even one as rich as this lord.

The door opened before Krampel raised his fist to knock, and a peasant boy of about thirteen summers led him inside. Apparently they had waited for his arrival, as the lord already had a meal readied for him.

"My master bids you to sit and eat," the boy said. "Lord Juniper will be with you momentarily."

Krampel nodded. He knew it was custom in some parts of the realms to make guests wait for the lord to arrive, but to have one fed before the lord arrived seemed quite odd to him. He stored this fact of Hanlin away for future reference, especially if he needed to take a job in this town again.

Luxurious scents wafted to Krampel's nose: His mouth turned wet as he inhaled deeply. He did not remember the last time he ate food such as this. Without a second thought, he dug in.

A few minutes later, the lord made his first appearance in the dining room.

"Continue eating, my good man. I have some other pressing matters on my plate before I may sup. Lutricia," he said, snapping his fingers. A blonde-haired girl approached. "Fetch him anything he so desires."

Without a look to Krampel, Juniper sped out of the room.

The blonde girl moved to Krampel's side and awaited instruction. Even though he ate quietly, he noticed that she was beautiful, wearing the dress of a maiden with her hair twisted into a bun. Krampel only glanced in her direction once more as he leaned back when finished with his meal. She moved in to clear his plate, and she looked into his dark face with a soft smile. He gave her a hard look in return, a natural, instinctive action that time had ingrained in him. No one had tried to break through his defenses in five years; he wouldn't allow it now, even if it was a soft smile from a beautiful serving girl.

As she walked away, a sweet scent lingered near the table where she bent over to clean it, and he struggled to find where he encountered that fragrance before. His eyes clouded with attempts at remembrance; it grated at his nerves.

The serving girl did not return, and for that Krampel thanked his gods. The lord, however, did return, and he found

Krampel deep in thought when he entered the room. He sat himself in a chair opposite the bounty hunter and did not inquire as to Krampel's deliberations.

"So you are the infamous Dark Falcon, I presume," the lord said.

"Would I be in your home had I not been him?" Krampel replied with a touch of sarcasm.

"Point granted, but let's not beat around the bush. Last week, my home was violated, a priceless bauble stolen. He was too quick for the town guard to catch, but we did get a good look at him, and he is a well-known thief throughout the southern kingdom. His name is Anfron Shivelpenny, approximately twenty-eight years old, about five small axe-lengths tall.

"This is a sketch of the necklace he stole. It is worth more than this house, more than our combined lives—"

"I place a higher worth on my life than on jewels, lord," Krampel said, interrupting.

"This bauble is priceless." Juniper had gone on as if he hadn't heard the bounty hunter speak. "It is many years old and has been in this family for just as long. It dates back to when the southern kingdom was ruled by kings, not Imperial Inquisitors. You can understand why I want the necklace returned to me—and the thief brought back to me alive."

Krampel nodded.

"So that you may execute him as you see fit?"

"No, so I can have his hands severed. He is a thief, and he must be given a punishment that none in Hanlin or the surrounding realm will ever forget."

Krampel's eyes glowed scarlet at the man's words. He quickly dismissed the fire with a thought. He also thought Shivelpenny deserved death for stealing something so exquisite, if the drawing was accurate. But that decision did not come down to him; he banished the thought from his mind immediately and didn't think about it again.

"So you want me to bring him back to you alive, I take it. How much is the bounty?"

The lord smiled at Krampel's question.

"It's more gold than you can spend in your lifetime," he said.

"I don't know, lord. I can spend quite a bit if I put my mind to it."

"Tell you what, bounty hunter. I will give you three things: A new scabbard for your sword, a sack of gold, and my most exquisite treasure of all," the lord said.

"And that is?" Krampel asked with a look of annoyance on his face. He didn't like it when those that hired him skipped out on deals.

The lord chuckled as he stood and walked around the table to stand in front of the bounty hunter.

"That, young fellow, is a surprise that only I know. Do not worry, you will not be disappointed in the least when you see what that treasure is. It will be far worth anything else that I could give you of tangible value," the lord said.

Krampel looked at the lord with a leery eye, but despite his misgivings, he trusted this lord. He didn't really know why: He seemed a man of his word, but Krampel remained on his guard as he shook the man's hand, swearing his skills to him. It was a handshake of fealty only for this hunt, and the man's grip was strong. Krampel did not sense deceit in him whatsoever—he would come through on his part of the bargain.

After providing Krampel with necessary documents—including the thief's known hideaways and recent sightings—Lord Juniper escorted him to the door and wished him good hunting. Krampel did not talk of expenses, for he needed none: He had already solidified his reputation in the southlands, and he had helped innkeepers dispose of vagrants and brawlers when in the area—even though he kept them on a short leash to avoid getting too close to them. He began the hunt in earnest. He returned the way he came, wrapping his cloak around him as he walked. Night's bitter bite nibbled on his skin; the seasons changed gradually in the south. He'd deal with it in his own way.

Krampel was no ordinary bounty hunter. Over time, he had developed skills that helped him surpass other hunters. Some of the skills he had already possessed, such as sword fighting—

he won countless duels with his prey—as well as the cunning he used with which to trap his bounties.

He also held custody of a talent that he didn't know was in him, a talent that he used every day since he left Cassimina long ago: The use of the trees. He found it ironic that the trap young Piety Crassnick had used against him, the same trap that started him on the road toward his destiny, would be the same trick he used to snare criminals and wrongdoers five years later.

He snarled at the memory. He wished for another try at Piety. It would be a sweet moment for the Dark Falcon if he picked up a bounty on his teenaged rival. He would strive harder than ever to collect it, since he already knew his target. He knew how he moved, how he fought—usually with one's back turned—and he knew his tendencies. It would be a spirited fight.

A few hours after he departed Lord Juniper's residence, he came face to face with the wall of Arborway. He saw no one from the watch holding a bow to stop him. He walked right into the wooded realm, which swallowed him completely.

It was as if the sounds outside the wooden realm turned off, and in its place, the sounds inside turned on to maximum. He heard the tweeting of birds and the snapping of twigs under his booted feet. He removed the cowl from his head and looked around, as if he half expected to find his quarry waiting at the entrance. No, Krampel knew that Shivelpenny would hide deep within the trees.

He looked back and forth, then looked up for the nearest branch. Bending his knees and propelling himself with quickness never before seen in a human, Krampel shot up and grabbed a hold of a thick branch. He swung slowly, gathering momentum, then flung himself across to another branch where he landed firmly on his feet. Krampel enjoyed this vantage point. Up here in the trees, he held a view of the surrounding area, one better than any other in the realms—except maybe the view from the summit of a mountain. No one knew of his presence while high up in the boughs, for the power of the Dark Falcon stilled the leaves with a look, and a calming voice to the trees kept the branches from collapsing under his weight.

In Arborway, the trees grew close together, so his natural talent for walking on branches would come in handy here. Arborway was different from other forests throughout the realms: There were narrow paths on which to tread, and there were some spaces in between the trees. But for the most part, Arborway's trees were stacked tree on tree on tree as far as one saw. With the agility of a creature whose habitat was in the treetops, Krampel walked from branch to branch, leaping lightly to keep his footfalls silent. He kept his eyes peeled for the watch as well as for Shivelpenny.

He leapt and landed on a higher branch, using his hands to steady himself and keep his balance. He walked along its length before hopping over to the next one.

He stopped when he heard a soft giggle coming from below, as well as the sounds of a babbling brook. Krampel looked down and saw a man kneeling at the banks of the tiny waterway, a rucksack next to him, his hands scooping up water to drink.

Curious, Krampel walked around to the other side of the brook, moving his feet cautiously on the branches while keeping an eye on this person. The man sounded slightly mad, as he continued giggling and sipped from the brook. Krampel, eyebrows raised, wondered what was so funny about the water.

Krampel crouched down with his feet firmly planted on the branch. He stroked his chin thoughtfully, rubbing his thumb under his bottom lip. He stared at the madman, getting a good look while measuring him up. Krampel noticed the man carried a sword, a thin blade from the look of it. He wondered why the man sat here all alone.

Then the man stopped drinking. The water continued to drip from his chin, and he quickly wiped his mouth with his sleeve. Krampel watched intently as the man reached for his rucksack, and the giggling returned in earnest.

The man opened the rucksack and began to laugh louder as he pulled a large necklace from it—the necklace that Lord Juniper had commissioned Krampel to return!

He stared at whom he believed was Anfron Shivelpenny now with narrowed eyes. Sizing him up, he figured he would get the drop on Shivelpenny before he even knew it. Krampel looked over to the trees where he stood earlier and saw a branch right above the criminal. He returned there quickly, and unsheathed *Flad-rul*.

Twirling the blade through his fingers, Krampel leapt and landed in a crouch behind Shivelpenny, coming up just as quickly and putting the edge of the greatsword up against the thief's neck.

Shivelpenny froze as he felt the blade come in contact with his skin.

"Fancy seeing you with that bauble, Anfron Shivelpenny," said Krampel, his voice icy and cold in way of a greeting. "I would have expected it to be with its owner, not with you."

Shivelpenny rolled away and came to his feet, his right hand pulling his sword out in the same motion. Krampel grinned as the criminal came into a fighting stance. He had the option of disarming him before he had the chance to pull his sword, but Lord Juniper wished to inflict the punishment himself.

He would not take away the lord's merriment. That's not what Juniper paid him to do.

"Who are you?" Shivelpenny said fearfully.

"You don't want to know," Krampel replied, turning his voice soft and low, before he moved in to strike.

Krampel's moves were quick, and he didn't pause to let the man catch his breath, either. The hunter slashed right and then left, each time narrowly missing the chance to damage his adversary. Each time Shivelpenny parried the strikes with ease, and Krampel knew it was time to adjust his tactics.

He stepped back slightly and twirled the sword between his fingers, taking a sharp breath before he attacked once again, crossing steel with the thief. Krampel moved his feet right, trying to keep the man off-balance, all while chopping away at his bounty's sides. It was all Shivelpenny could do to stop Krampel's attack, bending his wrist here and there and utilizing a one-handed defense while Krampel held the mighty *Flad-rul* in both hands.

"Why don't you die?" Shivelpenny said through clenched teeth.

"I'm prolonging the inevitable, since it looks like you need practice with the blade," Krampel taunted.

With an enraged howl, Shivelpenny tried a perpendicular slash, but Krampel wasn't there when the sword passed through air. Instead, Krampel spun and swiped low in an attempt at the criminal's legs, but his quarry deftly leapt over the swipe. Krampel rolled away in a backward somersault just as Shivelpenny tried to go for the kill with a two-handed chop, then came back up and attacked again without a breath.

The two traded swings, bringing their swords back and forth. Steel collided with steel, the sounds reverberating through the forest. Every time Shivelpenny attacked, Krampel parried and then counterparried with a move that Shivelpenny similarly stopped. But Krampel quickly tired of this game: Shivelpenny was a good swordsman, but he currently dealt with a sword greater than any he ever saw.

With a thought from its wielder, Flad-rul ignited and scared Shivelpenny out of his wits. He dropped the sword he held and fell down to the ground, landing hard on his backside. He looked up into Krampel's eyes, which reflected the fire that the blade gave off.

Krampel immediately kicked Shivelpenny's sword several axe-lengths away and leveled his own toward his face. The fire trickled away, but Krampel knew that Shivelpenny could see the remnants of the flames still dancing inside his pupils.

"Now let's try this again, Shivelpenny. I am the Dark Falcon, and you are my latest captive," Krampel said. "You are beaten. My orders are to take you back alive, so it would do neither or us good to force me to kill you.

"Get up."

Shivelpenny shook as he stood, while Krampel retrieved the man's blade and stuck it in his own belt. He then loosened a bit of rope and tied it around Shivelpenny's hands, then held the rest in his hand as he reached down and grabbed the criminal's rucksack and the bauble, which had dropped on the ground when Krampel pounced.

Krampel led him through the trees and away from Arborway, which stood as dark as the fall night. It was nearly the start of the next day, with the moon nearly at its highest peak in the southern sky.

The going was slow and Shivelpenny grew tired of walking, and that only delayed their trip. Krampel wanted to make it to Hanlin by sun up, which was only a few hours away. Krampel seemed certain that Lord Juniper did not anticipate him returning so quickly with the bounty and with the necklace that he wondered what the lord would say—or give—in response to such a fast delivery on the terms.

Twice they rested, if only to prevent Krampel from cutting out Shivelpenny's voice box. He believed Lord Juniper would take away some of the gold he promised if Krampel did that.

The hours passed as they walked, and soon the town of Hanlin came into view just as the sun started to peek over the horizon and into their eyes. Krampel believed that if Hanlin was like any other small town in the realms, he would have quite an audience when he brought Shivelpenny, defeated, back into the town at the end of a rope.

He smiled thinking about it.

Krampel heard the crowing of the cock as the pair stepped into the lane that led to the lord's home. He looked back to Shivelpenny, who did not look up at the house.

Within minutes they were at the front door, and Krampel knocked hard, just in case anyone was still asleep. He waited about two minutes before he knocked again, this time even harder. Another two minutes passed. Frustrated and scowling, Krampel had his fist up and ready to pound on the door when it opened slightly. Krampel said, "Finally!" as it opened, thinking that a servant would answer the door.

He was partly right, as it was the blonde serving girl from last night who came to see what the racket was about. Her hair was down, and she wore an extra-long tunic that came down to a few inches above her knees.

"Back so soon?" she said when she noticed who stood there. "We didn't think you'd be back for a few days." She looked to the criminal behind Krampel and scowled at him. Shivelpenny kept his eyes to the ground.

"Is your master available yet? I've done my job and now it's time to collect my fee," Krampel said coldly.

Slightly put off, the girl said, "Not yet, but I'll wake him. Come in, please."

Krampel dragged his captive into the house; Shivelpenny didn't put up a fight.

The serving girl walked them into the sitting room and asked, "May I get you something to eat, lord, to refresh you from your journey?"

Krampel waved her off rudely.

"Nay, just fetch the lord so I may be on my way."

The girl bowed her head, then turned and headed for the stairwell that led upstairs. She took one look at Krampel, who looked at her as she called up the stairs, "Father, your bounty hunter has returned with your prize!"

Minutes later, Krampel heard the heavy footsteps of the lord churning across the ceiling, then heard the echoes of the stairs creaking under his weight.

When he got to the bottom of the stairs and turned into the sitting room, Krampel rose and bowed, then reached into Shivelpenny's rucksack and pulled out the priceless necklace. Lord Juniper gave a boisterous laugh and nearly tumbled when he saw the jewels sparkling in the morning's candlelight. The sun had just begun streaming in, and Krampel wondered what the bauble looked like in natural light.

"You most certainly are the best bounty hunter around, Dark Falcon," Juniper said, grabbing the necklace from him. "This is definitely my necklace, and I cannot thank you enough for returning it!"

The merriment over, Juniper looked over at Shivelpenny and stared him down. The criminal continued to stare at his bound hands.

"Look at me, Shivelpenny," the lord ordered, but Shivelpenny didn't respond. Krampel reached over and tugged the man's hair back, twisting the length around his fist, forcing the thief to look into the eyes of the man whose house he had violated.

"That's better. I have spoken with the tribunal, and they agreed that you are to be executed for thievery of a Hanlin noble!"

Shivelpenny didn't even whimper, or plead, or show any emotion whatsoever. It seemed as if he knew his fate as soon as Krampel caught him. Krampel didn't understand it, but then again he tried not to understand the mind of criminals.

Lord Juniper motioned to the wall, and two well-camouflaged guards came away. Krampel didn't even see them; apparently Juniper relied on stealth, too. He handed the rope that bound the captive over to the guards, and they escorted the man from the room.

As soon as they were gone, Krampel turned to the lord.

"I'll take what's mine now, and I'll be on my way," he said, but the lord held up a hand.

"Please, you must be famished. Stay with us for the day, enjoy my hospitality, then we'll talk business," Juniper said with a boisterous laugh. Krampel noted that his client was a jovial man, and he didn't want to refuse. It was the first time a rich man actually paid him notice; his other rich clients never offered to break bread with him.

He accepted, albeit reluctantly.

***

Krampel ate his fill, and then some. The lord had a spread of hard-boiled eggs, muffins, crispy bacon, tomatoes, and pickles set out. The bounty hunter had a little bit of each before pouring himself a glass of something citrusy from a tall carafe in front of him. The lord's offerings had sated his hunger, he admitted quietly.

When he finished, Krampel turned to the lord and asked when he would be paid for this job. The lord gave another laugh.

"Why don't you rest here for the day, then I'll pay you. I'd hate to see a young man like yourself walking around without sleep."

Krampel blinked.

"I've done it before, I can do it again."

"But all that will catch up with you! I insist you stay here with us and sleep until you are ready to go on the road again."

Krampel couldn't say no to that. In fact, he did feel a little drowsy, and he didn't think the lord had poisoned his food. He then felt a hand on his arm, and it was the lord's daughter, helping him out of his chair and up the stairs. She led him to a sweet smelling guest room. The shades were drawn, he saw. Krampel's eyelids fluttered.

"Have a good sleep, Master Falcon," she said, then turned and headed back down the stairs. Krampel nodded in return, then fell, face-first, onto the bed. He barely registered the softness of the pillow or the breadth of the mattress. He was out before he knew it.

He slept like he hadn't slept in ages.

***

Nearly twelve hours later, Krampel awoke refreshed from his sleep. He thought that he could get used to sleeping in a bed instead of in a tree, but shrugged that thought aside. Like criminals, Krampel preferred to stay on the move. Complacency was just one of many ways to get yourself killed.

Sitting up, the aroma of meat caught his nostrils. His stomach rumbled, so he followed his nose.

When he reached the downstairs landing, the succulent scents led him left toward the kitchen. He passed through the dining room as if sleep walking, not pausing to say hello to the lord, who beckoned for him to sit and eat.

Krampel reached the kitchen and found a plate waiting for him; without further invitation, he sat down at the counter and ate heartily. A pheasant, fat and juicy, was the main course. Krampel hadn't tasted anything as delicious as this in at least five years; his heart quaked at the memory of stealing meat from the caravan's spit. He had to lick his fingers clean, catching every bit of grease from underneath his nails. There were browned potatoes sprinkled with rosemary, fresh rolls, and corn, boiled to perfection with just a touch of salt and sugar mixed together.

"You can join us in here, you know," the lord's daughter said with a smile. Frowning, he joined the lord and his daughter at the table. At a nod, the lord's daughter left the table. Krampel finished his meal there in silence, before Juniper stood and walked over to a small counter.

First, the lord picked up a long scabbard, then walked over to Krampel and handed it to him. It was made of gold and shined brightly in the candlelight. Krampel's eyes widened as he looked at it. Words had failed to come, so he bowed his head in thanks.

Then the lord returned to the counter and brought back a sack of gold, for which Krampel was able to thank him for vocally. Juniper nodded, returned to his seat, and continued to eat.

Confused, Krampel looked at the man, but didn't speak his thoughts aloud.

Wasn't I supposed to receive three things? The scabbard, the sack of gold, and the thing most precious to him. I hope I didn't misunderstand him.

He decided to wait until the dinner ended before he said anything.

When the lord dabbed his mouth with linen, he stood once again and walked over to where Krampel sat. Krampel heard soft footsteps above him.

"I know I promised you a third item as your bounty, but like I said, it's not an item of value as you'd see it. It is, however, something incredibly precious to me," the lord said, before he lifted his left hand and indicated the person standing at the foot of the stairs.

Krampel turned and saw the lord's daughter standing there, dressed for the road. She wore warrior's attire, with a coat of mail and a sword adorning her outfit. The trappings of wealth had disappeared. She looked like a hearty warrior now.

"My daughter," he continued, "has longed for the life of a bounty hunter. I have had her trained with the sword. But I would like it if you would train her in your field so she may live her dream."

All of this caught Krampel off-guard. It took him a second to process this information, but he thought he had heard the lord correctly. He wanted Krampel to teach his daughter to become a bounty hunter?

Who wanted that kind of life for their child? he thought. *Bounty hunting wasn't a career that one simply chose at a young age; it is an acquired talent, not one that a person just "became." Longing for the life of a bounty hunter?*

He had never heard that before. He had become a bounty hunter out of necessity.

"I work alone," Krampel said darkly as he stood up and slid *Flad-rul* into its new home. "It's better that way. Less collateral damage."

The lord's daughter lowered her face. Krampel looked at her, and for the first time in five years, his heart fell. He didn't know why.

"She won't be any trouble, I can assure you," Juniper said. "She can protect herself. She just wants the best to teach her the skills necessary to be a bounty hunter. We've heard you are the best: Your record of successful captures without killing or maiming your bounties is certainly impressive. She wants to learn from you, watch the way you handle your job, to see what it takes."

"Please sir," the daughter pleaded, stepping forward, "let me learn at your feet."

Krampel thought this over as he sat back down. There was still a beat of meat on his pheasant, and he reached out and pulled a bit of it away from the carcass. He tossed it in his mouth and swallowed without chewing. He shot a blast of air through his nostrils.

He didn't exactly want an apprentice. He had grown set in his ways over the past five years, and he had a routine that he liked to go through every day. An apprentice would want to know everything about their master's routines. Giving away secrets didn't exactly represent job security in the bounty hunting trade; giving away secrets led to the exposure of weaknesses.

That was something else that might get a bounty hunter killed.

But Krampel had another reason why he didn't want an apprentice: He didn't want an attachment, and he didn't want someone to get attached to him. Attachment led to poor judgment and bad decision-making while on a hunt. Most bounty hunters learned by doing their craft, not with someone looking over their shoulder to make sure they did it correctly. After all, each bounty hunter had a certain way of doing their jobs. None wanted their habits copied, or give away a tidbit so someone else thought they did a job when they didn't—unless it was a spectacularly heinous killing, which gave him a certain berth when walking in a crowd. With an apprentice, there was always a chance of the student turning on the mentor—especially if the price was right. He liked the way his head fit on his neck, and he didn't want a knife shoved into his back.

There was another fact that Krampel kept close to his vest: Should he die, he didn't want anyone to mourn for him like he did for Vossler. He had mourned for Vossler even after he burned down the home in Cassimina, doing so for several weeks until he decided to live his life for himself, not for anyone else. He had turned into a dark, brooding loner, with attachments to no one weighing him down. An apprentice meant someone looking up to him, someone to guide.

It wasn't the kind of life he wanted. Not at all.

"I insist you take her," the lord said, interrupting Krampel's thoughts. "I can give you a great amount of wealth for your services so that you don't have to ever hunt again. After you're done training her, that is."

Krampel felt his eyebrows arching, almost of their own volition, as he mulled over this latest offer. It was an interesting proposition, he had to admit. Never having to worry about money, living in luxury, and never having to hunt criminals again? It piqued his curiosity in several ways, and he knew it showed on his face.

"Okay," Krampel said, "I'll do it. As long as she knows her place and doesn't speak for me, then I'll do it."

And as long as she doesn't grow close to me, he thought. *I'll never grow close to another person. Not after what happened to Vossler.*

"Good! You've made me a very happy man, Dark Falcon. You won't be sorry!"

Krampel hoped that, too.

Krampel and the lord's daughter departed Hanlin shortly after; Krampel loaded with his new gifts and a heavy purse, while the girl carried provisions that should last the pair the next two fortnights, as well as her sword and traveling cloak. The girl had said her good byes to several people while Krampel calmly looked on. Some of the young ladies had giggled when they saw Krampel standing behind her, looking somewhat impatient; some of the elders thought Lord Juniper mad to allow his daughter to travel with a vagabond louse.

They did not speak a word to each other for the first hour of their journey together, with the only sounds being their footfalls crunching against the paths, and the chirping of crickets along the sides of the road. Grasshoppers pounced and bounced along, and the girl giggled when one bounded off her sword with a soft clink.

The pair made their first stop as soon as the moon met its apex. Walking for so long made both of them hungry and thirsty. They sat down on a small outcropping of rocks and ate for several minutes. They didn't stay in that spot for long: They departed several minutes later, for Krampel wanted to find a place to sleep soon.

And with Arborway still about ten miles away, they were in for several more hours of walking.

When they reached their first destination, the trees of Arborway surrounded them. It was darker inside the forest: the trees completely shut out moonlight and starlight. He watched the girl as she looked around and, even though it was dark, Krampel knew at once that this was not her ideal spot for camping out. The look on her face showed it, too.

Krampel dropped his gear—except his sword, which he always wore on his belt, and his shield, on which he laid his head—and stretched out against the base of a nearby tree.

"You take the first watch," he said, the first thing he ever said to her. "I'll wake myself up in three hours to relieve you."

Krampel soon fell asleep, leaving the girl alone to keep watch.

***

It's boring duty, she thought, with a sleeping bounty hunter and the sounds of crickets ricocheting around the wood her only company. She quickly attuned her eyes to the ever-enveloping darkness, but that also led to her growing complacency. She took a seat at the base of a tree immediately across from the bounty hunter and continued her watch there.

Within an hour, the girl was asleep, her head resting against the tree, tilted toward her left shoulder.

Chapter 8

Like clockwork, Krampel had leapt awake three hours later. It was still dark and only a short time into the new day, only a few hours until the rise of the new sun. He adjusted his eyes to the dark, pulled out a chunk of salted meat and began to nibble on it, trying to re-energize himself for the day. He would not rest again until the evening, no matter what the princess wanted to do.

He looked over to her sleeping form and snorted.

Some bounty hunter she'll make, he thought. *The first time she's out with me, and she falls asleep on watch. The criminals will slit her throat if she's alone.*

Which is exactly why he wanted to give her a swift kick in the side, but the idea had passed just as quickly. He would wake her in a few hours, when dawn broke and breakfast was ready; she would apologize profusely, he knew, and he would wave it off, even though he shouldn't.

But if it happened a second time—and he felt sure it would—then he would give her that kick. It would teach her the importance of staying awake and what dereliction of duty meant. This was the wild, and staying alert was not an option.

Staying alert in the wild kept one alive.

As his thoughts rolled from annoyance, he immediately saw the advantages to having the girl along with him on hunts. It was simple: She would use her feminine wiles to lure a male bounty into a sense of security before Krampel trapped him. He easily saw the possibilities—the increased benefits—of her continued apprenticeship.

And with her being an attractive girl, many men wouldn't resist her. That was a plus.

Krampel stood and walked a few feet to survey the area. He kept his left hand on the pommel of *Flad-rul*. He looked around with his night vision and didn't see anything that he considered a threat to either of them. He walked back to the campsite, where he sat down cross-legged and meditated.

He had turned to meditation as a way to gain self-control, something Vossler did not teach him in their short time together. He felt in control over every portion of his life when he meditated, focusing positive energy and storing it. He felt it helped him in sword duels and gave him an even more powerful swing, while it sharpened his concentration in search of wrong doers. He even used it to calm himself, and with the annoyance of finding the girl sleeping on watch still fresh in his mind, this was the opportune moment to cool down.

His meditation had lasted for several hours, and even with his eyes closed, he had kept himself fully attuned to the surrounding area. Nothing came close; not even an animal. With the sun about to peek above the eastern horizon; Krampel had snapped awake. He saw the sky had already turned a sharp pink, which meant an unseasonably warm day. Even with his cloak around him, he felt the air grow warm. He sniffed the air twice, then looked west.

A storm now brewed a few hours away, which meant the rain would more than likely catch them while in transit. But he knew the geography in these parts extremely well, and if they left now, they would make the next forest with time to spare.

Krampel shook the girl's shoulder and woke her up, looking at her with a scowl.

"We're leaving quickly," he said just as her eyes opened. She looked around as soon as she focused her eyes.

"The sun isn't even up yet," she said. "Why so early?"

"Because we're leaving," Krampel replied harshly.

"That's not a reason. We have to at least eat before we run."

That earned her a loaf of bread tossed to her, which she didn't catch. It smacked off her face and fell to the forest floor.

"Thanks," she said, annoyed at having food thrown at her.

Krampel didn't respond; he had simply turned and walked off. She picked up the bread and followed him out of the forest. Their footsteps—well, hers—crunched off the detritus of Arborway.

The pair walked approximately a mile north before the girl peppered Krampel with questions.

"So how long have you been a bounty hunter?" she asked.

"Five years."

"What does it take to be a bounty hunter?"

"Tenacity, strong will, quickness."

"You don't talk a lot, do you?"

"You talk a lot."

The girl blushed crimson as Krampel answered her third question with a light smile.

"So what made you decide to become a hunter?" she continued.

"I needed to eat. I needed gold to eat. Simple enough, isn't it?"

"True, but why did you choose hunting? Why not a tanner or a worker of metals? I mean, didn't you have a different profession in mind when you were younger?"

Krampel rounded on her.

"Why did you decide to become a bounty hunter, girl? You seem so keen on becoming one of us. You seem to be riding me hard for my vocation; why don't you tell me why you've chosen this line of work?"

The two had stopped in a clearing, facing each other, staring the other down. Krampel stood a full head taller than the girl, but she didn't back down in the slightest, even though Krampel's question put her back on her heels. The sun continued its methodical rise over the horizon, and the shadows of the pair streamed away from them, making them look like giants.

She kept her face calm as she looked at him.

"I wanted to see the realms," she replied. "Every part of it; the good and the bad parts. I wouldn't be able to do that being the lady of a house. I wanted action, adventure. I wanted to do something that would benefit the realms at large, not just myself. I wanted to give my life to something important, and fighting criminals and bringing them to justice is something I believe is important."

Krampel nodded slowly, seemingly accepting her reason, then turned and led them away.

"So would you like to know my name or are you just going to be calling me 'girl' while we're hunting together?" she asked.

"First names lead to attachment, and that is something I'd rather like to avoid."

"Why is that?"

"Personal preference, that's all. I have my reasons, and they are private. I'd rather not go into it."

They marched on, the clouds continuing to threaten off the coast of the Enchanted Sea.

***

She now questioned her father's wisdom in aligning her with this particular bounty hunter. *Not all of them were this moody, right?* she thought. She wondered about this and thought the Dark Falcon, underneath that rough and dark exterior, had some serious issues. She also wondered how long it would take her to chip away at his façade. If they were to stay together, she would need him to open up to her.

"Lutricia," she said.

"What?"

"My name is Lutricia," she answered with a smile. "So you don't have to call me girl all the time. Now, I know your mother didn't name you the Dark Falcon straight out of the womb."

"Don't talk about my mother!" he said as soft as he could, but she noted there was quite a bit of rage behind it. It definitely got her attention, and she dropped the subject of his name. He knew hers though, and for her, that was enough.

"Where are we heading?"

"We're heading to another place for shelter tonight," he said. "There are a group of trees near Oak Flats that we can stay in. The squirrellen won't mind."

"Squirrellen? I don't believe I've heard of them."

"There is a reason for that. Most squirrellen do not associate with other races, having been subjugated and enslaved by humans for centuries. However, some are trusting enough to help others. They are excellent navigators and love the sea; some of the greatest captains in the realms are squirrellen. They are fairly tall, thin, and walk upright like humans. They are a brilliant race and are also great warriors when they have to be; they prefer to do the attacking than be attacked, though. They run from invasions. They always get their revenge, though."

"I would love to meet one."

"You may, but then again, you may not. Depends on how things go in the future. I've been wandering the lands around here, and I've kept my eyes on Oak Flats' borders when I'm here. This profession takes me a long way from here, but news travels far when there are wars brewing. I hadn't heard of any trouble recently, so I don't expect to see any when we near their realm."

They continued walking, and within an hour the storm he had predicted let loose its contents on Obloeron. The Falcon raised the cowl of his cloak to ward off the rain, while Lutricia followed suit. They did that seconds before the first raindrops fell, and within a minute, the skies grew increasingly dark until a curtain of rain fell. The cascade continued for quite a while, and the Falcon prevented his apprentice from running.

"It is best to walk normally in a rainstorm. Running only soaks you further and faster. Do not worry, your cloak will keep your upper body dry. You won't develop a sickness."

Finally, after two more hours of walking, the pair reached the small forest just east of Oak Flats. Lutricia smelled the faint scent of salt water even on the rain-drenched branches. Under one of the boughs, the pair didn't lower their cowls, but they sat next to each other and ate, their bodies shivering as the fall rain storm continued to flex its muscle over the realms.

***

The rain did not stop for the rest of the day, and by the time the two moved again, their legs had cramped up from sitting in the same position for so long. The pair exchanged few words, as Lutricia had taken the hint that Krampel did not like to talk much.

Krampel had decided that it was too late for them to walk further. He told his apprentice that he'd take the first watch tonight. As expected, she was asleep within minutes.

A light, cool breeze wafted across the long meadow, chilling Krampel's bones. He wrapped his cloak around him even tighter in an attempt to ward off the cold.

There is another way I could keep myself warm, he thought. He drew *Flad-rul* from the golden scabbard, trying to keep the scraping of steel against steel to a minimum as the girl slept, then took off his cloak. He slowly paced the campsite, swinging the sword back and forth.

Hard work and a grueling training regimen, one that he kept secret from everyone, had hardened his body over the years. The regimen involved hours of sparring with shadows, much like he did in Vossler's training dungeon. But with so much of the wood around them wet, there would be no chance to light a fire to keep them warm, or give Krampel some shadows to spar against.

No one but Krampel heard the sounds of the wet grass crunching under his booted feet. He was now in Dark Falcon mode, and that training extended his senses beyond the levels of normal perception. Every little noise sounded like a cattle drive to him, but he shut it out as he swung *Flad-rul*. He remembered every little bit of his sword training with Vossler, and he mimicked the moves he practiced in the old man's dungeon so long ago. Using a two-handed grip on the magnificent sword, Krampel started with an old-fashioned style, protecting his center as he swatted away invisible enemies with a back-and-forth style that kept his wrists and elbows locked. This was a more one-on-one style, and he hadn't used it in a long time.

He breathed with every swing, exhaling and expelling the dirty air on a thrust and inhaling clean air with a parry. He felt clean and pure again within heartbeats.

Then Krampel switched the style, moving to a more circular style of fighting. Krampel moved the Flame Thrower around, spinning his body to deflect numerous attackers, each time moving in a different direction. First he'd move the sword right then left, then spun back the way he came, turning his wrists to block a non-existent strike.

He had worked up quite a sweat while he self-sparred, and he felt the heat seep into his bones, warming his body throughout. He felt content, but needed to spice up his fight a little bit.

He closed his eyes and sank into the power of *Flad-rul*, which ignited and bathed the entire area in light. The flames flew off the blade several feet into the air.

Lutricia awoke with a light yell.

"Sorry to wake you," Krampel said, not peeling his eyes from the heat of the blade.

"It's no mind. I watched you out of the corner of my eye. I can't sleep. Mind if I spar with you?"

Without looking, Krampel waved her forward. She got up, drew her sword and stood next to her mentor, then looked toward him so he could make the first cut. First he slashed down to the right, and she followed his lead. He then brought the mighty four-and-a-half foot sword up and around to the left, which the girl mimicked easily. Krampel then gave two quick crossing moves, going right and then left, but that ended when Lutricia spun to her right, bringing her left foot over to stand in front of the mighty warrior. In the same move, she brought her blade over and crossed steel with him, winking slightly. Krampel smirked.

Lutricia uncrossed her sword, brought it over her head and down to Krampel's right, which the bounty hunter brought his sword down to parry easily. Her strokes were soft and easy, not getting too far ahead of herself. The girl's fighting style eventually lulled Krampel into complacency.

That gave Lutricia an opening. She then turned into a ferocious beast, her eyes widening and focusing, her face rigid with concentration. She gave two hard slashes that Krampel just barely stopped, and the bounty hunter needed to step back to look fully at the situation. His apprentice had just unleashed a barrage of chops for which he was unprepared. His eyes had widened as he assessed everything, while Lutricia walked back and forth, swinging her sword low. She smiled wide, and even through the darkness, Krampel saw her teeth gleaming.

So she is trying to prove herself to me, Krampel thought. *She was trained just as well as her father said. Looks like it's time to get serious then. If she wants to be big and bad, then I'll show her what that means.*

Without warning her, Krampel came after Lutricia like wildfire. He pushed off with a blaze of speed, swinging his sword hard to the left. Lutricia's sword came up to block Krampel's, turning her body to the side, letting him sweep right by her. She spun around and slashed horizontally at Krampel's back, but Krampel avoided her attack, bringing his sword up behind his right shoulder, parrying her blade. Sparks flew away as they made contact.

He turned the moment the swords connected and quickly went on the offensive. He hacked right and left, going first for the upper body of his apprentice. Lutricia had blocked those without a problem, but then Krampel spun and swept low. Lutricia deftly leapt over the sword, then spun away without going for the killing blow. Krampel had righted himself in time to see Lutricia charging in, her eyes wide and bright.

Their swords clashed once again, Krampel stepping backward to let his apprentice expel all of her energy. He had turned his sword here and there, putting as much effort into stopping her as he had to without further draining himself. Even though she was well trained, she wasn't up to his standards of fighting. He was about to teach her the first lesson of fighting—being a defensive fighter.

As soon as she showed the first sign of tiring, Krampel had turned the tables against her. He kept up his attack until she fell, tripping on a loose stone and falling on her backside, her sword falling out her hands as she attempted to stop her fall. Krampel had quickly shoved the point of his greatsword toward her neck, signifying the end of the sparring session between the two.

Krampel pulled his sword away with a flourish and sheathed his blade, before he held out his hand to the girl.

"You fight incredibly well, but you have to remember one thing—it is best to be a defensive fighter," he lectured much with the same tone Vossler had used against him. "Let your opponent get rid of his energy by using only a minimal amount to deflect his attacks. Then, when he tires himself out, change the tempo of the battle and fight as viciously as you can, while staying in control of yourself, in order to subdue your opponent or cause your opponent to make a mistake. That is what I did to you, and you walked right into the trap."

Lutricia nodded as she sat up, reaching for her sword. She was about to speak, but Krampel cut her off by placing his hand over her mouth and quieting her. He stretched his hearing far, and then he heard something that worried him: The neighing of a horse, then the rumble of hooves on the ground.

"Quickly," he whispered, "gather your cloak and follow me!"

Lutricia did as he asked, scurrying about, while Krampel grabbed his and sprinted to an oak, the one next to their camp spot. He helped Lutricia into the tree, giving her a boost up with cupped hands, before he flung himself up into the boughs, following her to relative safety. He got close to the tree, and as he looked over to Lutricia, he put his finger to his lips to tell her to be quiet.

He didn't peek through the branches to see when the riders arrived: He was sure he would hear them easily enough.

Within two minutes, the riders arrived. Their horses streamed into the campground and paused while the riders dismounted.

From his vantagepoint in the tree, Krampel looked down and saw the leader walk toward the spot where he and Lutricia had sparred. The leader carried a torch in his hands, and he bent down and inspected the area.

"What's happening? I can't see. What do they want?" Lutricia whispered. Krampel turned and shrugged, then returned to his watch.

"These prints are fresh," the leader said, holding his torch low to the ground. "Within an hour they were made, I'd say. Spread out and search the area!" he ordered his troops, who tugged on the reins and guided their horses away. "The Lord of Myrindar wants to speak with that bounty hunter about something incredibly important to the Imperium. He must be found and brought before the Inquisitor. Make haste in your searches, but do not engage him if he has a sword out!"

Seconds later, another rider came up to speak with the leader, and they didn't bother keeping their voices down.

"Why does the Inquisitor want the Dark Falcon? Why can't he pick any bounty hunter at random in Myrindar?"

"Because he wants the best, and the Dark Falcon is the best at what he does," the leader replied with disgusting sneer. Krampel, above in the trees, smirked. "He will have no trouble capturing the three criminals the lord wants taken into custody. It is not our place to question the lord; he is the law of the southlands and has been for years. Our duty is to follow his orders explicitly.

"Now this is interesting," the leader commented. "Look here—another set of prints. It seems as though the two were in a dance of some sort. A fight, but there is no body remaining? A very strange development, I'd say. It is something we'll have to investigate further and let the lord know about when we return.

"Alert the men; we ride northwest."

The second man took out a small horn and gave it three quick blasts, signaling the horsemen to return. When they all returned, they headed off to the northwest to continue their search.

When they were long gone, Krampel and Lutricia still sat in the tree. Krampel looked down to make sure there weren't any stragglers minus their horse. When he felt sure there were no eavesdropping voices, he turned to Lutricia.

"This is very interesting," he said thoughtfully. "The Imperial Inquisitor wishes me to come to Myrindar and work for him. I had wondered where our next real meal would come from, and then this drops into our lap. This may be a very interesting day for us, indeed. We'll have to go to Myrindar and see what the man wants of me.

"All of those riders are part of the Inquisitor's Royal Brigade. They are his usual escort through the realms, when the Inquisitor is traveling abroad to other kingdoms. From what I've heard, though, the current Inquisitor is a recluse; he prefers to stay in his manor high above the city, and only uses the Royal Brigade as a message service. As you can see, that is their current task, and you could tell from the tone the leader of their party used that they are not happy at being relegated to being a bunch of well-armed couriers.

"Let us get down and make our way south to see what the Inquisitor wishes me to do for him."

With a leap, Krampel jumped out of the tree, his cloak billowing behind him. He landed cat-like on the ground. Lutricia, on the other hand, climbed out of the tree instead of leaping, her cloak in her hands.

The moon hung in the clear sky above them, the stars twinkling down on the realms. They departed southward, back the way they had come that morning.

"You're not tired?" Lutricia asked. "I didn't get much sleep, and I'm burned out."

"I slept a bit during the day, during the storm," he answered without turning his head toward her. "I have gone long nights without sleep while searching for numerous quarries. You'll get used to it. It's a part of being what we are. You sleep when you can, but those moments are few and far between."

Lutricia yawned. Krampel tried to stifle a yawn but couldn't, yet they did not stop to sleep. They continued south as dawn broke over them, bathing the path to Arborway in hues of yellow and gold. The storm was over here, too.

"It seems like we just left here," she said. "Maybe we should have just stuck around."

"If we didn't leave, we would probably not have received the summons," Krampel quickly replied, even though, in truth, the Royal Brigade did not hand him the summons personally. "Arborway is vast; if they had searched it for us, they'd still be searching. Finding us where they did was amazing, yet I'm sure they heard the clanging of our swords in order to detect us. That could be good or bad, depending on the way you want to look at it."

They entered the realm of trees without anyone stopping them, which surprised both the bounty hunter and his apprentice. They found a clear path through the towering oaks, weaving their way toward the great mountain city.

"I was supposed to go to Myrindar to study to be an artist," Lutricia said as they continued walking through the trees. "That was what my mother wanted long ago, before she died. She loved the arts and said an education in Myrindar would give me the realms at my feet. But when she died, my father said I would become a warrior instead of an artist. He hired a tutor for my lessons and a burly man who was very good with the sword to instruct me in the ways of battle. Then when I discovered that bounty hunting was a noble profession, I wanted to become one. That is when my father contacted you through his go-between."

"I never had that kind of opportunity, a wonderful education in a wonderful city," Krampel said, opening up slightly. "I hardly had an education when I was younger; I was orphaned twice and I use common sense, not what I would have learned in books, to guide me in my life. Maybe you should have taken the opportunity to have a great education; you would have been able to make something of yourself instead of becoming a bounty hunter."

"I didn't know you were orphaned," Lutricia said, ignoring Krampel's jibe.

"Yes, I was, and no, I don't want to talk about it."

"You don't like to talk about anything, do you? I told you about my life, and you can't tell me about yours. You're so unfeeling that you can't even tell me your name!"

"That is because I'm a very private person, girl," Krampel said, stressing the final word as he turned to face her. "When I feel you need to know more about me, then I'll tell you more about me. You haven't earned that right to hear about that side of me yet."

Krampel turned away, not caring that he hurt her: She seemed insulted that he refused to open up fully to her. To him, this was just another job; a different kind of job than he was used to, but it was still a job. Her father had paid him a great deal to teach her how to be a bounty hunter. When this job was over, he would move on to the next, while she would move from job to job. He didn't know her that well, and he didn't know if she deserved his trust regarding his innermost secrets.

If anything, Krampel was a cautious individual. He trusted no one.

"Look," Lutricia said, interrupting his thoughts, "we're going to be together for quite a while, so you might as well get used to having me around. I have to know what you're about, so you might as well tell me!"

Krampel paused in the middle of the woods, thinking over her last words. He turned to her and said, "You want to know what I'm all about? I'm all about me and the weight of my purse. That's it. I became an unfeeling individual when I saw my mentor murdered in front of my eyes by orcs. At that moment I snapped and killed every last orc that I could get my hands on. I mourn for him because I...I loved him like a father. I didn't want to take you on as apprentice to spare you your grief should I happen to die while we are together."

He stepped closer to her.

"Is that what you wanted to know? Is that the information you were looking for? Does that sate your curiosity about me?"

The fire in his eyes had ignited a little bit, and Lutricia recoiled slightly. She had pushed him here, he knew, and he saw that she now regretted every second of it.

"I'm sorry," she said softly. "I didn't mean to anger you."

Krampel turned away and walked off, not wanting to hear anything else from the young woman.

They walked in silence for the next half an hour, not saying another word to each other until they were out of Arborway, looking on the majestic mountain city.

"Myrindar, the chief city in the southlands," Krampel said to his apprentice, his anger apparently gone. "There will be a guard at the city gates, so keep your eyes open. I have no idea what to expect from these people. We must be on our guard."

Lutricia nodded, and together they set off for the northern gates to the city, crossing a long meadow. For fall, the air was slightly warmer south of Arborway. Krampel removed his cloak. Lutricia did the same.

It didn't take long for the pair to get to the gates, where, like Krampel had suspected, three guards stood at the stone opening. They had looked at the newcomers with wary eyes, their hands down by their weapons. The sight of Krampel and Lutricia's blades set them on edge.

Chapter 9

The two travelers took their hands off their weapons and put their palms up in a placating gesture, the realms-wide gesture of friendship. Krampel stepped forward and bowed.

"Greetings, gentles," he said, more in the manner of a lord than a bounty hunter. "I am here to see the Inquisitor. He issued an order for me to appear before him."

"Do you have the summons with you to prove your claim? We don't just let anyone up to the manor to see him," the guard on the left said.

Krampel grimaced.

"Well, no, I don't. We overheard a band of the Inquisitor's Royal Brigade as they searched for us. They didn't put it into our hand."

"Then I'm afraid I can't let you into the city," the guard replied. "No summons, no entrance."

"Please, send a runner to the manor. The Inquisitor will confirm this for you. I am the Dark Falcon. He'll want to see me; he has a set of jobs for me."

The three guards looked at each other as if to see who would leave the first level of the city and traverse the mountain to the manor. Krampel looked to each of them as they tried to make their decision, until he stepped forward.

"I don't want to make a stink about this, but could you hurry, please? My companion is a hot head and doesn't like to wait a long time," he said. Lutricia nearly stepped forward to contradict this, but Krampel stopped her with a look. He didn't want to give her another scolding for overstepping her bounds. She was the apprentice. He was the master. If he said she was hot headed, she was hot headed.

The two guards in the front looked at the third, who gave a resigned sigh. He mounted his horse and raced off to the manor to confirm Krampel's request.

He and Lutricia waited patiently for the guard to return to his post at the northern gate. They stood silently, even though Krampel knew his apprentice wanted to ask every question known to man. He would have to answer every single one, if he wanted to or not.

By the time the guard had returned, the clatter of hooves on stone had drowned out the sounds of the city proper shaking off its sleep: The people of Myrindar started their daily chores, so much so that it reminded Krampel of Cassimina, if ever briefly. He looked to the guard, who dismounted his horse.

"The Inquisitor confirms the man's story. He is to be allowed to enter," the young guard said as he walked forward. Krampel nodded to the guards as they waved him inside the mountain city.

As soon as they walked some twenty axe-lengths away from the gate, Lutricia finally let the hold on her tongue go.

"So I'm a hot head, am I?"

Krampel snorted.

"Relax. It got us what we wanted. We're inside now, and now we can see what the Inquisitor wants of me. It may be something major, or it may be something minor. We won't know until we speak with him."

"I don't appreciate you telling a lie about me."

"Get used to it. Master's privilege," Krampel said with a smirk. Lutricia huffed, but Krampel knew it was just bravado.

The pair wound their way up the paths that led to the manor, situated on the seventh level of the mountain city, just below the summit. The manor was a beautiful building and showed the advancement of modern Myrindarian architecture.

"Almost there," Krampel said.

"Doesn't feel like it. My feet are killing me."

"Another thing you must get used to."

Krampel grinned as Lutricia shot her mentor a look that would have killed a lesser human.

Once they reached the fifth level, another set of guards awaited their presence. Instead of stopping the pair, the guards each grabbed a door handle and opened the doors for them, bowing them through without pause. They found themselves in a large room with a staircase immediately in front of them, the stairs heading up.

The pair stopped at the top of the stairs, which opened into an audience chamber. Inside the room sat a group of about five people surrounding a tall, thin man with closely cropped silver and black hair. The five men all wore robes of blue, while the man in the center wore a half robe of blue that accented the white tunic he wore underneath. His trousers were gray, and he wore high black boots of a material Krampel had never seen before. The man dismissed the five others, and as they rounded the large table and headed out the door, passing Krampel and Lutricia on their way. The man came toward them, extending his hand in welcome.

"Greetings, Dark Falcon. I am Cairn Ford, the High Imperial Inquisitor," he said, shaking Krampel's hand, before he then bowed to Lutricia and kissed her hand. "I've not had the pleasure of meeting you before, my dear. And you are?"

"Lutricia Juniper, lord," she said.

Ford blinked.

"She is my apprentice at the behest of Lord Juniper, her father, lord. We've only been together for two days."

Ford, with a smile, waved off the explanation and invited the duo to sit down while he took a seat at the head of the table. Krampel pulled Lutricia's seat out for her, before he took the seat closer to the Inquisitor.

"I've heard of your great exploits over the past few years, Dark Falcon, and I must say that I am impressed with everything that has come to my ears here in Myrindar."

"Thank you, lord."

"I called you here because I wish to purchase your services."

"I figured." Krampel remained impassive with his hands folded in his lap. The Inquisitor grinned in response.

"Over the past year, I have hired several bounty hunters to capture a number of criminals wanted for crimes large and small. Every single hunter has failed to deliver these criminals to me. And since I hear that you are the best at what you do, I would like you to pick up the trail and catch these men."

"If you acknowledge my superiority over other hunters, lord, why are you waiting until now to request an audience with me?"

"From what I understand, you were away from the southlands for an extended period of time and were unavailable to work. When word reached me that you were back within the realm, I sent for you. I knew that you would be very interested in becoming affiliated with the Inquisitor."

"That's where you're wrong, lord," Krampel replied quickly, leaning forward. "I am aligned or affiliated with no one. I am a freelance operator, and I work for the highest bounties. To say that I am affiliated with anyone is incorrect and laughable."

"My apologies, Dark Falcon. However, I would like to extend to you a king's ransom for assisting me in the capture of these criminals," Ford said, looking straight at the bounty hunter. "I would like to bring them to justice."

"What were their crimes?" Krampel asked.

"Their crimes are numerous," Ford said, deflecting the question. "Only a well-trained bounty hunter like yourself can lay claim to these bounties and become wealthier than you've ever dreamed."

"I can dream quite a bit, Inquisitor."

Ford laughed.

"I'm sure you can. Do we have an agreement?"

"Let me consider it. Share with me the names of the criminals and I'll let you know in an hour."

Ford bowed with a smile, then handed him a list of three names. Krampel didn't look at the list until Ford left the room, closing the door behind him. As soon as the door closed, Krampel shot from his seat and walked over to a window. He unrolled the short list of names. His eyes darted to the first name, and remained riveted there accompanied by his sharp intake of breath.

It was a name from his past, a distant past. Krampel had not seen the man in more than five years, not since he sent the scoundrel running—

The Royal Brigade—and, presumably, Cairn Ford—wanted Piety Crassnick for stealing two foals. Krampel always knew his and Piety's paths would cross again.

The other two names did not even register in Krampel's head; he concentrated on Piety. He wondered how much larger the bully of Cassimina had grown. He remembered Piety had bolted town once word came of the death of his father in the first orc raid—*nay*, he thought, *pausing: Piety had left town before the orc raid.*

Krampel lowered the list and stared out the window, wondering where Piety was now. He longed for clairvoyant sight to see through the trees and long miles to where the man now hid from bounty hunters. Catching him, Krampel knew, would feel like he had achieved the sweetest revenge ever. He wanted to look him in the eyes again, knowing that he had, at last, gained the upper hand.

From behind him, Lutricia approached and took the list from his hands and read it. Her jaw dropped.

Then she dropped the list to the floor and strangled a cry.

That caught Krampel's attention. He turned to see if his apprentice was okay, but her face had turned ashen, as if she saw a ghost.

"What's wrong?" he asked.

She pointed at the parchment that now rested on the floor, as if laced with the worst wizard's potion imaginable.

"His name … his name is on there!" she panted.

His brows furrowed questioningly, Krampel picked the parchment and looked it over. It had Piety's name first, followed by another name that Krampel had never heard before. The third name, like it did to Lutricia, made the bounty hunter momentarily short of breath.

"Your father?" he gasped. Lutricia simply nodded, frightened about the immediate future. The Inquisitor wanted Lord Juniper for tax evasion, a crime punishable by torture in the prison of Karackstine, located deep within the mountain city.

Krampel returned his gaze out the window, looking toward Arborway. A few thoughts gnawed at him, but he tried to put them out of his head. He wondered if Lord Juniper's hospitality a few days ago was a way to keep Krampel off-balance, just in case this situation had come to pass. He also wondered if the lord had handed Lutricia to him as a way to keep her safe: Lord Juniper must have known that Ford had wanted him for his crime. Krampel couldn't blame the lord for wanting his daughter safe.

But then another thought crossed his mind—Hanlin was not that far away, and the Lord stayed there most of the time. Ford had said that the hunters could not track these three down.

Krampel immediately thought this was bunk.

Leaving Lutricia there, Krampel rushed out of the room and hurried down the stairs looking for the Inquisitor. He found him in the room below, speaking once again with his advisors in blue.

"Inquisitor, I'd like a word with you about your list," Krampel said, interrupting this confab. He gave less than a faint care when he saw Ford's advisors glancing at him with something resembling pure spite. He wanted to slice each and every one of them to tiny pieces; he wouldn't even blink an eye in doing it.

"Give me a minute, please," Ford said to the advisors and walked up to Krampel's side. "Yes?"

"How can you tell me that bounty hunters have not found Lord Juniper? His residence is not even fifty miles as the crow flies from this building!" Krampel said, his eyes turning a fiery orange. He didn't like having the wool pulled over his eyes.

"Ah yes, the Lord Juniper issue. As I'm sure you know, it is very difficult to get close to the lord, and for the past few months, he has not stepped foot outside of his manor to let any bounty hunters get a hold of him, or even a look at him. It's very difficult to apprehend a criminal such as he, so I was hoping—"

"You were hoping that I'd use my influence over his daughter to help you catch him," Krampel finished. "I can tell you right now that I would never do that to her."

"I thought you were a heartless individual," Ford countered, "an individual that holds no passion or prejudice when it came down to whom you took bounties against. I was under the presumption that was what made you the best at what you do."

"When it comes to families, I am very prejudiced."

The two men stared at each other, Krampel's eyes still tinged with orange. He would not take the job if Lord Juniper was on the list. He could not—would not, he corrected himself

—put Lutricia through the pain of having to track her own father.

"So I'm to understand that you won't take this job?" Ford asked.

"Not if Lord Juniper is to be a part of it. How much does he owe in taxes, Inquisitor?"

"Three thousand schills," Ford replied.

Just about the same amount that is in the sack that he gave me, Krampel thought. *So much for getting paid for training Lutricia; he's probably on the run already.*

"I'll pay it if you take Lord Juniper off your hit list," Krampel said.

Ford grimaced, but after a few nods of his head, looked back up to the bounty hunter once again and said, "Done. Now, about the others, Piety Crassnick is a very slippery fellow —"

"I have already dealt with Crassnick in the past," Krampel said, interrupting. "Finding him will be a challenge, but I can deal with him when I find him."

"Very well. Now, the other name, Jath Verbinks, is a very dangerous individual. Our last intelligence said he is in Salva. Do you know where that is?"

"Yes, it is the seafaring city on the peninsula south of here. It is somewhat similar to Oak Flats, minus the squirrellen."

Ford grinned.

"Correct. I expect him to be in the city's underground, so you may have to pay informants to help you. I can help you there."

Which is a good thing, Krampel thought with a brief smile, *since the money Lord Juniper gave me is now going to you to pay his debt.*

"When he is captured, bring him back to Myrindar for questions, trial and punishment."

"Sounds like a cut and dry case. Then I can move on to Crassnick," Krampel spat. Venom laced his tongue.

"Yes. How long do you think it will take you to complete the entire job?"

Krampel thought about the time it will take to travel to Salva and back with the prisoner, plus the time to find him and apprehend him. Then, finding Piety would be an absolute nightmare, since he had no idea where he was.

"For the first case, I'd say within a fortnight. For Crassnick's case, that may take longer. I do not know where he is, but I'll use my network to find him. Hopefully I can complete this task by the new moon."

Ford nodded as he took all of this information in and processed it.

"How much do you think you will need in expenses for this trip?" he asked.

After thinking it over, Krampel said, "Several thousand schills, I'd say, for bribes, food, lodging in Salva, as well as paying my network for information."

Ford looked at him silently and nodded. "You got it. I'll tell the treasury to give you whatever you require. Anything else?"

"Just torches for the night and provisions for the road."

"Done. I'll provide you with quarters for the evening and you can begin in the morning."

Krampel bowed and returned upstairs to Lutricia.

***

When he found his advisors waiting for him, Ford replaced the friendly façade he wore in Krampel's presence with his true countenance. His voice didn't change: Only his mannerisms did.

"This Dark Falcon thinks he's pulling one over on me; he's offered to pay Lord Juniper's fine if we leave him alone, but he's requesting that we give him several thousand schills to pay his expenses during these other two hunts. We'll take it out of his bounty, since he doesn't know exactly how much we're paying. I only told him a king's ransom to complete the jobs. Do we know if Juniper is still in his residence?"

"Aye lord, he was there at last check. Runners have been back from Hanlin since morning."

"Burn his manor and all inside of it. I won't need his sample for my creation," Ford ordered. "If you find him, kill him."

"Yes, my lord." The advisors bowed and departed, leaving the Inquisitor by his lonesome in his inner sanctum.

***

The night passed without incident, and as soon as Krampel had checked the supplies he had requested from the Inquisitor, they prepared to depart south for Salva.

Lutricia's mood had turned lighter since their meeting with Ford. When Krampel had returned to the audience chamber in the Inquisitor's manor, he had alleviated her fears about going after Lord Juniper. She had given a mighty sigh and had thanked her mentor ever so profusely. She did not have the heart to track down her father, he knew, even though she, too, thought her father had entrusted her care and training to the bounty hunter because of this reason alone. She told Krampel this. Like Krampel, Lutricia had surmised that Lord Juniper must have heard the rumors regarding Ford's cadre of bounty hunters, and subsequently took action.

Both Krampel and Lutricia strapped a bag to their backs; Krampel's bag was heavier than Lutricia's, and that forced the bounty hunter to wear his shield on his arm instead of across his back. He did not mind: if someone attacked, he had already saved precious seconds of preparation for self-defense. Both had their swords strapped to their hips and each wore their traveling cloaks. A look to the west and the Enchanted Sea far in the distance showed no signs of a storm over the next day or so, but Krampel thought wearing them was a touch prudent rather than walking out on the open plains without some form of protection against the elements.

Ford made sure he came out to watch the duo depart on their journey to Salva. He carried a sack of gold for them as well as two rolls of parchment. The first one Krampel unrolled, glanced at it for a few seconds, then rolled it up and handed it to Lutricia. The second one he did the same thing, but instead of handing it to the girl, he folded it and slid it into his breeches pocket. He made sure Lutricia saw this.

"Good journey, my friends," Ford said with a smile. Both Krampel and Lutricia bowed to the Inquisitor, then walked down the mountain paths to the gate.

"What was that second piece of parchment about?" she asked.

"I'll tell you later; it's information about our second hunt," he replied, and neither said another word until they had walked quite a ways from the great southern city.

When they no longer saw the peak of Myrindar several hours later, Krampel turned to his apprentice.

"The second parchment is about Piety Crassnick, a lad I once knew when I was younger. He is wanted by the Inquisitor for stealing two foals."

Lutricia giggled.

"What's so funny?"

"Two foals? That's it? There must be another reason why we're searching for him."

Krampel saw the reason for her laughter, since the crime sounded certainly laughable. But he didn't ask questions about why his client wanted the quarry hunted down. That wasn't within his purview.

"I don't know, and I really don't care, to tell you the truth. We've been hired to do a job for a well-paying customer. We'll do it without prejudice or passion."

"But you know the wanted man?"

"Yes, I do. He grew up in the township where my mentor lived and freed me from slavery."

"You were a slave?"

Krampel grimaced.

"Yes, for a time. That was until I broke free from their bondage and ran away. My mentor saved me in more ways than anyone can possibly fathom."

He sensed that Lutricia had gone deep into thought about this. Just from the look on her face, she obviously had feelings about her mentor's past life as a slave. She said nothing, though.

"So where are we going to find him?"

"That I do not know yet; we're searching for Jath Verbinks, and he was last seen in Salva, which is on the eastern side of the southern peninsula. It is a port town, so I'm sure there'll be plenty of sailors ashore. I haven't been to Salva in many months, though."

They continued walking south.

After three days, he had grown used to Lutricia's presence—he didn't know if he would ever fully allow himself to care for her as his mentor did for him, as his grief over the loss of Vossler still felt overwhelming five years later—but knowing she was close by gave him comfort in some aspects. Her constant line of questioning was a given, as she wanted learn as much as she could in a short amount of time. But as Krampel pointed out to her privately, learning to become a bounty hunter took a great deal of patience. Some took to it like a duck; some wallow in the lower levels of the profession for a great deal of time before they become part of the elite hunters. His indoctrination into the world of bounty hunting was rather quick, but that came from his natural ability with both the sword and with his sense of stealth. Not many had the ability to do what Krampel had with his sword, his powerful legs, and his nimble, quick-thinking brain.

Those thoughts floated away as they slowly made their way to one of the hardest portions of the journey south. They approached a rocky area, one with a pair of hills on either side of a plateau. This plateau, however, turned out to be more of a twisting cave that stretched for several miles in a north-south direction.

It also happened to be located right in the heart of orc country—southern orc country, for that matter. The southern orcs were a brawnier type of beast, unlike the orcs that attacked Cassimina so long ago. Krampel kicked himself for coming this way, but this was the only path to take without going too far west of their intended destination. Had they taken another path, it would have been another day on the road.

The craggy mountains and its dark cave represented a shortcut—a perilous shortcut, but a shortcut nonetheless.

"Be ready for anything," Krampel cautioned his apprentice. "Keep your eyes open for anything that may jump out at you."

"How many times are you going to tell me that?" Lutricia replied sarcastically.

"Until you understand what it means," he retorted. "I will keep telling you to be on your guard. Unless you want to sleep through the cave, do as I say."

"Are you going to keep throwing that falling asleep thing at me for the rest of my life?"

"That is my current plan, yes."

As they stepped ever closer to the cave mouth, Lutricia looked around at the tall, stony mountains and openly asked, "Where are we?"

"We are in orc country right now." She gasped, but he shushed her. "Don't worry. If we are quiet while passing through, they shouldn't bother us."

"Orcs only come out at night, correct?"

"Yes, but some do have the ability to come out while the sun is up. And since we are in the south, some can do that. That is also a reason why we should traverse the cave with intense care. I want to be far from here by nightfall; I don't know how far away the orcs will travel to find us if they catch our scent."

"That's not much of a relief to me; I haven't bathed in a few days, and neither have you."

"Exactly. Let us hope they don't smell us before we smell them."

Krampel made a torch, igniting it with the point of *Flad-rul*. He then led the way into the tunnel, and both the master and the apprentice walked with great trepidation as they entered the passageway. The torch brightened the gloom a little, but it was difficult to look back the way they came.

Only a black nothingness, one which no torch had the power to penetrate, lingered.

Chapter 10

Even with the torch, the darkness swallowed the two as they walked quietly through the cave, Lutricia's hand on her master's back.

Halfway through, the only sounds they heard were the sounds of their footsteps slapping on the rocky bottom. But soon, the scratching of nails on stone nearby met the hunters' ears.

"Falcon?" Lutricia whispered a little louder than she would have liked.

"Quiet," Krampel admonished, stretching out his hearing to determine what the other sounds were and from where they came.

The scratching continued and grew louder. Krampel's eyes widened.

"Draw your sword!"

"Already drawn," she replied. Steel scratched against steel, the collision long yet quick.

"Keep moving forward."

The glow of the torch aided them and kept the path clear, but within seconds the orcs had penetrated the light. With the torch in his left hand and *Flad-rul* in his right, he was ready to fight.

"Stay on my back or you'll be fighting blind," he warned his apprentice.

"I always wanted a challenge," she replied sarcastically. The shadows cast by *Flad-rul* masked Krampel's grin. He lunged forward and slashed diagonally from right to left, only feeling his sword stop as an orc blade blocked it. He turned the blade over with a twist of his wrist and quickly turned the attack around, delivering a backhand across the orc's throat. He heard the clashing of swords behind him and looked quickly to see Lutricia dispatching an orc with an uppercut that left a huge gash in it running from its right hip to its left shoulder.

"Quickly Lutricia, run forward as fast as you can and keep your sword out. We can make it out of here quicker if we don't fight every orc known to man," Krampel said.

He handed the torch to Lutricia, who sped forward quickly. He ignited *Flad-rul* once again, the magical fire dancing along the blade to its hilt, and followed her lead. The light of the blade filled the cavern.

The orcs spilled out of their catacomb hideaways to cut off their escape from the deadly cave. The snarling throng made the pair stop in their tracks. Each orc carried a weapon of some sort, along with the promise of a painful death.

Krampel stopped next to his apprentice. He twirled the blade in his fingers and stood in an en guard position, awaiting their attack. Then he sensed a second group of orcs closing in behind them.

"We're surrounded," he said to her. "You take these," pointing to the orcs in front of them. "I'll take the ones in the rear."

"Good, I want to look death right in the face."

This time, Krampel didn't smile, or grin, or smirk at Lutricia's reply. He didn't even hear her, as he prepared to defend himself and his apprentice from the rear attack. He turned and called more of the enchanted fire to the blade, giving him sight in the gloom. Most of the orcs recoiled, but some held their ground against the human warrior.

One foolishly attacked. Krampel easily moved his shield into position to block as the orc prepared to swing. Once the steel connected with the golden shield, Krampel drove *Flad-rul* into the orc's gut and, with a twist of his wrist, gouged the beast. Its death screams lingered in his ears.

Another moved in immediately. Krampel pulled his blade free, spun to the right with a quickness as yet unmatched by man or beast, and separated the orc's head from the rest of its body. Enraged, the orcs charged the bounty hunter en masse.

Krampel deftly moved into the pack and kept his feet moving through the orcs, while *Flad-rul* hemmed through the group. He slashed, chopped and stabbed the creatures, and soon their black blood covered him from head to foot. The five remaining orcs in the rear horde turned tail and ran.

Gritting his teeth and pushing off the balls of his feet, Krampel immediately gave chase.

The torch forgotten and on the floor, Lutricia swung her sword to and fro, blocking the swords of the orcs while sending stunning ripostes back at them. A brutal right-left-right combination knocked one orc's sword out of position before she rallied and swung parallel to the floor, her sword not stopping for the orc's neck, instead passing right through it.

When one remained, she circled the beast and awaited its attack. With a roar, the orc brandished its weapon and came after Lutricia's right side. She moved her sword down to parry, preventing the orc blade from coming anywhere near her. She then spun and brought the two blades around to her left, giving her a clear opening as the orc had its sword out of position. She only needed to utilize a small swipe to score a hit, carving a gash into the right side of the beast's abdomen.

A strangled howl came deep from within the orc, and Lutricia had heard enough. She wound up and leveled the orc, slashing its voice box before driving her sword into its dark heart.

She pulled it out and turned 360 degrees in search of more orcs, gasping hard, but did not see any more. The Falcon, too, had disappeared.

"Falcon? Where are you?" she called, her voice echoing in the rocky chamber of the cave.

She picked up the torch the Falcon had handed her and looked toward the way they had come. She didn't see a thing. She moved the torch back and forth, stepping forward, tiptoeing through the orc corpses and spreading the light into every nook and cranny of the cave.

"Where in the seven hells of the realms could he be?"

She got an answer two seconds later as she detected the sounds of boots slapping on the rock. She moved her sword up defensively, but when the Falcon strode into the light, she relaxed her sword arm and lowered it.

"Where'd you go?" she asked.

"Orc hunting," he responded shortly. "Not as profitable as bounty hunting, and a little messier."

Lutricia's mouth spread into a girlish grin. The bounty hunter motioned for her to make her way out of the cavern, just in case more orcs decided to crash their escape party. Within minutes they saw sunlight streaming through the mouth of the cave on the southern side. No orcs followed them.

"We must get as far away from this place as we can," he said. "We have at least eight hours until sundown, and that means we should be able to put thirty miles behind us in that time."

"You look disgusting."

He looked down. The blood of the orcs covered his entire body. Then he looked at his apprentice.

"You don't look so hot yourself."

She looked at herself and saw the orc's black blood had painted her, too.

"We should find a secluded area to bathe," the Falcon said. Lutricia's heart skipped a beat. He looked south and saw that a clump of trees that, by her judgment, looked approximately ten miles away.

"There has to be a river around here somewhere."

"I thought you knew all of this territory. Shouldn't you know this stuff?"

"I told you, I haven't been in this area for some time. I have to search my memory. We'll do that as we walk. Hand me the map I gave you."

Lutricia pulled out the rolled up parchment Ford gave them before they departed Myrindar and handed it to her mentor. The hunter unrolled it as they walked, and as she looked over his shoulder, she noticed a squiggly line running through what represented the trees.

"Yes, there is a stream there, and there are no towns in that vicinity, so we should be well secluded there. Come, let's make haste and get away from this accursed place. Remind me not to go back that way and to take an extra day of travel to return to Myrindar with Verbinks."

"You got it, master."

Their swords still drawn, they walked toward the wooden area.

Two hours later, they closed in on it. It was a small forest, but it held together like The Dark Forest outside the dwarven realm of Lowbridge, far to the north. They stepped into it without fear; the orcs hadn't pursued, and they had stashed their swords an hour ago.

Brushing past ferns and downed sticks, the Falcon and Lutricia made their way to the river he had seen on the map.

"You bathe first and I'll stand guard," he said.

"You'll stand guard from several axe-lengths away," Lutricia retorted. He nodded, then turned and walked away to scout out their new surroundings.

"I'll be within screaming distance," he said over his shoulder.

At the bank of the stream, which wasn't very wide, Lutricia undressed, taking off the heavy coat of chain mail first. She removed the rest of her clothing, and when nude, stepped into the shallow, slow-moving water.

The water was incredibly cool, so cool in fact that small goose bumps rose on her skin. Even though they were in the southern realm, Lutricia had never believed she would find such a refreshing body of water this far south. The pains in her feet and legs vanished just by the touch of the water on her skin. She waded into the middle of the stream and lowered herself to her knees, saturating her entire body with water. Then she stood up and began to scrub the dirt and grime and orc blood off her, turning her skin a deep shade of pink.

It is a shame that I don't have soap with me, Lutricia thought. *I could wash my hair and spend quite a bit of time pampering myself. But I don't think my mentor would appreciate that; he has a plan for today, and I don't think he wants to delay more than he has to. It is best that I bathe quickly.*

***

Krampel scouted out the area some twenty axe-lengths away from the banks of the stream. He stayed on that side, not able to find a downed log to cross over to the other side;

he wanted to make sure there were no people spying on Lutricia. She needed her privacy.

But still, the thought of the young woman bathing nearby piqued his curiosity; he had never seen a woman unclothed before, not even stopping in the whorehouses of the bigger cities, like Briskey Bucktooth. Women, especially the ladies of the night, had occasionally taken out bounty hunters while in bed: some cut their dalliances' throats, while others drove a shank into their lungs through the ribcage. It was easy enough to do, especially when one didn't have enough blood in their bodies to work more than one organ at a time.

He had managed to keep his gaze away from the stream for some time, even though his chest ached with indecision. Still, the prospects of seeing his first naked woman overrode his good sense.

Continuing his surveillance, he stopped at a large tree, one of the larger ones in the small forest, and looked around the side at Lutricia. There, Krampel stood mesmerized by her supple form, the curvature of her naked hips and bottom, which came close to touching the water even as she stood at her full height. She squatted a bit, her bottom dropping below the surface, and she tossed water over her shoulders and let it ripple down her back. The remnants of the road were there, he saw, as they mingled with the water trails.

He didn't look long: Blinking away his interest and his arousal, he pulled his attention away from the young woman's body and swallowed hard, then continued his search of the area, making sure there were no orcs or threats to either his apprentice or himself. He shook his head to clear it. He needed to remain alert.

Several minutes later, he heard the sloshing of the water as Lutricia got out of the stream. He waited until he was sure that she had covered herself before he returned to the stream bank. He finally detected that his cheeks had grown warm.

When he arrived, Lutricia had covered her body from the waist down, and her blonde hair hung over the front of her shoulders, covering her breasts from view. She had just put a fresh tunic on when Krampel walked around a nearby tree.

"I was just finishing up," Lutricia said, reaching for her sword and strapping it to her waist. "I can take the watch now, so you can bathe." She had a little twinkle in her eye as she walked away, a slight flush to her cheeks and a thin smile across her lips.

Krampel watched as she walked away and made sure that he had privacy before he undressed. He did not wear a coat of mail like Lutricia, so his disrobing didn't take as long. He removed his boots first, then his tunic, revealing a lean, chiseled chest. His breeches came off last, and he strode into the cool stream without worry of the water being too cold. At that point, he didn't care if the water felt like ice. He just wanted to get clean. He walked to the center of the stream and flung himself backward, sending a splash of water toward both banks of the narrow waterway.

When he stood, beads of water covered his torso and pectorals, clinging to each rippling muscle. He brushed his hair out of his eyes, slicking it back, before he sank back in and scrubbed. His dark skin turned lighter if by a shade as the dirt and black blood peeled away.

***

Lutricia didn't go too far from the bank of the stream. As soon as the bounty hunter had turned his back and walked into the water, Lutricia dashed for the nearest tree and hid from view.

She, too, felt entranced by her mentor. When she first saw him back at her father's manor, she immediately grew attracted to his dark, piercing eyes. She now saw that his rugged looks and the structure of his cheekbones certainly made him a desirable man. Of course, seeing the breadth of his back and the tight, chiseled globes that comprised his bottom sent heat radiating to her extremities.

He is quite the specimen, she thought as she bit her bottom lip. Lutricia admired his torso, especially his rippling back muscles. She felt herself growing flush in the face even more so than before, and it took everything within her to pull away from the scene in front of her.

And yes, as she thought about it, *he is moody and sometimes very standoffish. He has kept his past guarded, and he probably has good reason to be that way.* But she wanted to chip enough away, even if only a little bit at a time, to get him to open up to her. She would take a little and be satisfied with it.

When he had finished, she heard the telltale sounds of him walking out of the stream. She counted to ten to give him opportunity to cover himself, even though her young body had betrayed her. Her heart tapped nervously against her breastbone.

As she reached ten, she then stepped into the clearing and immediately saw that he had covered his lower body. The young woman had bit off a curse, and her distress showed. The Falcon's eyebrows had collided together as their eyes met.

"Are you okay?" he asked.

"What?" she replied as she looked up at him, startled by the sound of his voice. "Oh, yes. I am."

"Okay. Nothing has come around since my watch?"

"Nope, not a thing."

"Good. As soon as I'm dressed and armed again, we can resume our trek south."

He had dressed in no time, and after refilling their water bottles from the stream, the pair walked along the edge, which took them through the forest in a curving direction before the Falcon realized that it would be night soon.

"Let's put as much distance between ourselves and this place as we can. I'd say we'd have about five hours of daylight remaining before we have to settle down for the night. We're still in orc country, and I'd rather not be here when the sun goes down."

"I can't argue with that logic," Lutricia replied as soon as she shouldered her pack and followed her mentor out of the forest. She snuck several looks at him before smirking. He looked as if he remained oblivious.

The five hours passed quickly, as the pair alternated walking and jogging to make up the miles they had lost while bathing. When they had finally taken a rest, it had been after a seven-hour trip, as he had told her the more miles, the better.

They were now within two days of Salva.

"I'll take the first watch," the Falcon said. "You can get some sleep."

Lutricia soon fell asleep at her master's bidding, and he had remained stoically on guard for several hours before he lightly shook his apprentice when it was her turn.

When the sun rose over Obloeron, the pair ate some of the provisions Ford had provided them, drank more water to re-energize themselves, then hoisted their packs onto their backs and continued their journey to the south.

Chapter 11

From ten miles away, the two travelers watched as Salva's skyline rose into view. The smell of salt water wafted across the inland plains. Krampel breathed deeply and let the smell flood his nostrils, a slight smile slipping across his face as he inhaled the sweet coastal air.

The next two days of travel seemed a blur for the companions. No enemies had shown their faces to the pair; master and apprentice walked together in silence for a portion of the journey, before Krampel decided that Lutricia should take her sword out and practice positioning while they walked. As he watched the girl execute the moves, it reminded him of going through the same exercises in Vossler's training dungeon, so long ago.

The plain leading to Salva was a flat, grassy area, with nothing but green underfoot. The buildings in the distance seemed green, too, but Krampel knew that was an illusion of the sun as it beat down on them.

Like most of the larger cities across the breadth of the continent, a large wall surrounded Salva, designed to keep vagrants out; Briskey Bucktooth, far to the north, boasted a similar structure. However, the rules were lax in Salva, and over the long years it had turned into a haven for crime lords and those that wished to do their bidding. Some small-time criminals plied their trade on the streets, but the big players preferred to do their business in the underworld, unseen from what served as the law here.

Krampel knew in order to find Jath Verbinks, he and Lutricia would need to look in the sewers.

Krampel's stomach churned. He and Lutricia had last eaten several hours ago, and it had been a few days since they had slept indoors on real beds. Krampel recalled a small inn near the waterfront where they would be able to get a bed—*a bed each*, he thought, the memories of Lutricia bathing still fresh in his mind—and a hearty meal at a good price. He did not know how long they would have to stay in Salva; he thought it prudent to get bargains and not quickly dissolve their gold. That money needed to last until the hunts ended.

As they approached Salva, they saw buildings seemingly grow out of the ground like plant shoots, some large with rounded roofs, while some were small with slanted roofs. All housed businesses and homes—or were homes of crime businesses. No one knew exactly what their neighbors did on a daily basis, and sometimes it was best if they didn't. Criminals were everywhere, and even the most law-abiding citizens were under suspicion of being criminals themselves.

Within three hours of seeing Salva rise above the horizon, Krampel and Lutricia had entered the port proper through the northern gates, which, as Krampel had believed, were unguarded.

"Salva is a crime-ridden town, my apprentice," Krampel said quietly, as if reading her mind. "Anyone can come and go; even bounty hunters." He said this with a smirk. "If any criminal knew that a bounty hunter and his apprentice just entered their town, the town would go deathly silent and not a soul would walk the streets until they departed.

"The town does have a guard, though they are woefully inefficient when it comes to stopping crime. There is so much of it. The criminals run the town, for the most part," Krampel said with a dark look in his eyes.

"Looks like it's up to us to stop it," Lutricia said, looking up toward her mentor.

Krampel looked over to his apprentice and smirked again, laughing just a bit.

It feels good to laugh, he thought. *I haven't laughed in quite a while*.

They meandered through the throng of people at the northernmost market, where they saw dry goods at outrageous prices. Krampel steered Lutricia by the shoulder through this area. The aromas of sweat had mixed with those of the goods, resulting in a thoroughly unappetizing taste touching their tongues.

"Believe it or not, the area near the waterfront has the best prices. That is our destination," he whispered into her ear. Lutricia shivered.

"If that is so, why do these people shop here?" she asked.

"Districting," Krampel replied, "is a most unfair system if you ask me, but the people don't complain. If you live in a certain district, you must shop in that district. It's the law here. Visitors, however, have the right to shop wherever they like. For example, the place where I intend for us to stay has very good prices to keep ones' purse fat. The fish prices in that district are better than the southernmost district, and we can also purchase some information there."

"I don't see any sense to districting," Lutricia said. "Shouldn't people have the right to shop where they want?"

"Yes, but remember this town is run by criminals. You do as the criminals say or you find yourself in the gutter, surrounded by fish guts. That is why people don't complain about such things—they value their lives over their pocketbook. Now let us be quiet about this and keep our discussion of districting for a more private area. I would much like to make it to the inn without a sword sticking out of my back."

He watched as a shiver overtook his apprentice's body.

The two travelers wound their way through the human maze to the cobblestone streets of the northwestern district. Here they saw wooden buildings with beams framing the doors and windows, each wall a dull brown. The sea air smelled of brine. Lutricia held her nose to ward off the smell.

"This is where we're staying?" she said, her voice sounding half an octave lower than normal.

"This is nothing, especially if we have to search for Verbinks in the underworld. Imagine the smell and the look of what is down there."

Lutricia rolled her eyes and continued to follow Krampel, staying a step behind him to the right.

Two minutes later, Krampel found the inn. It was a simple structure a stone's throw from the wharf, and it, too, looked like every other building on that street. Shifting his cloak to cover the hilt of *Flad-rul*, Krampel opened the door and entered, followed by his apprentice. There were a few people imbibing in the parlor, and Krampel noticed them appraising the two newcomers with wary eyes, their drinks halfway to their mouths.

"I'd like two rooms for the next several nights," Krampel said as he approached the counter, where a wizened old man stood behind it. He had a bald head with a few wisps of silvery hair, and a jawline with salt and pepper stubble. His teeth, though, had seen better days.

"That'll be three schills," the man said a little too loudly for Krampel's liking. "Would you like a meal prepared?"

"Yes, we've been on the road for some time and we haven't eaten in several hours. We'd also like some information when we're done eating."

The man behind the counter nodded and handed Krampel two keys as Krampel handed over the coins. Krampel handed one to Lutricia, who walked behind her master.

"I'll meet you in the common room when you're finished freshening up from the road. Don't bring your sword, either. We don't want to alarm these folks."

Lutricia nodded and entered her room while Krampel entered his.

The room was quite nice, he decided, taking off the road-worn tunic and replacing it with a fresh one from his pack. He took *Flad-rul* from his belt as well as the shield, following his own advice. He went downstairs and found Lutricia already waiting for him at the foot of the staircase. She smiled up at him as he descended, and together they went into the parlor to eat.

As before, there were still a few people sitting in the parlor when they walked in. Many sailors stood or sat at tables while drinking, but neither Krampel nor Lutricia detected the presence of squirrellen there. They found an empty table, and soon a serving wench came over and served them: Krampel, an ale; Lutricia, water. Lutricia nearly gagged; her water had come directly from the sea.

Soon they supped on fish, broiled to perfection with spices that ensnared their nasal cavities. Lutricia had never eaten fish before, but she soon became a happy convert as she left nothing but the skin. Krampel finished his meal in silence, as he prepared to talk to the innkeeper about his mission there and where he might search for information about the whereabouts of Jath Verbinks.

"I'll be back in a few minutes," Krampel said, not waiting for an answer. He walked up to the counter where the innkeeper stood—not the older gentleman in the lobby—and leaned over to converse with him.

"I'm looking for a criminal," he said, which in turn earned him a laugh.

"Look around you, lad. There are plenty of criminals in this town. Pick one."

Krampel smirked. He knew he should have been more specific. Innkeepers were known for giving it to their customers straight, and this one was no different.

"The criminal I'm looking for is named Jath Verbinks. I … want him to do a job for me," Krampel said, fibbing slightly. He smiled and looked hard at the innkeeper.

"I haven't seen him lately; I do know the man you're talking about, though. But if you check at the *Sea Urchin*, they'd know more."

"*Sea Urchin*, eh? New place in town?"

"Aye. Opened about seven or eight months back. Rough clientele I hear, all from the sea, they are. If I were you, I wouldn't take that pretty little thing with you when you go there unless you want her taken away from you. Those men spend long months on the sea without women. It would be best to keep her here.

"And now that I get a good look at her, lad, you'd best be getting back over to her right now," the innkeeper continued, nodding toward where Lutricia sat.

Krampel had turned to look at her and saw two men, both sailors, sitting next to her. They sat close to her and each had a hand on her leg. From his vantagepoint, Krampel saw that she had grown extremely uncomfortable at the attention they gave her. Her face had turned pasty white as she had seemingly grown nauseated by their presence.

"Thank you for the advice and the tip, good sir," he said, pulling five schills from his pouch and handing them to the innkeeper. The man's eyes widened; he looked like he had just struck it rich—five schills bought two kegs of ale in his district.

Krampel calmly returned to his seat across from Lutricia, who looked at him with pleading eyes to do something about the ruffians that groped her. He simply sat there, looking back at the one to his right and then the left. They paid no attention to Krampel's return and continued feeling up his apprentice. One had his palm secured to her breast.

"Come on, love. Show us what you have on under that dress. Or is there nuffin' under there?" the drunk sailor on the left asked. Lutricia still hadn't found her voice, but she kept pulling the hem of her dress down as they tried to pull it up.

"Excuse me, gentlemen," Krampel finally said, the tone of an aristocrat instead of a swashbuckling bounty hunter. "The lady and I were finishing our meal. You've interrupted us, and I'd appreciate it if you'd leave us to enjoy our meal in peace."

"Beat it, pal. She's our property now. You left her alone," the sailor on the right answered. He had a little more sauce in his tone, but he was no less drunk than the other.

"Oh, I don't think she's anyone's property," Krampel corrected. "She is her own person and can make her own decisions regarding with whom she wants to acquaint herself. I'm sure you can notice by her countenance that she wants absolutely nothing to do with you gentlemen. Now, if you'll excuse us, we have a meal to finish." Krampel remained cool as a cucumber, alternating his eyes back and forth as he looked at them. He leaned back slightly in his chair, keeping his left foot firmly on the floorboards while he had moved his right up to the center leg of the table. He planted it right on the side of it, and just waited.

"Do you have a death wish, youngster? The lady is going with us, whether you like it or not."

"I don't think so," the bounty hunter said. "I'm giving you this last chance: Leave now, or you'll be very sorry indeed." Krampel's tone hardened, and the fire in his eyes began to kindle. His pupils rimmed with orange.

The drunk men laughed at Krampel, but the laughing suddenly stopped as Krampel—with the power of his foot alone —shoved the table into the stomach of the one to his left, dropping him and the table to the ground before he quickly went to his feet and head-butted the other, knocking him down to the floor. He then leapt over the table and picked up the drunkard by the throat, even though he weighed quite a bit more than Krampel did.

"Now apologize to the lady," Krampel said through clenched teeth.

The ruffian only squawked out a few indecipherable words, which only caused Krampel to squeeze the man's throat even more. Then with a burst of strength, Krampel hurled the man ten feet away. Krampel then heard a snarl coming from behind him. He turned swiftly to see the one he head-butted come after him, before he bent over and hip-tossed the knave toward his buddy's landing place. Both moaned as they got up and ran out of the inn as if their arses had caught fire.

Krampel looked to the innkeeper, who stared right back at him. He thought the innkeeper was about to throw both him and Lutricia out, but as Lutricia righted the table, the innkeeper walked around the bar with a smile.

"I'm glad you had the gumption to set those boys right," he said. "Not many would do that to a bunch of sailors. Are you interested in a job? I could use someone to throw the drunks out on their ear when they get too drunk and rambunctious."

"I'm sorry, my friend. I can't take you up on your offer; I have a few jobs currently. I'm training this young woman to become a bounty hunter, and I'm searching for Verbinks, not hiring him. He's wanted by Cairn Ford."

The innkeeper spat when he heard the name. Lutricia walked up and stood next to Krampel.

"Oy, you're workin' for him? He's not well liked around these parts, I can assure you of that. His taxation policies are incredibly strict; it's like his arm is growing across the southlands and none can stop him. He's a tyrannical, wicked despot who will stop at nothing to gain more and more power," the innkeeper said, as if his words were water running through a sieve. "If you can get out from under his influence, lad, and you too, lass, the better off you'll both be, I can assure you.

"I won't stop you from staying here since you cleared the ruffians, but I warn you: I won't allow you here again if you're still working for that insult of a human being!"

The innkeeper spat again, then turned and walked away from the pair as they stood there, completely dumbfounded by what they just heard.

"I don't know what to make of that," Lutricia said. "That was the first interesting thing that's happened on this trip."

Krampel smirked slightly, and he knew his apprentice's sarcastic streak had returned. It was only the tip of the iceberg of interesting things that have happened on this trip, as far as he was concerned.

"Apparently there are some who don't like our current benefactor, and that doesn't sit well with me. Do you know of anything that he was talking about?"

"I'm about as in the dark as you are on that one, Falcon," Lutricia said. "My father dealt with the tax issues; or didn't, as you already know." Lutricia shook slightly, and Krampel figured it was due to the near need to catch him for Ford. "As a nobleman's child, and a female child at that, I wasn't brought up to speed about the goings on of the realm. That wasn't my place, I knew that from the start. Now, if I had been a male child, I would have gone into training to run a city or town by the age of thirteen."

"I think we can presume that our benefactor's crimes are against the poor, not the rich," Krampel said, walking back to the table to pick up his ale glass, only to notice he had already drained it. He frowned, then brought it over to the bar. "To tell you the truth, I don't know what to think. That is the only opinion that we've heard about Ford, so let's generate a few more before we make any opinions of our own.

"The innkeeper told me about a place called the *Sea Urchin*, where a rough crowd hangs out. It's possible that we can find out more information about Verbinks' whereabouts there. Let us away and make good use of our time."

They moved to the door, but the two drunkards had returned to the inn—this time with two friends in tow. All of them held swords in their right hands, and all four looked ready to murder.

"Lutricia," Krampel said, "Hurry and make for my room and fetch my shield and sword; I have a feeling I'm going to need it." Without a word, Lutricia rushed off to the lobby, where she sprinted up the stairs.

"So you're the mangy mutt who knocked my comrades out," the taller sailor on the left said, brandishing a scimitar.

The innkeeper rushed forward and cut them off, his hands held up in an attempt to halt their progress. But before he said a word to them, the shorter sailor, one that wasn't one of the original miscreants, slashed the man across his left wrist, severing it. The innkeeper let off a blood-curdling scream and dropped to his knees.

Krampel had easily noticed the sailors only spoke with their swords, all four of which had sharp, angry voices.

"That's one!" the short one said, and all four sailors laughed. "Now to deal with this one!"

Lutricia barged in in the nick of time and gave Krampel his sword and shield, and she had her sword strapped to her waist, as well. Krampel grabbed it, drew the blade from the golden scabbard and tossed it aside.

"No time for the shield," he said quietly, twirling the sword through his fingers as he prepared to fight the four men. Lutricia also drew her sword and held it in both hands, standing at her master's left-hand side. She discarded the shield.

"Shall we dance, gentlemen?" Krampel said. As one, all four sailors attacked. Krampel and Lutricia were seriously outnumbered, but Krampel called the magical flame to *Flad-rul*'s edges, causing the four drunk sailors to take pause. Krampel grinned, then moved in two steps and swung. Lutricia followed suit. The rest of the inn's patrons scattered away, holding onto drinks as they dashed into the corners.

The clash of swords began, Krampel swiftly moving his sword to parry and block the blades of the sailors on the right. He turned his sword over his head and gave a hearty backhand that moved both sailors' swords into the other, knocking the two drunkards to the floor, one on top of the other.

Lutricia did her best to keep the two sailors on the left off balance. She crossed her sword left then right, parrying both before she rolled behind them. She got to her feet, spun, then leveled a swing at their midsections. Both jackknifed out of the way, but Lutricia corrected her blade and backhanded them, causing her drunkards to bend backward and nearly fall over.

Krampel stood over his opponents.

"Have you had enough of me yet, gentlemen?" he taunted. The sailor on top of the heap growled and launched himself at Krampel, swinging his sword madly.

Krampel, holding his sword two-handed, awaited his attack and moved the sword back and forth, first to the right and then to the left before spinning and swiping *Flad-rul* down low to cut at the drunkard's legs. Surprisingly, the sailor leapt over the sword, but the bounty hunter corrected quickly and came back up to block his counter. He twirled the sword through his fingers and hacked hard at the sailor's left shoulder, then backhanded the other sailor, who quickly came off the floor and chopped with all the power he could muster. Krampel spun away and bumped into Lutricia's backside, as she too spun away from her opponents.

"How are you holding up, girl?"

"As good as I can, boy," Lutricia replied.

Krampel gave a tight yet short grin, then went back to the fight, ready to end it quickly. Lutricia stayed put and awaited her opponents' attack.

He charged in and left his feet, knocking the one on the left, the shorter of the two, to the ground with a heavy boot to the face, all while holding his sword parallel to the ground and along his leg. The other sailor quickly made to chop off Krampel's foot, but with *Flad-rul* plunged to the floor, his opening evaporated rather quickly.

Krampel landed the initial move with the sole of his boot standing on the sailor's sword hand, preventing him from making a move of his own, before he turned and raised the Flame Thrower, slashing at the other sailor in the same breath. He knocked the sailor's sword out of his hands, sending it flying across the room, coming to rest near the flames of the hearth. The flying sword nearly took Lutricia's face off, the girl ducking just in the nick of time and spinning away, but it also gave her an opening, as her two opponents stupidly watched Krampel gain the upper hand.

Lutricia took the opportunity and rushed in, taking a hearty swing at the newer of the two sailors, the one who hadn't tried to get frisky with her. She swung low, severing his left hand, taking the sword with it. He gave off a mighty howl as the pain surged through his arm. She didn't stop, though, and instead of killing the one that tried to take advantage of her, put her sword right up to his Adam's apple, pricking him in the small depression of the throat.

"Try to defend yourself and I'll cut out your voice box," she said, looking at him with a devastatingly hard look. The sailor didn't know what to do; he dropped the sword, which hit the floor with a shrill clang.

That left Krampel to deal with the other original sailor. He stepped off the sailor's wrist and let the man get to his feet.

"I gave you one last chance earlier to leave my companion alone, yet you and your friend decided not to heed my warning. Now you've brought two others into this: One has lost his hand, the other his sword. I'll give you the choice now, for all three of them—surrender and you'll be placed under arrest for causing a disturbance, or I'll kill you now and you'll burn in the ninth circle of hell!" Krampel said in no more than a whisper.

The sailor thought it over for a moment, but his brow furrowed and he grinned maliciously at Krampel. He struck.

Krampel blocked two quick swings, moving to his left as he circled his opponent. The two held their swords aloft as they studied the other. He met the sailor's eyes and widened his own, then quickly exchanged two blows, a short right-left combination, before both retreated. Krampel swung his sword over his head toward the left and came back at the sailor hard, aiming for the right flank. The sailor moved to parry, but not before Krampel swiped his right leg underneath his opponent and knocked him to the dusty floor. Krampel righted himself and quickly stuck the point of his sword toward the sailor's throat.

"You have this thing for the floor, lad," Krampel sneered. "Maybe you should stay there."

The sailor, defeated, dropped the sword and put his hands up in surrender. Krampel didn't let go of the breath that resided in his lungs.

"Lutricia, help the innkeeper call the town guard, then fetch me some rope to tie these vagrants up. I'm sure their captain will love to know that his men were carousing and got into a drunken brawl. It will be nice to see them hanging from the gallows."

"Yes, master."

Lutricia eased her captive sailors toward Krampel, who then held all four at sword point. She helped the innkeeper, who held the bloody stump of his wrist, to his feet, then escorted him to the bar, where he rang for the local law enforcement. She then brought over enough rope to bind the four sailors together until the guard arrived.

The guard came to the inn several minutes later to take the sailors away. They were also ready to take Krampel away, but the handless innkeeper stepped in.

"It was them who had stopped them earlier," he said. "Let them stay here."

The guardsman bowed, and called for a medic to tend to the innkeeper as he gave his statement. The guardsman turned to speak with the bounty hunter and his apprentice.

"Apparently you've won over the great barman of this district. What are you in Salva for anyway, bounty hunter? What quarry has you far from your home?"

Krampel didn't bother asking how the guardsman knew he was a bounty hunter. He simply leaned back against the wall and smiled at the questioner.

"I have no home, guardsman. I am searching for a criminal known as Jath Verbinks. Do you know of him?"

The guardsman looked at him with an approving eye and nodded.

"Aye, I know of him. He's one of Regent Currance's most agile warriors, and not an easily captured person. I'm sure you've heard he's as slippery as a snake."

"I've not heard," Krampel answered. "Please tell me about him."

The guardsman led Krampel and Lutricia to a table while the rest of the inn's patrons either left the parlor for their rooms or left the building entirely. Obviously a few people wanted to profit from the information they held, especially if they overheard Krampel's conversation with the guardsman.

"Verbinks is known in these parts as one of the fiercest battlers the guard of Salva has ever fought. We've been unsuccessful in capturing him; he has injured several of the best guardsmen we've had, even killing two."

"Where in the underworld can he usually be found?" Lutricia asked. Krampel nodded sharply to the guardsman.

"He has been known to frequent the easternmost portions, near Regent Currance's home. It's not that hard to find."

"The innkeeper told us about the *Sea Urchin*. Will we find him there?" Krampel asked.

"I don't believe so. Our surveillance of that particular establishment is not in his district; but then again, the criminals care not about the districting plans. They do as they wish."

Krampel leaned back in his chair.

Finding Verbinks sounds like a most rewarding chase, he thought. *He has already given many bounty hunters the slip.*

Krampel wanted to be the one to bring him to justice—or whatever method Cairn Ford considered justice.

"My most important question, though," the guardsman said, "is why you're looking for him?"

Krampel leaned forward, which preceded the guardsman leaning forward. He didn't want anyone else hearing this information.

"Cairn Ford, the High Imperial Inquisitor of Myrindar, wants him for questioning. Verbinks has many crimes to answer for. The criminal has eluded capture, so the Inquisitor has asked me and my apprentice here," he gestured to Lutricia, "to capture him. Have you heard if he is in the city proper, or are we on a wild goose chase?"

"He entered the town yesterday, but disappeared just as quickly. We presume that he is at the Regent's home, seeking asylum. Of course, Currance would give it to him without question."

"Naturally."

"The guard will give you all of the necessary intelligence we have on him, but I'm afraid it won't be much."

"Any information you can give us would help."

"We'd also like to assist in capturing him for you, especially after his treatment of my brothers."

"Thank you. That won't be necessary; young Lutricia and I can apprehend him by ourselves."

"I'll take my leave then, and I'll return here shortly with that information." The guardsmen stood and bowed, then departed without another word to the bounty hunter or his apprentice.

Krampel slumped slightly in his chair, the question and answer period over. He looked deep in thought.

"Master?"

He didn't answer immediately, but ended up looking toward her after several moments.

"Are you okay?"

He nodded.

"Unfortunately it had to come down to a fight. They weren't equipped to fight us, but I must say you did a wonderful job in disarming that one sailor."

Lutricia beamed at her mentor, accepting his praise for her fighting efforts.

Krampel looked out the window and noticed the sun had already dropped to the western horizon, and that night would soon approach. It had been too long since he had slept in a real bed. It had been that long for her, as well. He felt himself grow drowsy.

"You look incredibly tired, master. Up you get; we can search for the criminal as soon as we both get some sleep," Lutricia said, helping Krampel to his feet. Grabbing his shield and the golden scabbard, Krampel allowed the girl to help him upstairs to his room.

At the door, she gave him a soft smile.

"Good night, master," she bid, before he entered his room.

Chapter 12

Morning came early for the two travelers, although slightly earlier for Krampel. He awoke as soon as dawn's first light had broken the horizon, even though he knew the town guard wouldn't come to speak with him for some time. He began his day with several morning exercises, which he hadn't done since before Lutricia came into his life. Soon, sweat covered his torso, as he did several hundred repetitions of sit-ups, helping to keep his abdomen in shape.

When the church bells rang seven times—which surprised him, since there weren't many regular church-goers in Salva—and after he strapped *Flad-rul* to his waist, he went to Lutricia's door and knocked on it with three quick raps of his knuckles.

A few moments later, the door opened. Lutricia stood there with her blonde hair tousled, her eyes half open, wearing only her tunic. It hung loose as she had it unbuttoned, the bottom of it ending halfway between her waist and her knees; it drew plenty of attention to the bottom half of her supple thighs.

"Yes, master?" she asked.

Krampel stared and didn't realize Lutricia had asked a question until her eyebrows raised slightly. She snapped her fingers once, right in his face. He blinked.

"You wanted to say something to me?"

"Uh, yes. Get dressed; we'll be expecting a visit from the town guard soon. Meet me downstairs to break our fast," Krampel ordered, trying to keep himself under control. He turned quickly and headed down the stairs. Lutricia's door snapped shut, and Krampel let out the breath he had held for several seconds. He wiped away a heavy bead of sweat which had gathered on his brow.

Ten minutes later, Lutricia quickly rushed downstairs, sliding her belt through the loop on the back of the scabbard. She entered the parlor at a brisk gait, trying not to bump into any of the sailors, who, even though it was a little after seven o'clock in the morning, already had a drink in hand before they returned to their ship's berths. She found Krampel sitting alone at a table nearest the back corner, as far away from the door as possible, drinking juice. She sat down with her back to the already drunken patrons. Krampel noticed from the look on her face that she could not believe these men caroused just as badly—and just as early—as they had the afternoon before.

"What is our plan for today?" she asked her mentor.

Krampel slipped warm bread into his mouth.

"The guardsman should be here momentarily, and he should have information for us. Then we search for Verbinks, and hopefully apprehend him to bring him back to Myrindar," he said after swallowing.

Lutricia ate her breakfast, which included bread, eggs and fish.

Krampel soon looked beyond her. The guardsman had arrived and meandered his way through the drunken sailors.

"Greetings," he said as he pulled up a chair between the duo. "I put out a few feelers during the overnight. I believe we have a good bead on Verbinks."

"Does that mean that you've found him?" Krampel asked with a piercing gaze. The bounty hunter tried to look through the man to detect a lie; he saw no deceit within him.

"Nay, at least not yet. We have several contacts—trustworthy contacts, mind you—that travel through the underworld proper and hear things."

"So you're going on hearsay? Not exactly proper law enforcement protocol, don't you think?"

"These contacts are reliable!" the guardsman said, raising his voice slightly. He caught himself when he heard all conversation in the parlor cease and heads turned to the small table in the corner. He grimaced and turned back to Krampel. "I'm sorry. They are very reliable contacts; they've led to the arrest of several different criminals in the past. I trust them implicitly, and their information is worth more than you think."

Krampel took this all in and processed it through his mind. He hardly knew the guardsman, but trusted him regardless. Most guardsmen were trustworthy, and this one fit the mold. He wanted to hear the information that the guardsman had, but he hoped he wouldn't be charged for it; after all, he only had so much coin to spend on bribes, and the less he had to hand over, the better.

But still, free information was better than no information at all.

"Where have they said he is?"

"In the northern section of the underworld, and that surprises me, to tell you the truth. That area is miles from Regent Currance's holdings. But I do believe that he has done other work for other Regents in that area. I'll have to check on that when I return to quarters."

"There is no time," Krampel said, interrupting the guardsman's thoughts. "I want to have Verbinks in custody within the day. It is imperative that we are back in Myrindar before the week is out. It will take us four days, possibly five, to make the return with Verbinks in bondage, and I do not want to tarry here more than I have to. I do have another bounty to apprehend to complete the contract, then I have to begin my apprentice's training in earnest. Waiting for you to confirm what the criminal has done for other Regents is unnecessary and will delay me further. We will begin our search for him momentarily.

"Now, how do we get into the underworld of this city?"

"Find the easternmost building and go to the rear of it," the guardsman said at a whisper as he leaned forward toward the bounty hunter and his apprentice. "There is a staircase hidden behind the garbage bins. That will take you straight to the underworld."

"I thank you for all the help you've given us already."

Krampel stood as he finished speaking, followed by his apprentice and the guardsman. He began to walk out of the parlor with Lutricia on his heels to the left, while the guardsman walked to the right of him.

"If you need support, the guard will help you at your word."

"It is not necessary, but thank you." Once again, Krampel sounded more like one with exemplary breeding than a bounty hunter.

"I wish you luck on your hunt," the guardsman said before leaving the small inn. Krampel then turned to his apprentice.

"Let us not waste any more time. Go retrieve your cloak so that we may go into the underworld like any other person would—like a pair of bandits."

The duo both vaulted the stairs and into their rooms to fetch their cloaks. Krampel also retrieved his shield, which he slid over his wrist to his forearm, keeping it hidden under his dark gray cloak. As soon as he walked out and locked his door, Lutricia also came onto the landing in her own cloak. She even tied her hair back further, showing off her eyes. Krampel stared into them for the briefest of seconds, then shook himself awake. He wasn't sure, but he never recalled her eyes being so bright before.

Once they got outdoors, Krampel looked to the sky. The cloud cover made the day seem grayer than normal, and it looked to be a passing thing. Krampel sniffed the air and didn't detect an approaching storm. Down the cobblestone street they walked, headed east.

There were quite a few people already out and about this morning. Shadows that lurked in corners stretched as they passed.

The duo turned left and then right, heading down a long, busy cobblestone boulevard with many shops lining both sides. People bustled here and there, darting into shops without looking up at the other people in the area. Krampel noticed that the people in Salva lived in great fear every day, and he pitied them.

"How long do you think it will take us to get over to the other side?" Lutricia asked.

"Not too long, I think. The easternmost district is the largest, so most of our time walking will be through that district. We should be there momentarily."

They continued to stroll across the stones, their eyes taking in everything. They saw women in shabby clothes pleading for food for their children, while the passersby walked quickly by them without dropping a coin in their hands. Krampel quickly diverted his pace, strolling over to them. He dropped several gold coins in their hands. While the women were grateful, Lutricia beamed at her master.

"That was kind of you, master. What made you do that?"

They walked a little further before Krampel finally answered her.

"Everyone deserves to eat; no one should go hungry. I went hungry too often as a child, and I don't want to ever see someone starving."

Krampel's eyes misted over as he remembered his time with the caravan. He thought those feelings were buried deep, but they rushed forward. He felt a phantom pain surge through him, as if the whip of the masters came down on his back as he remembered his youth. He fought incredibly hard to keep his emotions hidden.

He failed; he felt Lutricia's hand on his shoulder, and for the first time in a long time, he didn't shake off someone who had touched him. He looked over to her and saw the concern in her eyes.

"Are you okay, Falcon?"

"Yes, I will be," Krampel replied, taking a deep breath. "Let's continue walking and find the entrance to the underworld."

***

Lutricia felt put off as the Falcon still refused to open up to her. She had tried her hardest to crack those walls in these last few days, even though she had unknowingly made a dent in them. He didn't recoil at her touch or look at her with flaming eyes. It was a start, and she would have to live with that.

Twenty minutes later, the pair found their way through the eastern district, meandering through the crowd. He looked at the tall buildings and tried to locate the farthest one to the east.

Soon, he found it and frowned.

"We are nearly at our goal, my young apprentice. I can feel him in my bones."

"I didn't know you were possessed."

The Falcon smiled, then continued: "It's a feeling that I always get when I'm close to a bounty. I get a tingling in my bones, like an adrenaline rush through my bloodstream. It is an indescribable feeling, Lutricia."

Lutricia nodded, looking ahead for the building the Falcon sought out.

"Where is it, master?"

"Just ahead: That building there, with the green spire." He sighed. "It is a house of worship. The underworld begins at a church."

"Doesn't that make you sick?"

"Aye, it does," he spat.

The Falcon and Lutricia walked toward the temple, without a crowd slowing them down. The crowd thinned considerably as they drew closer to it.

As they walked, they tried to conceal their weapons under their cloaks. Lutricia had no problem doing so as she wrapped her cloak tighter around herself. The bounty hunter, though, had a little more difficulty as the four-and-a-half foot blade stuck out from the rear as he kept his left hand on the hilt of the greatsword. They darted down the alley on the left-hand side of the temple, avoiding trash bins and broken cobblestones until they found the staircase which the guardsman had mentioned. It wasn't well hidden; it was practically out in the open where anyone had the opportunity to access it.

The Falcon peered down into the staircase's depths. She did, too, and saw plenty of light.

"I'll go first," he said; Lutricia didn't put up an argument. "We're not going to be hostile—at least not at the beginning. We'll scope out the area and throw around enough coin to find our bounty."

"Do you think that'll keep them silent, though?" Lutricia blurted out. "They'll probably cash in on our wanting to know about Verbinks to anyone that will pay for information, and they will be the ones getting richer! That will tip off our quarry to our presence."

"I *want* Verbinks to know we're on his tail. I want him to attempt to run. I want a challenge on this hunt," the Falcon explained, his tone somewhat defensive. "It'll be good practice for when we go after the next bounty."

Lutricia rolled her eyes at her mentor as soon as he turned his back to walk down the stairs.

"I saw that," he called without turning his head. Lutricia smiled as she followed her master down into the underworld, neither of them noticing the impish stranger peering at them through the curtains of the adjacent building as they descended.

***

Torches dotted every few feet of the walls, keeping the corridors of the underworld surprisingly well lit. However, that stopped once Krampel and Lutricia turned the first corner, where the lighting had grown increasingly dim with each step. Krampel figured that meant to disorient any newcomer or undesirable into the lavish underworld of Salva's criminal network. He took several moments to compose himself and get used to the difference in lighting, while Lutricia held her hands out by her sides to feel her way down the corridor. She bumped into the back of her mentor.

A minute later, both had regained their bearings and continued into the narrow passageways.

They were the only ones in the corridor for what seemed like many minutes until a large, brutish-looking fellow stopped them. The fellow's tunic didn't seem to hold the engorged muscles protruding from it. His hair was closely cropped and he had a square jaw with light stubble running along it, matching the long healed cut that went the length of his left cheek.

"What d'you want 'round here?" the guard asked the pair.

Krampel looked to Lutricia and nodded, letting her know to keep her mouth shut until he asked her to speak or was otherwise spoken to. Krampel knew the guard's type—they only spoke to males.

"We're looking for someone," Krampel said. "A criminal."

The guard's laugh seemed to come from below what served as his feet.

"We're all criminals here, buddy. Take your pick of the litter."

"We're looking for Jath Verbinks. Can you tell us where you've seen him last?"

The guard mumbled something unintelligible that echoed down the musty, dark corridor. Krampel caught Lutricia looking around to make sure the guard wasn't attracting any unneeded attention. Needless to say, they were all alone, just the three of them.

"I saw him yesterday," the guard said.

Krampel waited for the guard to say more, but only got a vacant look in return. He raised his eyebrows in anticipation of more words, but none came.

"Where did you see him?" he prompted after several seconds of silence.

The guard scratched his chin as if deep in thought.

"I think it was over by the Regent's place, but I'm not too sure. Why do you want him?"

"I want to make sure he finishes a job I asked him to do," Krampel lied.

"Are you a criminal? I've never seen you before."

"I'm not from around here. We came a long way to make sure he did the job I've paid him for."

"If you've paid him for a job, then it must not have been a big job. He doesn't look like he's eaten in weeks; he looks like a waste of his former self, like something is eating him from inside."

It is probably fear that someone will actually catch him and bring him back to Myrindar that is eating him alive, Krampel thought. *Let's see what else I can get out of this guy.*

"Tell me, since you know all about this area, if you were Verbinks, where would you go?"

The guard scratched his chin again. From behind, Lutricia blew out a hasty sigh. Krampel, meanwhile, kept his arms folded as he waited.

"Well, he has been known to hang out at the fish market," he said. "That is his, um, how do you say it? 'Legitimate' business is the term, I guess. He just got out of prison not too long ago, so I'm sure he wants to lay low to keep away from the ... authorities."

Krampel grinned at how the guard said the word; he said it with such distaste that it must have rankled his bones to admit that to someone he had never seen before. There was some new information here, though: Verbinks had been in prison, which accounted for why Cairn Ford's other bounty hunters hadn't caught him yet. The underlying question was whether or not Verbinks broke out of prison or if he had been released; the latter was more than likely, or the town guard would have been more adamant in assisting with he and Lutricia's search.

There was also the fact that if Verbinks owned a fish market, why had he looked like he hadn't eaten in weeks? Krampel had a nagging sense that the guard, as dumb as he appeared to be, looked to quickly throw him off the trail.

Krampel, however, wasn't as stupid as the guard looked.

"Thank you for your information. We appreciate it," Krampel said with a curt bow, then turned on his heel and led Lutricia out of the underworld.

***

Lutricia, for her part, stayed silent far longer than she wanted to. As she followed the Falcon out of the dingy darkness of Salva's underworld back into its lighted corridors, Lutricia adjusted her eyesight, blinking away the cobwebs, so to speak.

It would be perfect timing for someone to jump us while our vision isn't as keen as normal, she thought. Once she adjusted her eyes to the brightness, she hurried after the Falcon, who also shaded his eyes from the glare.

"Not a word until we are far from here," the Falcon admonished quietly.

"I wasn't planning on speaking until you brought it up," she replied, her tone as sharp as a knife edge.

Neither spoke a word as they meandered through the crowd once again, but this time the bounty hunter and his apprentice walked south toward the fish markets. The smell grew slightly more pungent as they closed in on their location, and it took a great deal of restraint for Lutricia to prevent her hand from holding her nose.

It wasn't until they had traveled several blocks away from the temple before the Falcon chose to speak to his apprentice.

"Disguising true intentions with a lie is one way us bounty hunters can seek our prey. Never forget that, young one."

"Will you stop calling me 'young one?' It's not like I'm that much younger than you are," Lutricia said through clenched teeth so that no one but he could hear her.

He sped up a step and whirled on her, his face right up in hers. His eyes, she saw, had turned menacing and it looked like he would scream at any second.

Instead, he used a more calm approach than his demeanor belied.

"Until you've gone through the pain and torment I've gone through in my life, Lutricia, you will always be 'young one,'" he said at nearly a whisper, his face inching even closer to hers, if that was possible. "You don't have half the experience as I do, so until you gain that experience, you will be a child in my eyes."

The bounty hunter turned and walked away from the girl, leaving her standing there for the minutest of moments. She then walked toward him again, trying her hardest to keep her tears from flowing. She had felt his walls immediately go back up, even though she had seen a chink in his impenetrable armor within the past few days. She had the sneaking suspicion, though, that another opening would present itself. She took a deep breath and exhaled quickly, getting her emotions under control before she returned to his side.

"What is our plan now?" she asked.

He didn't respond at first, and Lutricia's heart fell slightly. She felt he ignored her on purpose after his rebuke, and her face turned slightly pink: the words were still fresh in her mind.

He said, "We'll speak with the merchants around the fish market to see if they've seen Verbinks. If what the guard said was true, Verbinks will be known to them, and they'll be able to give us more information about him and his whereabouts. This should be an easy apprehension, despite what we've already been through to find him."

The Falcon and Lutricia found their way by following their noses. Soon, they found themselves at the heart of the market, where folks bought their share of fish for the night.

"Verbinks is probably making a killing today," the Falcon mused to no one but himself, but Lutricia heard every word.

"I wonder if they know he's a wanted criminal. Some people don't like to buy from criminals," she said as she looked at all of the people milling about, making purchases.

"True, but if he's got the best fish, they'll go to him even if he were a dwarf," the Falcon said. "When it comes to quality, people do not care who you are as long as you put out a good product. Remember that ... young one."

Lutricia gritted her teeth at his taunt, but let it slide down her back. They continued walking deeper into the market, not stopping to talk to any of the merchants.

She found this odd.

Didn't he just say we are going to talk to the merchants? she thought. *Why aren't we talking to them?*

She looked up to her mentor and saw that he scanned the crowd, looking at faces. He looked at the simple sidewalk stands the proprietors set up to sell their daily haul, and Lutricia had no idea what the Falcon looked for; she figured he would know when he saw it.

Lutricia walked to the nearest stand and looked at the fish, trying not to gag at the smells. She had never eaten fish before yesterday: living so far inland, getting fish to Hanlin would take several days, and by then the fish would spoil. Inland people ate beef and vegetables; what the ground gave, the inland people took in great amounts. She looked back at her mentor and noticed that he had not moved an inch, other than to scan the crowd. She rolled her eyes and turned back to the display of fish. A rather thin man with beady eyes and untidy brown hair guarded the stall.

"Excuse me, I'm looking for Jath Verbinks. You wouldn't happen to know where he is, would you?"

"Aye dear lady, he is three stalls down. See him there," the man pointed with a bony hand, "the one carrying the box toward the back. That is him."

Lutricia followed the man's finger and saw the undernourished criminal carrying a box load of who knew what toward the back.

He is a scrawny character, she thought as she got her first look at their bounty. He barely had a hold on the box as he carried it, for he kept stumbling on. Fish guts covered his gray tunic. Sweat stains cascaded from the underarm area.

She thanked the man before she hurried over to her mentor's side.

"Falcon," she said, "I've found Verbinks!"

This snapped him from his scan of the crowd and looked at his apprentice.

"Where is he?"

"Over there," she said, turning to point at the booth three places down from the thin man's stall. "He's in the back, carrying boxes. He doesn't even look to be the owner—why would the owner do grunt work?"

"A very good question, but it's one that doesn't need to be answered just yet; it is unimportant to our mission. Let us capture our quarry and be done with Salva."

The pair walked toward the criminal's booth and waited for him to make a re-appearance. They even ignored the attendant's inquiries to help them, choosing to look past him at the door that led into the back. The attendant finally gave up, throwing his hands in the air in frustration before he went to assist another customer.

It was a few minutes more before Verbinks returned to the stall. He held another box, this one looking much heavier than the one he had just carried to the back. Lutricia saw that it was a box of fish brought for the attendant to restock the stall. His face had the color of a beet.

"Jath Verbinks!" the Falcon called, "Under the name of Myrindarian law, you are under arrest for crimes against the Inquisitor!"

The criminal looked up with a look of pure shock registering across his face, his eyes wider than the moon. He dropped his box of fish without thinking, the wood cracking, the fish spilling onto the ground. He moved right to the doorway, disappearing in a flash.

"I'll get him!" Lutricia said with a yell, and without waiting for approval from her master, sprinted after the criminal, rushing through the side curtain of the stall. She knocked the attendant over and disappeared through the doorway that Verbinks ran through a split second earlier.

"Lutricia, wait!" the bounty hunter called after her, but he did not get a response from his apprentice.

***

"She is daring, I'll give her that. Crazy, but daring."

Krampel took off running down the cobblestone street. He tried to get through the people, but once they saw him rushing toward them, they quickly gave him a rather wide berth. He rushed around the corner with speed behind him, trying to find a way to cut the criminal off.

He didn't have to wait long, as a commotion from two streets over guided his feet toward the sounds.

Chapter 13

Once inside the rear portion of Verbinks' fish stall, the overwhelming smell assaulted Lutricia, but the bounty hunter's apprentice had kept her wits about her. She was in pursuit, all alone, of a criminal she had never heard about until four days ago, a criminal that might be armed to the teeth, a criminal that knew Salva like the back of his hand. All she had was her nerve and her sword. She hoped to simply count on the former; if she had to use the latter, so be it.

She dodged doorjambs as she sprinted full throttle through the building and outside into Salva proper, gathering her bearings as she found the criminal running north. She gave chase again, moving her body like a fluid entity as she ran, trying not to run into pedestrians. They did not know that a foot race—one for survival, another a bloodhound—passed them. Lutricia turned and squeezed through a small opening between two people, brushing them by and nearly knocking one of them over. She didn't lose her balance as she continued her pursuit.

She watched the criminal turn right into an alley and followed him. As she turned the corner, she saw him duck into a small passageway a few feet away from where she stood. She lunged for him, but he quickly disappeared into the crevice. She silently cursed to herself as she saw his body vanish, but then she heard the sickening sound of bones breaking and soon saw the criminal fly backward out of the hole in the wall. He hit the ground hard and rolled around, clutching his nose as his fingers went from dull gray to crimson. Lutricia turned to the crevice and stared.

Two seconds later, the Falcon stepped out of the wall and drew his blade, while Lutricia drew a deep breath and sighed at the sight. She followed suit after she had regained control of herself and walked up to the criminal. Both pointed their swords toward the now-moaning man. Blood streamed from his nose. He rolled over a quarter turn and sneezed. Blood and mucus flew out and nearly landed on Lutricia's boots. She didn't jump back, holding her ground as she saw the phlegm spray out across the cobbles.

"So as I was saying," Falcon said, looking down at his captive, "you are under arrest for violating Myrindarian law, Jath Verbinks. You will now come quietly with us so the Inquisitor can deal with you as he may."

"No," the man panted through a mouthful of blood and saliva, moving into a kneeling position yet still prostrate on the ground. "Don't take me to Ford. The man is a lunatic!"

The Falcon, Lutricia saw, cared not for the man's ravings, even though it was the second time during this trip that they had heard bad things about their current employer. Lutricia disregarded this outright, for the Falcon never believed the derision of criminals. They usually said anything to get out of trouble.

"Keep your tongue still or I'll cut it from your mouth! The bounty is alive only, but I don't think the Inquisitor would mind if I maimed you."

"You're as sick and twisted as he is!" the criminal screamed. He tried to get up, but Lutricia's boot came up and kicked him right in the chest. He went down like a child's rag doll.

"Tie him up," the Falcon ordered, handing his apprentice a length of rope from his right hip. "Bind his hands and feet. If we have to drag him to Myrindar, so be it. I'm sure he'll like tearing his flesh open on the city's cobblestones." The Falcon grinned at the prisoner as he said this. Verbinks, Lutricia saw, cowered in fear, as if trying to shrink in size.

Lutricia had secured the prisoner and had him up on his feet. Once they walked out of the alley and back into the streets of Salva proper, Verbinks resumed his ranting of Ford's evil, and how he would pay them more money than Ford would if they released him.

"I would rather witness your execution than take your filthy coin!" the Falcon said as he turned and sneered at the man. "Now be quiet or I'll make good on my promise!"

The Falcon had Lutricia hold onto the rope by wrapping it around her waist, then gave the rope a sharp yank. Verbinks toppled to the cobblestones as a result, but soon got up and made a run for the bounty hunter. The bounty hunter simply gave the criminal a running lariat across the throat, which knocked Verbinks right back down to the ground.

Verbinks didn't make another stupid move for as long as he was in custody.

They returned to the inn to retrieve their belongings, and the Falcon sent word to the guardsman that they had caught Verbinks.

"Now," he said, "we have to hope that Regent Currance hasn't heard of this, or we may have difficulty getting out of Salva. Let's get away quickly, or this will be a very short trip!"

With all haste, the bounty hunter, his apprentice and their quarry walked out of Salva and started the long trip to Myrindar.

***

A day out of Salva, Krampel and Lutricia ate a good deal of the provisions that Ford had prepared for them before the trip. They gave Verbinks enough to keep his strength up for the next day of marching. He looked as if the fear of his capture had gnawed away at him, and Krampel had asked him if the Regent had turned him away when he went to see his old employer. Verbinks said nothing, only to avert his gaze. He made a mental note not to trust anyone in Salva when it came to information about criminals, as he received so much that conflicted with everyone else; he figured it best to use his own power of observation. At night, he and Lutricia took turns on the watch, guarding the captive with their blades drawn, just in case a brawny, southern orc came calling.

The next day the trio passed the small forest where Krampel and Lutricia had taken turns bathing two days prior. Krampel fondly remembered guarding his apprentice while she bathed in the brook, remembered seeing her naked form for the first time. He smiled inwardly and then recalled how he had scolded her before they captured Verbinks. That wiped the smile from his face, and even though the reasons for his anger with his apprentice were many, he felt he owed her an apology.

Lutricia reminded Krampel of his desire to avoid the orc cavern that day, and they immediately walked east to skirt the mountain pass. They walked through the night. He noticed

Lutricia didn't seem to mind the continuation of their journey in the evening.

By the time they saw the mountain of Myrindar, the trip had exhausted them; it had exhausted their provisions, as well. They finally reached the city a few hours later, where the guard escorted them and their prisoner to the summit and into the manor.

Ford greeted them with a wide smile.

"Ah, I see you had no problems with this one. He came quietly, I take it?"

"Of course I didn't," Verbinks replied, then spat at the Inquisitor's shoes. "I told them about your evil ways, Ford. You may kill me, but the message will spread!"

"Take him away to Karackstine; I'll be down to administer his punishment," Ford said with a snarl. As the guard led him away, Ford turned to the bounty hunters. "Thank you for apprehending him; you have my thanks for a job well done. Please rest before you go on your next hunt; I'll have the chambermaid show you to the rooms you had a week ago."

Both Krampel and Lutricia bowed before the chambermaid escorted them to their rooms without a word.

***

The guards of Karackstine had stripped Verbinks of his clothes and his dignity before strapping him down to the raised platform in the darkened room. Verbinks had screamed for them to release him, this last gasp effort unheard by the guards. One guard had smacked him hard across the mouth with a gauntlet-covered hand, busting open the left side of his lip and shattering two teeth. The guards chuckled to themselves as they eagerly watched the prisoner spit out teeth and blood onto the already blood-strewn floor.

A strong light streamed into the room as a door opened with a long creak. Ford and two other individuals entered it, blocking out a portion of the light. One carried a torch to brighten the gloom of the torture chamber.

Ford sauntered up to the side of the platform that held Verbinks to it; the criminal appeared immobile as the High

Imperial Inquisitor looked down on the condemned man. Ford wore a look of triumph on his face, his grin unerasable.

"Comfortable?" he taunted.

Verbinks replied by spitting in the Inquisitor's face.

Ford simply smiled, then turned and paced in front of the platform, only walking four paces before he turned and walked four paces the other way.

"How does it feel, Verbinks? How does it feel to evade every bounty hunter I sent after you, only to be captured by the best in the realms?"

"Shut up!"

"You were beaten even before you knew it," Ford said as he continued his pacing, not taking his eyes off the prisoner. "You are not worthy of my attention, yet you have it anyway. You committed a crime against my rule, and for that you shall pay!"

"I stole a pig!"

"That pig belonged to the Imperium, not to you. You shall be punished for your crimes. You may even die for your crimes." Ford snickered until his laughter turned into a sinister cackle. "Oh, yes. I expect you to die."

Verbinks had screamed a blood-curdling bellow that reverberated throughout the small torture chamber, but to Ford it was the sweetest music ever conjured in this city.

When it finished—both Verbink's screams and his struggling—Ford motioned for the other person who had entered with him to step forward. A man with short, dark brown hair had stepped into the torchlight. He had a square jaw and a sharp, thin nose and looked to be about twenty-five summers old. He wore dark wizard's robes, as his white tunic showed in between the folds of his robe.

"This is Danolf Jenson," Ford said. "He is a young wizard, but please do not be fooled—he is very powerful, indeed. He will perform the first part of my plan to blood share and create the ultimate warrior, the prototype which will become the model of my army, the army that will take over all of the realms."

Verbinks shuddered.

"You... you... you are insane! I knew it! You are evil incarnate!"

"I said be quiet!" Ford hissed.

"I can quiet him," Jenson said as he raised his hands and pulled back the sleeves of his robes, as if ready to cast a spell of compulsion. But Ford had stopped him before he muttered a single incantation.

"That won't be necessary, Danolf. I want our friend awake when everything occurs." Another smile had flashed across Ford's face as Verbinks went pale in less than a second. He almost let out a pathetic whimper, his fear eating him from the inside. "Send in the clerics!"

The guards opened the doors and in walked two hooded clerics, each carrying a different object—the one on the right carried a vial, while the other carried a knife.

"What... what are those for?" Verbinks said, whimpering.

"They are for the blood sharing process," the wizard had said with a smile. "Your blood will be the first we use to create the prototype. You should be honored."

Verbinks' mouth moved, but nothing had emerged save whimpers and mews. White-faced and horrified, he couldn't come up with words to express his displeasure.

The wizard looked to the Inquisitor for the go-ahead, and soon received it in the form of a stiff nod. Jenson had smiled, then turned to the clerics and gave them a nod, too. They then moved in on the prisoner, doing so with slow, measured steps.

The criminal blithered, his protest unrecognizable.

"No, please no, don't do this, no," he said, his body quivering against his bonds as they approached him. "I'm sorry, forgive me, lord!"

"It is too late for forgiveness, Verbinks! Your punishment will be carried out!" Ford yelled over the criminal's pleas for mercy.

The cleric with the knife looked back to the wizard, who then reached into his robe and pulled out a small bag. Jenson handed the bag to the cleric with a wicked grin on his face.

"What's that? What are you doing?" Verbinks had said, his tone frantic, his head raised off the platform.

"Nothing you'll care about in a few minutes," the wizard had replied, his tone lacking emotion.

"I'll leave you to our combined work, Danolf. I'll expect your report soon."

The wizard bowed to his master. Ford turned and departed the room, but not before throwing a peek at the platform. The clerics had poured the contents of the bag, a white, powdery substance, on the criminal's left upper arm. Verbinks' eyes rolled slightly, then he gave off another powerful scream.

Cairn Ford grinned maliciously, then shut the door behind him. He heard another scream as the clerics plunged the knife into Verbinks' arm, drawing the criminal's blood with cruel, malicious force. He didn't need to witness the deed; he knew his henchmen would do their jobs as he had ordered.

As soon as Verbinks' screams had ceased and the room grew intensely silent, Ford gave off a short laugh and walked forward several paces.

"My lord," Danolf Jenson said, bowing to Ford as soon as he had exited the chamber. "The criminal is now minutes from death."

"Good, Danolf. Is our treasure secured?"

"It is being secured as we speak, lord. The clerics are now draining him. It shouldn't be more than a matter of minutes, then they'll perform a simple spell to preserve it until we use it in the blood sharing process."

Ford nodded and allowed the wizard to walk with him. Passing cells and the moans of agony from the prisoners, Ford leaned to the wizard and spoke to him in an undertone so no others overheard them.

"Did you scry the orb as I asked while our friends were on the hunt for Verbinks?"

"Aye, I did, lord. An interesting pair, the bounty hunter and his apprentice."

"And what did you see?"

"It seems that whenever I saw them, they were at each other's throats. Constantly bickering, they were; the apprentice did not take too kindly to her mentor talking down to her, obviously because of her breeding, and the bounty hunter did not appear to want her there with him, as he appears to be a loner by nature. A peculiar pair, if you ask me, lord.”

Ford’s eyes widened slightly at this knowledge.

“An interesting development, wouldn’t you say, Danolf? Two people who work so closely together, yet can’t stand the other’s presence? Yes, I’d say that is an interesting development, indeed.”

“If my lord believes it to be interesting, than it shall be considered so.”

“Consider this, as well—we have something to use against them, should the need arise.”

“I understand, my lord.”

“Good. Keep your understanding silent, and make sure none hear of this. And make sure that we get the sample from the hunter tonight. It is critical for the prototype project.”

“It will be done.” The wizard gave another curt bow to his master.

“I will be with my grandson for the next few hours. Go and watch them through the orb and keep me apprised of Crassnick’s progress and his whereabouts.”

“As my lord commands, it shall be done immediately.”

Chapter 14

The wide trunks of the trees of Arborway had swallowed Krampel and Lutricia as they took off into the wilderness the next morning. They had felt rested after having spent the night in relative comfort.

The duo had kept to the path and crossed through the wooden realm in a few hours. By then, the noon hour approached, the sun high in the sky. Its rays tried to beat through the leafy canopy above the travelers, but darkness prevailed, for the most part. They decided to rest there and eat a meal, saving their energy for the moment that they came face-to-face with Piety Crassnick.

As they sat and ate, Krampel pulled out the parchment documents that Cairn Ford had handed him prior to the start of the hunt for Jath Verbinks. He unrolled the scrolls and looked over the information, which he figured gave him an edge over his quarry.

Ford had incredibly detailed information, including a listing of all Crassnick's haunts and places he had visited in the past five years. Krampel held Piety's history from the last time he had seen him in Cassimina in his hands.

He considered it interesting reading. He had learned that Piety had filled out over the last few years—at least that's how the sketch represented him. His hair had thinned slightly and he had filled out in the face, arms and legs, while he had developing a broad, muscular chest. It also said he had led raiding parties of men who, at one point or another in their lives, had done time in Karackstine. Piety seemed proficient with a sword and small daggers, his main weapons of choice, but he had also dabbled in archery, as well.

Krampel processed everything. His newest and oldest adversary had turned into one in the same, and he had obviously improved in every way, shape and form. It would take every bit of the cunning he possessed, Krampel knew, to subdue and defeat Piety Crassnick. This wasn't like Cassimina when they were young. This was a much deadlier arena, where the slightest mistake may lead to a scarring injury, or worse. This was for keeps.

He had read the parchment scroll for what seemed like ages, as he tried to commit every word, every paragraph, to memory. He wanted to check and double-check each letter to make sure everything added up. Before now, Krampel had used patterns in criminals' habits to find and capture them. He loved criminals with routines, and he certainly hoped he'd expose Piety through his habits.

Lowering the parchment, he stared off toward the northeast, toward the area where he knew Cassimina lay somewhere beyond the horizon, taking a deep breath as his thoughts rolled. He had said even then, when he had swiped Flad-rul from his masters grave, that he would never return. From what the parchment said, Piety had never returned there, either.

That's a relief to me, Krampel thought. *I don't ever want to go back there, not unless I'm arresting one of those buffoons who hid from the orcs.*

His thoughts turned to the six months he had spent there, where Crassnick and his cronies had harassed and had bullied him until he finally couldn't take it anymore. He absent-mindedly reached down to pat the hilt of *Flad-rul* while continuing his vigil. He knew that if he had not turned the tables on that particular day, there probably would be no chance of him wearing that sword on his hip right now.

And Vossler would probably still be alive, he thought.

He took another deep breath as he brought his emotions under control. Thinking about Vossler brought about old feelings from deep within him, feelings he had thought buried forever.

Thinking about Piety Crassnick had simply re-awoken those feelings. He looked over to his apprentice, who sat next to him eating an apple. She appeared to have no idea of the internal conflict her mentor endured at this moment, and she simply looked ahead while nibbling away at the fruit, the wind slipping through her long, blonde tresses. Her skin looked as if to glow in the sunshine, and Krampel had suspected she snuck a bath while in Myrindar.

He looked at her with a soft smile.

Lutricia turned to him and noticed his stare. She paused mid-bite and asked, "What's wrong? Are you okay?"

"Yes, I am," he said after several seconds of silence. "I'm just making a plan for today."

"So what is the plan?"

"We march. The closer we get to Piety Crassnick, the quicker we can end this mission and begin your training. Pack up and get ready to leave Arborway," Krampel said, who stood and stretched.

The pair took their time heading northeast. As Krampel noticed, this was the same route they had traveled after leaving Hanlin nearly ten days ago. Several things had occurred in their lives since then; several interesting things, at that.

When night came, Krampel built another fire in the same spot they had camped the night they heard the horsemen coming for them. It seemed like forever ago. They ate and rested, each taking a turn on the watch while the other slept.

After they broke their fast, they had left the small forest and had continued their journey northeast. But within a few seconds of venturing into a soft meadow, they heard gruff voices coming from the west, singing and chanting as they marched. The duo stopped in their tracks and looked into the direction from where the sounds came.

"What in the nine—wait, sorry—the eleven hells is that?" Lutricia asked.

"I have no idea; either it's an army of balladeers or a plain old army. Let's go back into the forest!"

They retraced their steps back into the trees, hiding behind two of the largest oaks they found, yet still able to see what happened in the meadow.

"Isn't this what happened when Ford's Myrindarians—" Lutricia had started to ask, but the question died on her lips as the singing voices were now within fifty axe-lengths of them.

Krampel knew what she wanted to say, but had a feeling these weren't Myrindarian guards. He looked toward the group as it came over the distant hill and noticed an army of dwarves, each one armed with an axe, marching into view. He saw a standard with a red flag emblazoned behind a golden mug, and wondered from what realm these dwarves originated. He didn't recognize them, although he had conversed with many over the last five years. Talkative was not in the nature of a dwarf, except when soused.

"Let's go," he said, and he led his apprentice out of the copse of trees to await the band of dwarves.

Within a few minutes the dwarf army had finished their approach, and they slowed at the raised fist of their leader, a rugged dwarf with a long black beard and weathered, sun-baked skin. He looked no more than 350 years old, but Krampel knew that with dwarves, appearances were deceiving.

"Greetings, dwarves. May I ask where you're off to, so far from home?" Krampel asked.

"Nay, yeh may not ask," the lead dwarf with the long black beard replied. "Yeh don't have the look o' a highwayman; besides, yeh may not ask of tithes o' the Lowbridgian dwarves if yeh are!"

Lowbridge, Krampel thought. *Yes, I have heard of that land.*

"Indeed you are far from home, friend. And aye, you are correct. I am not a highwayman, but I am a bounty hunter. I know of your kingdom and that you are always on the side of good. Again, I ask what your purpose is in these lands; I know them well. Perhaps I could be of assistance to you, lord."

Krampel's voice once again had the tone of one with incredible breeding.

The lead dwarf looked at Krampel with narrowed eyes, and Krampel only smiled in return. He did not show any threatening gestures to the dwarf. After all, by his count, three hundred dwarves marched along with the black bearded one. Krampel knew he might be somewhat reckless at times, but he wasn't a stupid man. He wouldn't get into a fight with odds so stacked against him.

"Aye, yeh probably could, lad. We've heard o' scuffles near the borders o' Cassimina. Have yeh heard anythin' that would be able to help us?"

The mention of Cassimina nearly boiled Krampel's blood, but he resisted the urge to scream. He became somewhat intrigued by the developments at his old home. His left eyebrow inched upward.

"Nay lord, I have not heard of a thing going on there; we've only just come north from Salva. What do you know of events there?"

"Bad doin's are happenin' there, friend. We've heard the Cassiminians called out for help, and it was nearly a week ago that word reached our king, Ricanack Rosar's, ears. I am his son, Radamuck Rosar, the future 24th King of Lowbridge, and I command these hearty dwarves."

"If you're going to Cassimina, then I'd like to join you on your quest. My name is the Dark Falcon, a bounty hunter of the south, and this is my apprentice, Lutricia. We'd be honored to assist you."

Krampel watched as the dwarf thought it all over, running his thick fingers through his black beard, twisting and twirling the hair between the pads of his fingertips.

The dwarf had grinned slightly, seemingly coming to a decision.

"Aye friend, we'd like the assistance o' yer size on the trip, and yer knowledge o' the lay o' the land would be quite helpful. Yeh may march with me at the front, and tell me about yerselves. We march, lads!"

The dwarf army gave a mighty cheer and marched away, heading east first to avoid a long swamp, then turned northeast, straight toward Cassimina.

***

Two days later, the company had stopped at the base of the Falls of Dannin, well within shouting distance to Cassimina, Krampel knew. The falls consisted of only a ten-foot drop, as the river that ran above it from Timber Lake was narrow. These lands were his old stomping grounds, as he spent many an hour, when not in training with Vossler, fishing along the banks of the river. Cassimina proper sat approximately five miles away.

He sat down on a worn rock on the shore as he watched the dwarves set up their camp, while Lutricia had busied herself with setting up her own camp near her mentor's belongings. As he sat and looked on, the memories of his former life rushed back at him once again, like a large, round boulder rolling down a steep hill. The memories of the girl with whom he had fallen in love back then—*what was her name again?* he thought —and meeting Vossler came foremost to mind, and the day he left Cassimina, leaving it with *Flad-rul* on his hip, he recalled vividly.

I've said I would never step foot in this town again, he thought, *and here I am, less than five miles from it! I must be out of my mind.*

His torment soon showed on his face and Lutricia had noticed it as she put the finishing touches on her bedroll. She looked over to her mentor and frowned, then smoothed out the bedroll before she emerged from her crouch and walked over to where he sat.

"Are you okay, master? You have been acting very strange these last few hours."

Krampel looked at her and shook his head.

"Nay, I'm not okay. This town we are coming on, it is known to me. I know it all too well. I haven't been here in five years, but things that happened here continue to haunt me."

***

Lutricia had crouched down in front of him with a look of concern on her face. The great warrior shook. The thought that he was about to open up to her frightened her, but she had steeled herself for whatever he said.

She wasn't his student right now; she was his confessor.

"I lived in Cassimina when I was younger, although 'lived in' shouldn't be the term I use. I was pretty much indentured to the town."

"How?"

"I told you that I was an orphan and a slave. That much is true. What I haven't said is that my mother sold me to a slaver, who in turn sold me to a gypsy caravan." He took a deep breath as he let his explanation tumble away from his lips. "I basically cleaned up the muck their horses left, and the food they gave me was about as healthy as the stuff I shoveled. Then," he said, standing, "one day in the autumn, we had come rolling into Cassimina. I don't remember exactly what I did, but I earned a beating at the hands of the caravan master. Later that night, after we departed the town, I figured out how to loosen the bonds from my wrists. I vanished into the darkness, eventually making my way back to the town. I was hungry. I tried to steal bread and the town guard caught me. The next day, a man by the name of Vossler came to my aid; he freed me. I worked for him as his apprentice; he was a tanner and a cobbler.

"Within a few months, Vossler sat me down and said that I had a talent deep within me, a talent he saw when he caught the caravan master beating me that day. He said he wanted to unlock it. Within his training dungeon, he showed me how to fight with a sword, then with the shield I wear. These were gifts from him; in fact he said that he had to pry the sword from his own master's dead fingers.

"Which is what I ended up doing: Vossler died in an orc raid only a few months later. I fought back-to-back with him, and orcs killed him. He slumped into my back, and when I saw his body lying prostrate on the ground, I snapped: as my rage rushed through me, feeding my strength. I had never felt so full of potent energy, yet so empty emotionally."

Moving next to him, Lutricia put her hand on his shoulder in a comforting gesture. He didn't flinch at the touch. She looked into his eyes and nodded for him to continue.

"The day after, I prepared his body for burial, and I put the sword I used on his breast: I figured the sword that saved Cassimina should be buried with the man who organized its last stand. But the town leaders, who holed themselves up in a house when the orcs invaded, overruled me and thought his sword should be buried with him. I protested, but they went against me after I embarrassed one of them following the battle.

"So I burned the home we lived in, I robbed the grave and replaced *Flad-rul* with mine, and I departed Cassimina for what seemed like the last time. I never thought I would be back here, and here I am."

The Falcon lowered his head, but didn't cry. Lutricia looked at her mentor with a new understanding and a much deeper respect for him than before. She now understood his wariness about taking her on as an apprentice, and his refusal to lower his guard.

"I'm sorry," she said softly. "You've gone through so much. I didn't know you had so much pent up inside. But you've gotten it all off your chest; maybe now you can move on from your fears."

"Aye, maybe. I don't know. There is just so much pain within me that it would take a lot to ease it."

"I'll be with you every step of the way," she said with a smile. "Now, let's get something to eat. I'm famished."

He chuckled a little, then stood up and followed his apprentice to the pot where the dwarf cook ladled out a hot, creamy substance that looked like porridge. When they received a bowlful each, they sat next to the riverbank, until Radamuck came up to them with a bowl of his own.

"Yeh seem to be troubled, lad. Are yeh goin' to be okay?"

"Aye, your highness, I should be. Thank you."

"What was it that had yer beard in a knot?"

"I thought about my time in Cassimina long ago, my old mentor, and a lad who used to bully me around when I first arrived, until I turned the tables on him one day. His name is Piety Crassnick, and we're on a hunt for him. He's wanted by the High Imperial Inquisitor of Myrindar for crimes against the southern kingdom. I intend on bringing him back alive."

Lutricia watched as Radamuck's eyes widened.

"Piety Crassnick, eh? What do yeh know o' him?"

"Not much, actually. The Inquisitor gave us information about him. The last time I saw him was more than five years ago, but never a day passes when he doesn't enter my mind, seeking to torment me."

"I must admit to yeh lad, that we are on the hunt for Crassnick, too. It is his band that is organizin' against Cassimina, and shortly, I'm sendin' scouts ahead to find out what is going on in the town."

The Falcon looked dumbfounded at the dwarf prince as he revealed this.

"It will be different knowing that Piety Crassnick, the lad who tormented me so while I was there, is still in the area. It must be fated for me to find him here. If you don't mind, your highness, I'd like to join the scouting party to see if Crassnick is there."

Radamuck nodded.

"Aye, it is okay with me. I'll send yeh over to me scoutin' leader, and he'll ask yeh what the best-case scenario would be to scout."

The Falcon looked at Lutricia and said, "Our hunt just grew nine times more interesting than it was. Prepare to join the party; I believe this will be an insightful mission."

Chapter 15

Stalking through the trees in the dead of night, Krampel, Lutricia, Radamuck and another dwarf tore through the underbrush. They went about their mission without a torch, just in case Piety Crassnick's army or scouts were about. Krampel had told the dwarf prince that he would take care of any scouts, and he had patted the hilt of *Flad-rul* to emphasize his point. Radamuck had grinned through his beard; Krampel had seen two rows of white.

They had approached Cassimina from the south, only an hour away from their waterfall-side campsite. Krampel's heart raced as they ran, and not because of his cadence: he now moved closer to the life he had set aside. He didn't know if he would even recognize Cassimina, but seemed more worried that someone there might recognize him.

Krampel now relied solely on memories as he took the point, leading the other three through the wild. Adrenaline coursed through the rivers under his skin. He now tread on the vales he had once frolicked in. He had built the stamina he now possessed on these lands. He sidestepped a fallen tree and felt his heart skip a beat.

Lutricia followed him, keeping her mentor within reach. Radamuck was next, followed by the other dwarf, a rather obnoxious-looking fellow with a large protrusion in the middle of his face. The dwarves fought to keep up with the humans, but as Krampel noticed, they, too, had quite the energy reserve stored deep within them.

"That's what we dwarves get for drinkin' the gods' blessed ales!" Radamuck had said with a laugh. "They give us the strength to do such great feats that many humans would blanch at!"

At a tall ash, Krampel halted the others and looked off toward the east, where he saw an orange glow settling in near the horizon. He knew sunrise was a few hours away.

This could be something interesting, he thought.

The dwarves noticed the glow before Krampel said anything, but he was the first to speak.

"I think this is something we should check out, Radamuck. This could be Piety Crassnick's campsite up ahead."

"Aye lad, I agree. It could be a slight diversion or it could be what we're looking for. We'll follow yer lead," Radamuck answered.

With a nod, the bounty hunter led the trio away from their intended direction and headed for the eastern horizon, where the orange glow grew slightly larger as they approached. Krampel knew a path which would let them pass over the river —he had the feeling the dwarves wouldn't be too keen about hopping across it on rocks—and take them to a small clearing to get their bearings.

The bridge Krampel had led them across was of sturdy construction and consisted of a fallen tree trunk wide enough to allow the foursome to cross it single file, one foot over the other. There was a pair of handrails running along each side, so at first glance, the bridge looked like a horizontal V running across the river. Taut rope kept everything together. Krampel wondered if Vossler had woven it in the years before he had died. He had never said anything about it.

They had crossed to the other side of the river rather easily, so easy in fact the quartet ran right across it and didn't stop as they continued their trek. A few minutes after the crossing, they had found themselves within two hundred axe-lengths of the large orange glow. They came on a crest Krampel knew overlooked a valley that stretched a good distance in either direction. They now stood in a small, hilly area that marked the southeastern borders of Cassimina's territory, several miles from Cassimina proper. They dropped into a crouch.

The sight that met their eyes was a mix of awe-inspiring and terrifying at the same time. Throughout the valley stood hundreds of tents surrounding a large bonfire, cutting the darkness and reaching to the heavens with orange-tipped fingers. Krampel figured that at least four hundred warriors slept in that valley right now.

Krampel took a deep breath and let it out slowly, almost as a whistle. If it came down to a fight, he knew it wouldn't be an easy one. Then he grinned, knowing he liked a challenge.

"Are we sure this is where Crassnick is?" Lutricia whispered as she knelt next to the bounty hunter. "This could be one of his diversions."

"It's as large as we've heard," Radamuck said, "and it's near the Cassiminian borders, as we've heard. This has to be it."

"The only way we're going to be absolutely sure is if we can hear him. He'll be in the largest tent down there," Krampel replied, leveling a calloused finger at it. "And I'd bet my sword that is his tent right there."

The other three looked down toward it. The glow of the fire caught a pair of guards nearest the opening of that tent, making them clearly visible to the scouting party.

Krampel backed away from the edge of the cliff, followed by the other three.

"I'm going down," he said. "I know Piety's voice, I would recognize it anywhere. I've heard his taunting voice in my nightmares for years, even though I defeated him long ago."

"I'm coming with you," his apprentice said. "You can't go alone, not without someone to back you up in case something happens."

"Nay, lass," the dwarf prince said. "Yeh won't be goin'. Me word is law."

"You're a faster runner than the dwarves," Krampel countered. "If something happens, you will be able to run and get help."

"They wouldn't listen to me even if I did!" she said, slightly raising her whisper to emphasize her point. "You know how dwarves can be: stubborn, pig-headed, overly masculine. Their patriarchal society doesn't allow them to listen to women."

"Aye, we can be stubborn, pig-headed, and overly masculine, but lass, me dwarves would come runnin' to me if yeh gave them the password."

"There is no need for you to do this," Krampel said, turning to her. "You don't have to prove anything to me."

"I have to do this! I told you I want to experience everything you do as a bounty hunter! This whole 'apprenticeship' would be a farce if you didn't let me go with you," she said. The look on her face was not one of pleading; she was serious. "I'm going whether you like it or not!"

Krampel looked down at his apprentice and felt the pain in her words. She had proven herself worthy of being his apprentice this last fortnight. His face was set, and his frown was not meant for her.

It was for him.

"She's right," he said to the dwarf. "She has to come. It's part of her training. It'll be easier if it's just her and I going down to see what we can see."

"All right, Falcon. I'll trust yer judgment. But get back here as quick as yeh can!" Radamuck said, shaking his finger at the pair.

"We will," the bounty hunter said, "don't you worry about that."

The mentor and apprentice crouched down and darted down the path, bushes and ferns grazing their trousers as they walked. They found themselves at the bottom of the hill, but it took several more minutes for them to find an opening into the camp.

"I appreciate the confidence you show in me," Lutricia said. "It means a lot."

"I wouldn't say it if I didn't mean it." Krampel's voice was serious, with that dark edge to it which had made the bounty hunter a mysterious entity.

They walked into and through a dense clump of trees that blotted out the moonlight but didn't do much to dampen the light of the bonfire. They tried to keep their movements slow and even, and they tried not to step on twigs or downed, browned leaves. Lutricia tried to keep her footfalls silent, much like Krampel's; she didn't have a pair of elven boots. Every time he heard a branch snap or leaves rustle close behind him, he knew his apprentice came close to broadcasting their arrival in Piety's camp.

Krampel walked up behind a wide tree and peeked around to see if there were any guards in this western end of the campsite. He grinned when he saw none.

He nodded to Lutricia, who also hid behind another nearby tree, and led her out into the sea of tents.

"Do everything I do, mimic my movements. The more you do that, the better chance we have of getting out of here alive," he told her in a whisper as they walked out of the woods together. She simply nodded.

They walked softly and carefully as they reached the first tent. Krampel sidestepped a tent hook, which nearly tripped up Lutricia. Krampel looked back at her with a stern warning; she put her hands out at her sides in apology. From there they crouched down and walked a little faster between the rows of tents. They had not seen or heard any of Piety's men passing or talking among themselves, and that, Krampel knew, was a blessing in disguise.

A long space between the tent rows approached. He had paused for a second, looked both ways and saw none of Piety's underlings on either side. He waved Lutricia across before him, then followed with his hand near the hilt of *Flad-rul*. They inched closer to the center of the encampment and the bonfire. They still needed to pass some twenty rows of tents before they reached the large tent. It was located in a center ring, which was how Krampel saw it from above.

He held Lutricia back with a hand, then crouched low and walked toward the rear of the large tent.

From above, he saw guards on the other side and purposely came into the valley the way he did because of that reason alone. He put his hands out to keep his balance as he crouched to one knee, then put his left ear up to the tent.

He wasn't shocked to hear Piety Crassnick's voice—albeit a little older, a bit deeper than he remembered—through the tent. He looked back at Lutricia and smiled while nodding.

"It's him," he mouthed to her, then turned his attention back to the tent.

***

"We've already decimated Cassimina, and tomorrow we will march toward the south. Our ultimate goal is Myrindar, but we need to take out any resistance to our efforts."

Piety Crassnick had paced the length of the tent while his advisors—cronies, in truth, fellow criminals who had resisted

Ford's arresting efforts—stood at attention on the northern side of the tent. Piety wore a broad, armored chest plate with a sword dangling at his left hip. He also wore brown trousers and black boots that went up to his knees. He wore his short hair parted down the middle, so it looked to cascade off his scalp as it fell on either side of his head.

"My lord, does anyone know of our takeover attempt? No disrespect meant, but I do not believe Ford knows we're coming for him," one of the cronies said.

"That may be true, but I am sure that Ford knows of our intentions. He has sent bounty hunter after bounty hunter after me, and I've held off each and every one of them."

"Why didn't you tell us of this?"

"I didn't tell you because you didn't need to know," Piety answered. "I've dealt with the hunters and kept it from you. As you can see, I have the unwavering fealty of the guards. They have kept it quiet because I ordered them not to talk about it to anyone. You are all on a need-to-know basis, and you don't have to know all of the things I've done now or in the past; you would blanch if you knew what I did to my own father." He laughed maniacally, and each of the five men inside the tent looked at each other with bewilderment on their faces.

***

Krampel couldn't believe his ears.

Did I hear what I think I just heard? he thought.

He felt the blood rush out of his face until the flesh tingled; his eyes bulged as he replayed Piety's words in his head.

No, it couldn't be, he thought. *Piety's greatest ambition was to be just like his father. What did he do to his father that made him laugh like that?* The laugh alone sent shivers up Krampel's spine.

Swallowing the bile that had threatened to rise, he stood and returned to Lutricia's side.

"He is in there, but he's not alone; he has at least one other person in there with him."

"Then let's grab him and be done with it."

"Nay, we can't do that. Two of us, four hundred or more of them. The odds are not in our favor."

"All right. Let's go back to the dwarves and report what we've found. At least with the dwarves it will be better odds."

"Let's do it quickly and quietly; we've come in undetected, let's leave the same way."

The duo had turned and walked back the way they came, but Lutricia only walked three feet before she had tripped again. This time, she did not keep her balance: she had hit the ground hard, her sword slapping against the tent hook. The sound had reverberated around the camp like a massive cannon explosion.

Krampel had turned at the sound and, with wide eyes, saw his apprentice sprawled on the ground, a look of intense fright on Lutricia's face. He made a quick move to her, but then he heard the unmistakable sound of bedcovers thrown aside and light sleepers reaching for swords, yanking them from their scabbards.

Without asking if she was okay, Krampel had picked her up hastily and had pushed her away from him.

"Go! I'll deal with them, get as far away from here quick as you can!" he had said when she had turned and looked at him. He had *Flad-rul* drawn in anticipation of what was to come.

He wasn't, however, ready for what Lutricia did next.

***

With widened eyes, Lutricia ignored the metallic taste which had coated her tongue. She then looked from the Falcon's face back toward the wooden area, then back to her mentor. She wasted time, precious seconds that meant life or death, but she had to do this. The urge was just too great, the feelings too urgent.

She took two steps forward and flung herself into his arms, burying herself in his chest for the fleetest of seconds. She then reached up and gave him a very soft kiss on his lips. She broke away with a smile and said, "Just in case."

The Falcon had grinned slightly, before he had regained control over his emotions.

"Quickly Lutricia, get away from here," he said, just as two of Piety Crassnick's men left their tents. "Go!" he had ordered a second time, this time a little louder. Without another word, Lutricia took off, running down the middle of the lane, avoiding the sides where the unseen tent hooks were placed.

***

Her scent still lodged in his nostrils, the taste of her blood on his lips, and his heart swollen for the first time in years, Krampel didn't bother to see whether or not Lutricia had made it to the woods, because he now had bigger problems on his hands. Holding *Flad-rul* with his right hand and with his fiery golden shield strapped to his left forearm, he turned to face the new arrivals. They stood there in their dressing gowns and bore no armor, but each had a sword of similar length.

The one on the bounty hunter's right side came after him and started chopping across his body, chops Krampel had parried easily with slight twists of his wrists. The other fighter came in at that moment and, with a spin of his feet, he turned over and led his defense with the sword, parrying the first fighter's blade with the golden shield.

Keeping his feet moving and his sword swinging, Krampel had deflected everything these two mercenaries threw his way. But within minutes of the opening salvos, the number of men he faced went from two to several hundred, as the sounds of blades clashing against each other and against his shield had alerted them to danger in the camp.

Time to dispose of these two and get out of here, Krampel had thought as he slashed low on the first fighter, severing the fighter's left leg at the knee before he spun once again and with a flash of magical flame tore the other fighter's wrist, hand and sword away. The sounds of bloodcurdling screams had echoed throughout the valley. Krampel had turned and ran for the woods, the shouts of mercenaries following him until they caught up with him at the camp's western edge.

***

Radamuck and the other scout, Herdly Noseminer, had assessed the situation as soon as they heard the swords clanging against each other from their cliff top perch.

"The lad's gotten himself in a heap o' trouble now," Radamuck said.

"Should we go down after him, yer highness?"

"Nay, not right now. The odds clearly wouldn't be in our favor, and he's a big lad. He can take care o' himself."

A few minutes later, a panting Lutricia had returned to the dwarves' perch. Her face, Radamuck saw, was flushed.

"How did yeh get away, lass?" Radamuck asked.

"The Falcon shoved me away," she had replied, before she broke down. "It's my fault! I tripped and alerted everyone in the camp to our presence there! Now he's down there alone against all of them!"

"There, there lass, it'll be okay. The Falcon is a tough one, I can tell yeh that much. Hopefully he'll get out o' there soon, and we can get back to me dwarves."

"He said that Piety Crassnick is down there. Then I tripped as we prepared to leave, and that's when everyone came out of their tents."

Radamuck had patted her back as she wept, but soon that was the only sound he had heard—the sounds of swords colliding with each other had soon stopped, but a raucous cheer rose up from the valley a split second afterward. He had turned to regard it and had frowned inwardly.

"Herdly, help the lass down the hill please," he said gravely to the other dwarf. "We'll come back with the dwarves on the morrow to free him—or pick up what's left o' him."

Lutricia had tried to keep her crying silent as the dwarf had escorted her down the hill, while Radamuck, not hiding himself from the eyes of the enemy, had stared down on the campsite and spat, before he too turned and walked away.

There would be a day of reckonin' coming for Piety Crassnick, Radamuck had thought as he walked down the hill. There was too much at stake for him to go free.

Chapter 16

Blows rained down on Krampel, the attackers' knuckles digging into both flanks. They had tied him to a cross, his belly rubbing against the wood. The mercenaries had used whips, leather switches and their fists to pound their captive, who took everything they had dished out in punishment for treading into their campsite.

Once captured, though, the mercenaries had dragged him by the hair back toward the center ring nearest the bonfire, where Piety Crassnick awaited him. Piety did not know that his old enemy was anywhere within a league of this place. But when the men had forced Krampel to show his dirtied face, kneeling in front of him, his tree-trunk-sized arms held behind him, Piety had gasped at first, then grinned when he recognized him.

"Tie him up and torture him like you would a slave that has disobeyed you," he had spat, earning cheers from his men. Piety kept eye contact with his old adversary as his men dragged Krampel away.

Krampel had recalled what Piety said to his men, and they carried out his orders to the letter. He had winced as pain tore through his body, but he had tensed his muscles up to dull the pain. The punches he withstood, but once the brutes began to use the switches, agonizing screams left his lips as easily as a confession.

After a few roundhouse rights had collided with his kidneys, the torture had stopped. The tent grew deathly quiet, until all he heard were the soft footsteps of booted feet on the grass. He waited for the person to speak, but no voices had penetrated the silence.

Then he saw the person responsible for his discomfort, the person responsible for ordering his beatings. Piety Crassnick had come around from Krampel's left side to face him, smirking as he looked his old adversary in the face.

"Krampel Paddymeyer," he said; it was the first time Krampel had heard his own name spoken aloud in five years. "I wish I could say it is a pleasure to see you again, but I would be lying."

Krampel had grinned, even though grinning felt painful to him. His cheeks had burned. The mercenaries had rubbed his face into the ground when they caught him trying to escape the campsite.

"Oh come on, Piety. We both know how much you like to lie," Krampel had chuckled, but the chuckle ended when Piety stepped up and slugged him across the jaw.

"Why are you here, Paddymeyer? Haven't I given you enough beatings in your life?"

"You forget the one where I turned the tables on you, the one where I beat your face to a pulp. I remember that you ran home to your father crying. Wasn't he the one who came to Vossler's door demanding my hide afterward?"

"Your memory seems to be failing you, Paddymeyer. Maybe I should rearrange your brains so that the correct memory comes back to you," Piety had whispered menacingly to his prisoner.

"That would be just like you—beating up a defenseless person while he's tied up."

Piety laid another smack across Krampel's face, and this time, it stung. Krampel tried to stave the pain away, but instead he licked his lip where it had started to plump.

"Why are you here?" Piety demanded once again, his anger rising. His face was fully flushed.

"You should watch that temper, Piety. It will be the death of you." Krampel stared at the man in front of him with a hardened look, despite the pain it caused.

Piety circled his prisoner slowly, as if stalking him for a kill.

"You know something Paddymeyer, this is how I've always wanted to kill you. I've waited a long time to get you like this, and I want to enjoy your death. I'm sure that having you hang here for a month without sustenance and with regular beatings will satisfy my hatred for you so that I can finally be rid of you. Apparently, informing the caravan that you were in Cassimina didn't get the job done."

Despite this new piece of information, Krampel didn't speak. He wanted to wait for the right moment to respond. Piety, though, was full of words and he relished delivering every one of them.

"Oh yes, I've always wanted to kill you from the moment you came into Cassimina. You were lucky not to be killed that morning; if it wasn't for the old man, you would've been sentenced to death immediately, and it would have been my father to carry it out! The old man bought you five more years of life, Paddymeyer. I hope you thanked him for that before I had him and practically everyone else in Cassimina killed."

Krampel hid his grin. This was it, he knew. This would confirm everything he heard outside—and everything he had believed for five years.

"What do you mean?" he asked, feigning stupidity.

Piety simply laughed.

"You don't seriously believe that it was a simple orc raid, do you? It was I who organized the orcs to attack that worthless land of my birth. I sought them out days before it happened. I had heard the clatter of swords inside Vossler's little dungeon hideaway, and since you weren't in the tanner's room doing your 'apprenticeship,' I simply put things together and discovered you were training with him. I decided to end your training before it progressed any further. I sought out the orcs, told them what I knew about Cassimina's defenses, then told them when to attack."

"Your father died in that attack, Piety! How could you do that to your very own father!" Krampel screamed.

Piety simply shrugged.

"He was not teaching me a proper trade, so I needed to get rid of him so I could pursue my own interests."

"He was the butcher; what else couldn't he teach you except how to chop meat?"

Piety ripped a right cross across Krampel's mouth. Krampel felt a tooth break, and he soon tasted copper flooding his mouth. Piety leaned down to cackle in Krampel's face, and Krampel took the opportunity to spit blood at his captor.

"It is no matter," Piety said as he backed away, wiping the blood from his face. "I've leveled Cassimina twice—first in the orc attack, the second time earlier this week. I did everything but defile the graves." He cackled once again.

Krampel struggled against his bonds as he tried to get to Piety. He knew what Piety meant by defiling the graves;

Krampel wanted to defile him before Piety thought about going near Vossler's final resting place.

Piety continued to laugh.

"So tell me something, Paddymeyer: What does it feel like to be made an orphan again? I don't think it feels so bad, especially when it's brought on by oneself." Piety smiled through stained teeth.

Krampel looked at Piety and felt the fire in his eyes burn. He wanted to break free of the wooden cross and strangle the man standing before him. He wanted to wrap his hands and fingers around Piety Crassnick's throat and finish off what Vossler had interrupted so long ago. He wanted to kill Piety right then and there.

But then he remembered his mission for Cairn Ford, and that he wanted Piety taken alive. He tried to calm himself, but it took all of the will power he had to do so.

Piety must have read Krampel's mind. He grabbed Krampel by the throat, the ball of his palm digging into Krampel's esophagus.

"I'll ask you one last time, Paddymeyer. Why are you here? Old adversaries don't run into each other without reason, so I know that you have a reason to be here. What is it? Tell me why, and I'll spare your pathetic life—for now," he whispered.

Krampel began to choke out the words as Piety's squeezed.

"I'm here... to arrest... you," he said through clenched teeth.

Piety let out a small "Hmph" before he let go of Krampel's throat. Krampel wished he could rub his neck. "Cairn Ford must have sent you after me, did he not? He is a foolish old man. He is paranoid and utterly delusional. I could tell you stories of what he wants me for, but I'm sure he's already let you in on that secret."

Krampel nodded.

"I can tell you right now, Paddymeyer, that the only way you leave this tent with me is if you were to overpower me. But since you look like you are in no condition to do so, you'll have to forgive me if I decide not to follow you to the Inquisitor's hellhole." Piety walked around Krampel and headed for the opening of the tent, but not before he turned around to regard the prisoner one more time. "You've lost, Krampel Paddymeyer. You've lost like you've always lost to me. I will not submit to you, no matter what your brain is telling you. I have grown in size and strength while you are still a puny thing. I will eventually see to killing you, but I'll let you think you will escape from here."

One of Piety's mercenaries came through the opening before Piety turned around to depart. He saluted sharply.

"I'm sorry for interrupting your interrogation of the prisoner, lord, but I thought you should know that an army of dwarves has been spotted heading this way. They are all armed, and there is something strange about them, lord."

Piety waited for the man to speak, but when he didn't, he prompted him with slightly wide eyes and raised brows. "Well?"

"There is a woman with them, and some of our people thought they saw a woman leaving the campsite from afar when he was captured," the mercenary said, pointing at Krampel's back.

His back turned to Piety and the mercenary, Krampel's eyes flew open.

Lutricia! Radamuck! His heart soared. They were on their way to rescue him!

Piety turned to regard Krampel and smirked.

"Give the prisoner lashes until he spills his guts—whether he talks or you actually cut him open with the whip matters not to me," Piety told the mercenary before he made to leave, but as he stepped through the tent opening, he paused and turned back around. "On second thought, give him the lashes after our army decimates the dwarves. Maybe it will prompt in him a change of heart. He is skilled one way or another. Maybe we'll use him as a slave." Piety laughed hysterically as he said this, then departed the tent. The mercenary followed him out, laughing as well.

With no other alternative, Krampel stayed put. He focused his energy on relaxing, since he needed every fiber of his being and every ounce of strength he had to separate Piety Crassnick's head from his body when he finally freed himself from the wooden cross.

***

The hour-long return trip to the dwarf camp took less time than they had thought, as Lutricia, Radamuck, and Herdly practically ran the entire way. They didn't stop to take water or food, because saving Krampel was far more urgent than replenishing themselves, at least at that moment.

Once they had arrived at the camp, the dwarves knew there was something wrong, especially when Radamuck pulled Colonel Roding into his tent to explain the situation. Lutricia, who didn't want to be alone, followed them inside.

"Wilhaut, our human friend has been taken prisoner by Crassnick and his band o' thieves, so we're assemblin' the army and goin' after him. Once he's free, we can go after Crassnick, capture him, and bring him before me father," Radamuck said.

"Aye, your highness, very understandable. When do we leave?"

"Immediately. Rouse the troops and have them assemble in the green. We march within the hour."

Roding saluted and left. Radamuck stood surprised that his second didn't give an argument about saving Krampel, since Krampel was only a mere human.

Perhaps it was the mention of me father that kept Roding's tongue silent, he thought.

Radamuck shrugged.

"We're leaving so soon?" Lutricia asked.

"Aye, lass. The quicker we rescue him, the quicker we can bring Crassnick to justice."

"We have a contract to bring Crassnick to Myrindar."

"That's all well and good, but he will be brought to Lowbridge first. He will answer to charges there, and I will convince me father to release him to yers and Falcon's custody. I'll even give yeh a dwarven escort to Myrindar, and then we can go our separate ways."

"I hope the Falcon will agree to it."

"I don't think the Falcon has any choice to agree or not to agree. Right now, he's bein' held prisoner and is probably bein' tortured by Crassnick's men. He will be in no condition to fight, so the treasure will be ours as soon as we catch him. And like I said, I'll convince me father to let him go with yeh to Myrindar. He only has to answer to our charges, then he'll be yers."

"What did Crassnick do to the dwarves that has you all searching for him?"

Radamuck sighed.

"Lass, he murdered nearly an entire township just south of our realm. The survivors had nowhere else to turn to except to us. Only three people were left alive in a township of one hunnerd. Crassnick and his men have ninety-seven lives to atone for, at least. Who knows how many other lives he has taken."

"Probably more than we can fathom."

"Aye. Take some rest and food. We march soon, lass."

Radamuck left his tent after handing Lutricia a sliver of meat and water, just to build her strength up.

***

As she ate, she thought about Krampel. She hoped he was okay, because she felt guilty for putting him in such a position in the first place. She commanded tears to come, and she wept briefly.

An hour later, the dwarf army set off after Roding had assembled them to march. They headed up the hill and through the woods nearest the campsite, before crossing the river. Lutricia chose to walk over the thin bridge Krampel had led them over a few hours ago, instead of wading across the river like the dwarves.

Lutricia recalled Radamuck's speech to the dwarves just before they had departed. Radamuck spoke of giving thanks to the dwarven war god during the upcoming battle, and giving thanks to him many times over. He spoke of the people in the township that Crassnick and his forces murdered senselessly. It was only fitting, Radamuck said, that they get a dose of the same medicine. He spoke that the enemy should not be underestimated, but make sure they underestimate you. Then he lifted his double-bladed axe into the air, and as one the dwarven army thrust their axes into the air and cheered heartily as they did so.

Dawn slowly approached as they marched, and as a group the dwarves chanted a dwarven war song. Lutricia felt her spirit soar and her heart swell twice its size as the dwarves sang their tune, which had filled her with hope and had erased her despair. She wore a smile on her face for the first time since she kissed the Falcon.

But her smile erased when she noticed Radamuck leading the dwarves away from the cliff, instead bringing them to a nearby glen.

"Why are we headed this way?" she asked the dwarf.

"We want to attack from an easier place than the hill. Flatter ground, lass. We dwarves need flat areas to fight in, even though we'll fight anywhere if we're attacked! Nay, we are choosin' the battle ground, and it'll be on our terms." His explanation made sense.

Then she heard a few mutterings coming from the dwarves nearest the head of the pack, and she looked at them curiously.

"Bah, what are women doin' fightin' anyway? Shouldn't they be home takin' care o' the younglings?" one of them said.

"The woman fights because she must," Radamuck scolded the dwarf, "just like we fight—for honor and for what we believe in. She fights because it is her callin'." The dwarf who spoke out of turn had blanched at the dressing down from the next king of Lowbridge.

"I'm sorry that some dwarves are prejudiced against non-dwarves. They have been taught that since their own younglin' days. Why me father permits it is beyond me. I can assure yeh, lass, that practice will be stopped when I become king," the dwarf said.

"It matters not, your highness. I understand the role women are supposed to play, but that's not the role I am going to play —at least not yet. I have quite a bit of living to do before I settle down."

Radamuck smiled at her in response.

With Lutricia and Radamuck at the head of the army, it meandered around the cliff side and increased the volume of their dwarven song. They didn't want to sneak up on the band which held her master prisoner: They wanted them all to know that a fight was on its way. Their song reached its climax, and Lutricia's chest rose with pride at the sounds of the words and their deep meanings. With the repetitious chorus, Lutricia joined in.

A few minutes later, the dwarf army rounded the cliff and looked on the sea of tents. Morning's first light crept over the eastern horizon and even though it shone into the eyes of the dwarves, the army had hardly flinched at the rays.

***

Krampel hung in the tent, staying as still as possible. Gravity had pulled his weight down to the grassy floor, his muscles stretched and taut as he waited for the next round of torture, whenever Piety decided it was time for it to begin. An hour had elapsed since Piety departed when word of the dwarf army approaching reached his ears. Krampel had attempted to recharge his batteries and his defenses. He felt the raised welts across his back, the cuts the whip made into his flesh. He felt like a human punching bag.

The past few hours reminded him greatly of his former life. Piety had ordered his men to treat Krampel like a slave, and did they ever treat him as such. Thinking it over for the hour or so since Piety had left the tent, he'd have to say the caravan masters were kind compared to the criminals who had attacked Krampel's body.

Now, with the tent quiet and no one inside of it, Krampel had looked around as far as his head would move. It was non-descript, but he saw *Flad-rul* to his right rear, just visible as far as he could turn his head.

What would Vossler say if he saw me now? Krampel thought. *He would probably rap my knees with his cane if he knew that my sword was away from me and I was tied up. The old man would have a lesson or two to teach me, I'm sure.*

Krampel smiled to himself. He missed the old man greatly.

But then his memories turned to fresher ones: Piety's admission about the night Vossler died suddenly shouted at him, Piety's voice rang and echoed in his brain. The smile evaporated, only replaced by a tick in the skin over the left side of his upper lip. His brow had furrowed, and he had felt his eyes growing dark. Then the fire Vossler saw so long ago had ignited within him, burning his soul and setting every inch of him ablaze. His body turned incredibly hot, as if the adrenaline rushed through him at a breakneck pace.

Soon he saw that the tent began to fill with smoke. He coughed as the realization came to him that he might possibly suffocate.

But then he looked around and saw *Flad-rul*—it had come alight! It ignited as the power rushed through Krampel's veins and caught the material of the tent, sending it into flames and billowing smoke.

Krampel wished he could get to the sword, but he could not get free, not without assistance. The bonds around his wrists dug into the flesh and rubbed against the bones. Trying to free himself, he knew, was a fruitless and tiresome endeavor. He already decided to save as much strength as he could for when he met up with Piety again.

The flames and smoke nearly consumed him when one of Piety's mercenaries entered and untied Krampel's hands; the mercenary stupidly turned his back to the prisoner. Once free, Krampel had leapt from his knees and lunged at the criminal, catching him in the small of the back. The criminal fell down with Krampel on top of him, the criminal smacking his face on the ground with an audible crack. Krampel rolled off him to the left and found breathable air, then grabbed *Flad-rul* and his golden shield. He found an untouched portion of the tent and rolled under it, letting the mercenary burn inside it.

The sun's rays rose above the tents, the dew soaking the grass. Krampel stood and watched the backs of the criminals marching between the rows of tents, headed off to face the dwarves. The anticipation in the air was heavy with anxiety as they headed off toward the small glen on the eastern edge of the campsite.

He saw Piety Crassnick standing at the rear of the pack, his cape waving in the early morning breeze. He had his back turned to Krampel, but Krampel saw the style of Piety's hair.

Krampel's hand squeezed the handle of *Flad-rul* as his eyes had turned a shade of magenta. He stalked in on his tormenter, ready to drive the point of his sword into Piety Crassnick's guts. He drew to within ten feet of his childhood rival when Piety turned around and, on seeing him, he grinned before drawing his own sword, a shining steel blade just as long as *Flad-rul*.

The two men marked each other, circling to the right. None of the other mercenaries saw their leader, unless they turned around.

The two spoke not a word between them as they circled each other. They merely kept eye contact, each with their sword in the en guard position. Krampel held *Flad-rul* in his right hand, the fiery golden shield fixed to the left forearm, while Piety held his sword with both hands.

Then, without provocation, Piety stepped in forcefully just as Krampel moved to strike. Their swords met once and then twice as the blades clashed between them, Krampel answering with a one-handed parry and riposte.

Chapter 17

The dwarves didn't wait for the mercenaries to advance.

They marched forward en masse, their axes at the ready. They sang praise to their war god as they strode across the glen, the voices carrying throughout the valley so the humans in the rear heard it as clear as a bell. The dwarves wanted them afraid of the pack which now headed their way.

Lutricia had her sword out, ready to fight, even though her insides squirmed and her palms had grown sweaty. As she walked, she thought of nothing but her mentor. She got herself involved in several close calls with him, and she saw several glimpses into his scarred psyche. She had also seen him at his most vulnerable—both while bathing and while he remembered what happened to his own mentor. It had touched her heart to have him finally open up to her.

And now, less than a few hours later, she was closed off to him.

She kept her tears held back, for she didn't want to hear the snickers of the dwarves. But as she looked around at her comrades, their faces showed incredible determination and she figured they wouldn't notice her crying, or be distracted from it, period. She took a deep, calming breath and concentrated on the task at hand.

The army now stood within fifty axe-lengths of the enemy, and Lutricia wanted to run in. Her stride lengthened so much that the dwarves nearly sprinted to catch up with her. On the other side, the mercenaries ran toward the attacking dwarves, and they held their blades aloft as they ran.

In minutes, the distance between the two hordes had closed considerably. Within seconds, the two parties had engaged, steel crossing steel—and sometimes, steel against flesh.

Lutricia swung her sword with such grace and elegance that it was, at first, hard to believe that her swings held such deadly accuracy. She crossed swords with a man twice her size, but she was undaunted. She swung left and parried his attempt at a killing blow before swinging around to the right with a thunderous riposte that knocked the man's sword aside, if only by an inch.

Gritting her teeth, Lutricia went on a blistering attack that the mercenaries had no chance of defending. Her quick strikes, comprising a right-left-right combination, ended with a spin to the right and a slash across the man's left thigh, opening up the quadricep muscle. The man screamed and dropped his sword, lunging for his leg. Lutricia made sure he never got that far, backhanding him across the throat, splitting his jugular. He dropped like a wet rucksack.

Lutricia stepped over him and continued the fight.

She moved to parry low on an attacker who tried to take out her legs. She swiped him with a backhand and ripped a deep, bloodied trench across his pectorals. Smiling, she drove the point of her sword into his gut, twisting and removing it before positioning the blood-stained steel in front of her, preparing for the next attack.

It came quickly—a burly man was next, holding his sword above his head, ready to drive it into her skull. She had raised her sword to block, feeling the vibrations as the swords connected. With a twist of her wrists she had pushed her opponent's sword toward the ground, then spun and drove her heel right between his eyes. He saw a flash of light and staggered backward, and that was all the distraction that Lutricia needed. She quickly went on the offensive, snapping off a brutal left-right salvo before ending it with a thrust that pierced the man's side.

She ran forward and lunged. Her blade caught an unsuspecting mercenary battling a dwarf—the same dwarf who said that women shouldn't be fighting. The man had dropped hard, leaving the dwarf to look at Lutricia with a mixture of shock and fury on his bearded face. Lutricia, on the other hand, had already turned and went off to find another fight.

"Yeh takin' 'way one o' me kills, lass!" he yelled after her. Lutricia hadn't heard a word. The blood pumped in her ears, blocking out all the extraneous noises around her, lost in concentration in her own little world. She fought with everything she had and then some. She had already taken out four enemies.

She wanted more.

Several came at her with lumbering strides. She sidestepped them and slashed away, cutting into them deeply and causing them to fall.

If only the Falcon could see me now, she thought. *I know he would be very proud of me.*

Lutricia put the thought of her captured mentor aside and concentrated. She fought against somewhat weaker competition, and it surprised her. She swung her blade and caught the flesh of many enemies. Those that approached her stopped and stepped backward, a step Lutricia used to her advantage. She chased them down and made them pay for hurting her mentor, even if they had nothing to do with his torture.

A look of pure fury wrenched Lutricia's face. She swung with such strength that belied her lithe, supple frame. She fought men sometimes three or four times her size, and she dispatched them with ease. She had used quick movements and footwork that kept her moving, never in the same place for more than a second. It had confused her opponents and left them vulnerable to attack, and she took advantage of the openings.

This is getting too easy, she thought.

***

The two swords clashed against each other, far from the main battle. Krampel and Piety fought all alone, with no one to help them should they get into a bind. This long-awaited swordfight would be to the death—at least to Piety. For Krampel, he only needed to subdue and disarm his opponent. Death was not an option, he reminded himself.

It was a fast and furious battle between two opponents who clearly loathed each other. Each rained skilled and merciless blows on the other, only for the opponent to meet them with equal skill in blocking, followed by a brutal counter. Relentlessly, the fight progressed.

Despite the ache in his muscles from hanging for so long, Krampel had willed the pain away and concentrated on this fight. He was at a great disadvantage: Piety was much more rested. Krampel had to rely on his skill with a sword, his cunning, and his quick thinking. To Krampel's mind, it meant that he had Piety seriously outmatched.

The pair had exchanged vicious strikes; sending sparks flying off the sides of their swords. Krampel had ducked and spun and brought his sword around with such speed that Piety almost failed to get his wrists turned in time to block it. Krampel had pulled his blade away and, keeping his feet moving, regrouped.

One deep breath later, he had returned to the fight, attacking with a high chop toward Piety's left shoulder. Piety had slashed upward to block, then both spun in place and swung their blades, connecting in the middle. Both retreated, Krampel twirling the blade through his fingers before he attacked again.

This time, he ripped off a flurry of swipes, crosses, and slashes, leaving his opponent breathless and wide-eyed.

"Maybe I should have had you beaten harder, Paddymeyer. It doesn't seem like you've learned your lesson," Piety said while swinging.

"If you had me beaten harder, I would have recovered much quicker than this," Krampel retorted sharply, parrying Piety's blade with the shield before plunging the tip of *Flad-rul* toward his right deltoid.

Piety saw the attempt and ducked, feeling the breeze of Krampel's sword and arm pass him by. Krampel spun out of the way quickly, closing up the opening he had unknowingly handed his opponent. Piety swore.

The two circled each other and waited for the other to make a move. Krampel unstrapped and dropped the shield and proceeded to hold the Flame Thrower in both hands, giving him better leverage against Piety. With the two-handed grip, he stalked his opponent and leveled two swings, both going to opposite flanks. Piety had stopped both of them, before he let an onslaught of moves drive Krampel backward, passing the tents and heading west, away from the brawl between Piety's men and the dwarves.

Krampel grinned as Vossler's teachings came back to him.

Krampel had blocked Piety's attempts at killing blows. Twenty axe-lengths, then thirty, then all the way up to fifty before the sounds of the battle between the dwarves and the mercenaries turned into distant memories. It was just the two of them, and Krampel couldn't have been happier.

Piety had slashed at Krampel's thighs but couldn't get through the firestorm that was Flad-rul. The bully of Cassimina had grown frustrated, and deservedly so. He had tried to one-up Krampel for quite some time before Krampel beat him up long ago, and he now simply looked for a way to make him pay for that beating.

One swing later, their swords locked against each other, the hilts rubbing together.

"Why can't you just die like my father or Vossler?" Piety said through gritted teeth.

Krampel didn't rise to the bait, but had an old, scathing remark on the tip of his tongue to enrage his opponent.

"I'm only prolonging the duel, Piety, because I see you need the practice."

With a scream, Piety raced at Krampel, who simply sidestepped him and slapped him on the rear end with the side of his sword. Seeing his adversary cracking, Krampel had rushed over and chopped at his opponent, first to the shoulders, then a spin and a slash to the waist. Piety had blocked the first, twirled his sword, and moved it down to parry Krampel's attempt at his waist, but he couldn't correct in time as Krampel's right foot came from out of nowhere to crack against his temple. He dropped his sword and fell to the ground, clutching the side of his head.

Krampel stood over him and placed the point of the sword near his neck, but had to hold his hand from plunging it into Piety's throat.

"You are beaten, Piety Crassnick. Surrender now and call off your army. You're under arrest for crimes against the Imperium, and Cairn Ford will deal with you however he so chooses."

Panting and prone on the ground, Piety wanted to lunge for his sword, but the proximity of Krampel's sword was too close for comfort. He put his left hand up in a plea for mercy.

Krampel kicked the pommel of Piety's sword behind him, sending it a few axe-lengths away.

"I should kill you," Krampel said. "I should take your life for what you've done. I should kill you for the people of Cassimina that died on that day. But I will be merciful and hand you over to the authorities in Myrindar, so they may pass judgment on you."

"Handing me over to them is like a death sentence, Paddymeyer. Ford is a lunatic who is trying to put everyone under his heel. I have information that he doesn't want to get out—he's ready to take over the realms. Spare me and the information—all of it—is yours."

Krampel spat his disgust.

"Spare me your lies and innuendo. You're incredibly evil, you always have been. Don't expect me to fall for your ploy when you're staring at a death sentence!"

"It's not a ploy!" Piety screamed. "It's all true. Ford is not to be trusted. He is a power-hungry tyrant."

"Sounds like someone else I know," Krampel said, looking at Piety with a smirk.

Piety sighed, then looked up at his old nemesis.

"You never learn, do you? Cairn Ford will be the end of the realms as you and I know them."

"Spoken like a true criminal; many others have said as much to me."

"Then you know of his horrible deeds!"

"Nay, I believed them not. Most of them were criminals, and I do not trust them as far as I can throw them."

"You're making a mistake if you don't listen to me, Paddymeyer. Ford is evil, and he intends on making the realms —not just Myrindar—his. Our spies told us this is so," Piety pleaded. "Believe me when I say this is true."

"I don't believe a word of anything you spew, Crassnick. As long as we knew each other in Cassimina, you seemed hell bent on making my life there one of agony and despair. You made me feel worthless, and just today you had me beaten to within an inch of my life; why should I heed your warnings now? Give me one reason to believe you."

"Because I know things! The things I could tell you of Ford's treachery and deceit would make your skin crawl."

Krampel immediately reached down and grabbed his prisoner by his hair, dragging him to his feet. He pressed *Fladrul* to Piety's throat and led him toward the battle some one hundred axe-lengths away. He picked up his shield—he forced Piety to bend over, kicking him in the back of the knee, to prevent him from making any sudden moves—and saw the mercenary army's numbers had dwindled.

Krampel smiled.

Those men have already paid the price for aligning with Piety Crassnick, he thought. *Now it was time to bring Piety to justice.*

***

Radamuck had dropped his axe into the head of a mercenary Lutricia had sliced the legs out from under when the dwarf prince saw Krampel leading his prisoner toward them. On seeing the prisoner, he called a halt to the fighting. The mercenaries wanted to keep fighting, but when they saw Piety captured, they turned tail and ran for it.

"Let them all go!" Radamuck cried, even as a dwarven axe felled one, the axe embedded in his back. "There will be plenty o' time to round the rest o' them up. We got the one we came for!"

The dwarves all cheered at their leader's proclamation, and at Radamuck's gesture, dwarves pulled ropes from rucksacks to bind Piety's hands together. Krampel had sheathed his sword when the dwarves took possession of the prisoner.

"You're a fool for following Ford, Krampel Paddymeyer," Piety said as the dwarves led him away. "You'll rue the day you ever took his money!"

"I don't follow Ford, Piety: I follow no one." Krampel looked at his old adversary's back. Piety was struggling now that *Fladrul* was away from his neck, but one of the dwarves slid his axe up to the human's neck. That quieted him considerably.

"Why did he call yeh Krampel Paddymeyer, Falcon?" Radamuck asked.

Krampel sighed.

"It's my name."

Lutricia, who stood off to the side while the dwarves bound prisoner, sheathed her sword. She walked up to Krampel and wrapped her arms around his neck. Krampel returned the gesture.

"Are you okay?" she asked.

"Yes, I'm fine. My back stings a little, but that's what happens when you're beaten with whips."

"It's all my fault, Falcon. I'm truly sorry."

"Nay, it is not your fault," Krampel said. The dwarf, who stood next to them, patted the girl on the back. "It was a risky endeavor in the first place. It is something we need to work on, your stealth. It will take time, but I believe it is something that we can improve as soon as we better your sword fighting. Do not concern yourself with what happened last night."

"I don't think the lass needs help there, Falcon," Radamuck said. "She did a fine job of moppin' up these mercenaries. I think she was the one who really wanted to make sure yeh we're okay."

Lutricia smiled up at her mentor and nodded.

"I'm fine. A little sore, but it's nothing that will put me out of action. We still have to return to Myrindar to deliver Crassnick, after we bring him to Lowbridge first," Krampel said, remembering his deal with Radamuck.

I may not be loyal to the dwarf, Krampel thought, *but I remember bargains. And he came for me… I should be thankful.*

Krampel extended his hand to the dwarf.

"Thank you for coming after me. I'll never forget that."

Radamuck bowed and said, "Think nothin' o' it, lad. We Rosars look out for our own."

Radamuck's words touched Krampel. Here with him were two beings who cared very much for him, even though they had recently met. Krampel didn't want to get close to them, but he felt that his resistance to that one ideal, his life's mission, weakened with each passing moment.

***

Radamuck ordered that the dwarves who lost their lives in the battle be burned, as according to custom. Once they had piled the bodies on each other, he gathered the surviving members of his army and spoke comforting words to them: They all knew the risks of being a member of this force. They all offered prayers to the dwarf god of war and asked him to welcome the warriors into his vaunted halls.

Krampel had never seen the dwarven ceremony before, and it moved him. He was curious about many of the different customs of the races, and he figured this one was quite possibly the only one of its kind he would ever witness. He knew there was no chance of seeing an elf, halfling, or orc ceremony such as this.

And as he stood and watched the dwarf prince ignite the bonfire and smelled the burning flesh, he was reminded of Vossler. Now that he knew who had set up the orc raid, he finally felt closure about his mentor's death. He took a deep breath as he tried to control his emotions, but one lonely tear trickled out of the corner of his right eye and streamed down his cheek.

Maybe I should pay the grave a visit before we return to Lowbridge, he thought.

Within an hour of burning the dead dwarves, the rest of the dwarf army plus Krampel and Lutricia started the long march to Lowbridge, Piety Crassnick in tow. Krampel requested that the army make a stop in Cassimina proper. The dwarf prince allowed it.

After visiting Vossler's grave, Krampel considered the mission to capture Piety completed. Now he needed to convince Radamuck's father to honor their bond, and then he could move on to other bounties—with Lutricia next to him.

He wondered how easy a task that would be.

Chapter 18

The red standard flag of the Lowbridge dwarves made its first appearance in its homeland five days after the Second Battle of Cassimina, leading Radamuck, Krampel, Lutricia and the rest of the army across the grassy plain. The mountain city of the dwarven realm loomed ahead.

The past five days seemed a blur to Krampel. Radamuck took him off the watch so he might rest and recuperate from his injuries. Even though he fought Piety Crassnick and won through sheer nerve, his body ached, the pain gnawing at his bones. Radamuck told him to see the dwarven clerics for an antidote when they reached Lowbridge; by antidote, he meant blessed dwarven water.

"The golden ales o' Lowbridge can put a man back on the road to good health in no time!" the dwarf prince had exclaimed.

While walking, Krampel and Lutricia conversed over what had happened in the campsite, and he chose to be completely honest about his past. He wanted to trust her, despite how difficult it was for him to do so. He knew that if he taught her the bounty hunting trade, he'd have to learn to trust her. He told her that what happened in Piety's camp wasn't her fault, and he meant it sincerely.

And the kiss in Piety's camp... the kiss had turned into multiples over the next few days.

Soon they came on the large gates to the mountain city, which opened swiftly and swallowed the army. They dragged Piety behind Radamuck, Krampel and Lutricia and brought him in front of Ricanack Rosar, the 23rd King of Lowbridge, who awaited his son to arrive inside his Main Audience Chamber.

Radamuck bowed to his father, who rose and walked over to his only son, embracing him. An elderly dwarf of 500 years, Ricanack's vigor and stamina supplemented his wisdom and his patience of others. His hair looked as white as the snow of the northlands, his eyes as crystal blue as the Enchanted Sea to the west. A hefty dwarf he appeared, but that didn't stop him from engaging in occasional sparring matches with members of his army.

After their embrace, Radamuck introduced his guests to his father.

"Me king, may I present to yeh the Dark Falcon," he said, waving to Krampel, who bowed low, "and his apprentice." Lutricia did her best to curtsy.

"Welcome to me home!" the king boomed with wide open arms. "And I see yeh brought me a present, me boy." Ricanack referred to Piety, who looked to be a present for the king, all tied up like a package.

"Aye father, we did. In fact, this is the criminal yeh sent me to apprehend for yeh. I must tell yeh that Falcon here was the one who captured him; he is a bounty hunter o' great renown in the southlands, lord. Actually, it was by chance that we ran into him; he was on a mission to capture him for the Inquisitor."

Ricanack took all this information in with widened eyes.

"Lord, I've made a deal with him that I believe we should honor," he said.

"Aye, what is the deal?" Ricanack asked.

Taking a deep breath, Radamuck said, "I promised him I'd talk to yeh about letting him fulfill his bounty and taking the criminal to Myrindar as he wanted to—after yeh deal with him here."

Ricanack stroked his long white beard for a moment. He looked from his son to the bounty hunter and nodded.

"Aye, a Rosar's word to a gallant man is always upheld. Let us commence the trial, and then our bounty hunter friend can uphold his part o' his contract," the dwarf king said.

***

Within an hour of the start of the trial, Ricanack found Piety guilty of crimes against the realms and ordered him put to death. However, he suspended the sentence pending charges against him in Myrindar. Krampel somehow knew that the king did not want the blood spilled in his realm. If Myrindar did the actual act, it would be all fine with him.

Krampel took possession of the condemned man. Radamuck stopped him and Lutricia before they left.

"I'm goin' to come with yeh, lad," he said.

Krampel looked confused.

"Why would you want to do such a thing? You have a kingdom to help run with your father."

"Me father can run this realm virtually blindfolded, and I'll tell yeh somethin' else—I think he does, sometimes," Radamuck said with a wink. "I want a little adventure in me life before I take over as king. I'm sure that I won't have as many adventures when the Crown of the Golden Mug is passed to me."

Krampel chuckled more to himself than anyone.

"Aye, that's probably true. We need to get going soon if we're to deliver Crassnick to the Inquisitor."

***

After another five-day march, Krampel, Lutricia and Radamuck delivered Piety Crassnick to Myrindar. Many watched intently as the bounty hunter, the apprentice and the dwarf dragged the criminal up to the fifth level, where Cairn Ford awaited them. By the time they arrived, Piety's body had nearly broken under the strain—apparently he would rather lose all of the blood in his body on the cobblestoned roads of Myrindar's twisting paths to the summit instead of in Cairn Ford's laboratory deep within Karackstine.

"Well, if it isn't Piety Crassnick. It's about time you made your appearance here," Ford taunted with a grin as wide as the valley Piety's campsite was in.

Piety had answered with a big, wet glob of saliva directed at Ford's feet.

"Burn in the fifth layer of hell, Ford. You may kill me, but not before the realms find out about you," he said, "and what you're planning to do."

Ford had only grinned wider. Krampel only stared at Piety and didn't look at his part-time employer. He really didn't care for what Piety had to say about Ford—or about anyone, for that matter.

"Take him away, and make sure the prisoner is… comfortable," Ford said. Three guards had rushed forward to take possession of the prisoner, and Piety had screamed and kicked his feet in protest as they took him into the manor.

Ford had seemingly ignored the yells and the sounds as he turned to Krampel.

"Again, I must thank you for ridding the realms of another worthless criminal who is no use to anyone. I will pay your contract in full, and I'll let you be on your way."

With a grin, Ford extended his hand for Krampel to shake, but when their hands met, an electric shock ran through Krampel's arm as they locked eyes. Ford broke the handshake and then entered the manor, closing the door behind him.

For some reason, Krampel didn't like that look.

***

Ford had replenished Krampel's account with the coin he had promised in the contract. The trio then left Myrindar soon after, not bothering to look back on the mountain city.

His purse full, he felt its weight on his right hip and wondered what he, his apprentice, and their new friend should do now. As if reading his mind, Radamuck asked, "So what do we do now? Look for another adventure?"

Krampel had grinned and looked to his friends.

"I don't know about you two," he said, "but I'm interested in finding a warm bed and relaxing for a few days. This sleeping in the open is all fine and dandy, but every once in a while, a bed would come in pretty handy."

Both Lutricia and Radamuck had laughed with Krampel and his rhyme, and soon the three travelers were en route to Arborway and the realms beyond.

***

Deep within Karackstine, the screams coming from the torture chamber seemed to overwhelm even the stench of fear that came out of every cell, the fear palpable and ever-present.

But the man who walked the long passage between the cells didn't feel the fear emminating from inside the cells. He felt no fear whatsoever. Instead, he relished the fear he instilled in others.

Cairn Ford kept his eyes on the door to the torture room and paid no attention to the prisoners he had condemned to die. He strode past them, taking great glee in ignoring their pleas for mercy. He took even greater glee in staring them down with his wicked eyes and ordering their immediate execution.

He had walked through the door and found Piety Crassnick strapped to the table, technicians milling about. The wizard, Danolf Jenson, also stood by, ready to proceed with the next step in the operation.

Ford looked down at Piety.

"You certainly do know how to perform."

Piety simply grinned.

"It was an honor to perform for you, lord."

"Are the others dead?"

Piety nodded.

"Good. That is a help. How much did you tell the bounty hunter?"

"As much as he would listen to, and that wasn't much. Paddymeyer has too much of a good streak in him; he considered everything I had said about you, and wouldn't listen to a criminal like myself, as I'm sure you've already guessed."

"It has been told to me by others that they have told him about me, but as it stands, he did not believe them, either. It will be too late before he can do anything tangible against me; the people will look to him, but they will fail. I have foreseen it. It shall be this way for some time before I can fully inflict the pain I wish to hand the realms, and I can assure you, Piety Crassnick, that you will be a part of it."

"I am honored that you have chosen me for this, lord."

Ford only smiled thinly and nodded in return.

"Of course you are honored. Not many would so willingly go to their deaths before their time, but you are different and I know this. You know what is at stake. You see the greater picture, Piety, and for that, I will give you the highest honor anyone can possibly imagine."

Piety had taken a calming breath as he rested his head back against the table. He closed his eyes and sighed.

"Thank you, lord."

Ford turned to the wizard and nodded. Danolf Jenson stepped up to Piety's side and chanted his incantations, his hands placed on Piety's chest, right over his heart. He then sprinkled a substance over the body, another incantation followed. The candlelight dimmed, then shot toward the ceiling as the wizard's speech reached peak volume.

Not needing to see what he knew would eventually happen, Ford had turned and departed the room without another look at his servant of several years, Piety Crassnick. Many of Ford's atrocities Crassnick handled, and Ford would need to find someone else to do his dirty work once Piety was gone.

But as he walked down the passageway to continue to run the public face of the Imperium, he thought it over—*as soon as everything is ready, Piety will once again to do my bidding.*

And soon, everything would be completed, he knew. The necessary components were there. It would be a masterpiece, as soon as everything came together.

Ford smiled as he envisioned his plan once again. He smiled even wider when the next set of screams emanated from the torture room.

It was the sweetest music he ever heard.

TO BE CONTINUED

Like what you've read? Sean Sweeney has something for every member of the family: check out more books and stories!

For young adults:

Zombie Showdown

For adults:

The Jaclyn Johnson, code name Snapshot series
Model Agent: A Thriller
Rogue Agent: A Thriller
Double Agent: A Thriller
Promises Given, Promises Kept: A Jaclyn Johnson novella
Federal Agent: A Thriller
Literary Agent: A Thriller
Jail Bird Jenny: A Jaclyn Johnson short story
Travel Agent: A Thriller
Chemical Agent: A Thriller
Ticket Agent: A Thriller
Scouring Agent: A Thriller

Redeemed
Royal Switch: A Major League Thriller
An Invitation to Drink… and to Die
The Lone Bostonian
Freedom (with David Wood)

The Ricky Madison series
The Long Crimson Line: A Thriller
Persuaded By The Reflections: A Thriller

The Peg-Legged Privateer: A Tattered Sails novel

The Alex Bourque Small Town PI series
Cold Altar
Voir Dire

Beach Blanket Bloodshed

The Obloeron Saga
The Rise Of The Dark Falcon
The Shadow Looms
Krampel's Revenge
The Quest For The Chalice
The Return To Lowbridge
The Fall of Myrindar

Short stories
Belief Debt: Paid In Full (Part of Christopher Nadeau's Not in the Brochure anthology)
C is for Coulrophobia (Part of the Phobophobia anthology)
Red Christmas (Part of the Bump in the Night 2011 anthology)
Refugees: A short story of survival

Writing As John Fitch V

One Hero, A Savior
Turning Back The Clock
A Galaxy At War
The Mastermind: A novella

Short stories
Sidetracked
Amber Twilight
Vuvuzombie

Writing as D.L. Boyd

Scollay Love: A Romance

The Glorious series
Glorious Slip
Glorious Rise (coming soon)

Visit Sean online:

www.seansweeneyauthor.com

Join Sean's mailing list and get updates on his work straight to your email!

Email Sean!

seansweeneyauthor@yahoo.com